~ That Mad Ache ~

A novel
by Françoise Sagan

~

Translated from the French
by Douglas Hofstadter

BASIC
B
BOOKS

A Member of the Perseus Books Group
New York

Originally published as *La Chamade*,
copyright © by René Julliard, Paris

Translation copyright © 2009
by Douglas R. Hofstadter

Published by Basic Books
A Member of the Perseus Books Group

Books published by Basic Books are available at special discount rates for bulk purchases within the United States by corporations, institutions, and other organizations. For further information, please contact the Special Markets Department at the Perseus Books Group, 2300 Chestnut Street, Suite 200, Philadelphia, PA 19103, or call (800) 810-4145, ext. 5000, or e-mail special.markets@perseusbooks.com.

A CIP catalogue record for this book is available from the United States Library of Congress in Washington D.C.

LCCN: 2009922415
ISBN: 9780465010981

2 4 6 8 10 9 7 5 3 1

À mes parents

PART ONE

Le Printemps

J'ai fait la magique étude
Du Bonheur, que nul n'élude.

— Arthur Rimbaud

I've probed the magic of Bliss,
A path that no one can miss.

Chapter 1

She opened her eyes. A brisk little breeze had impudently slipped into the bedroom. Already it had turned the curtain into a sail and bent the flowers in their tall vase on the floor, and now it had set its sights on her sleep. It was a spring wind, the very first one, and it smelled of thickets, forests, and soil; it had swept unchallenged through the *faubourgs* of Paris, through their streets choked with traffic fumes, and now it was arriving softly but brashly at dawn in her bedroom, intent on reminding her, even before she emerged from her drowsy state, of the pleasure of being alive.

She reclosed her eyes, flipped over onto her front, and with her face still buried in her pillow, groped around on the floor for her alarm clock. She must have forgotten it — she always forgot everything. She carefully rose from bed and thrust her head out the window. It was dark, and the windows across the way were shut. This breeze should have known better than to go blowing at such an hour! She lay down again, wrapping herself tightly in her sheets once more, and spent a little while pretending to be asleep.

But it was of no use. Now the cocky breeze was strutting about her room, and she sensed its irritation with the limpness of the weak-willed roses and the obsequious swelling-up of the curtains. It was sweeping over her coquettishly, urging her with all the power of its rural fragrances: "Come out, come out — come stroll with me!" Her sleepy body just wouldn't go along, though. Little shards of dreams kept returning to fog up her brain, but ever so slowly a smile started to form on her mouth. Dawn, the countryside at dawn... the four plane trees on the terrace, their leaves so crisply outlined against the pale sky... the crunch of gravel under some dog's paws... eternal childhood...

Was there anything left in this world that could still imbue childhood with some charm, after all the sad wailings of novelists, the obscure theorizings of psychoanalysts, and the fatuous out-pourings of random souls encouraged to vent themselves on the theme "When I was a child"? Only the nostalgia for those days of utter, absolute irresponsibility, now long gone. But for her (and this she would never have admitted to anyone), those days weren't gone at all. She still felt totally irresponsible.

This last thought made her again get out of bed. She scanned the room for her dressing gown but didn't find it. Someone must have stuck it somewhere, but where? She opened the wardrobes with a sigh. There was no way she could ever get used to this bedroom. Nor to any other bedroom, for that matter. Decor in general left her completely indifferent. Even so, this was a lovely room, with its high ceiling, its two big windows opening onto a small *rive gauche* street, and a grayish-blue rug that was easy on the eyes and on the feet as well. The bed struck her as an island flanked by two reefs — the nightstand and the low table between the two windows — and both of them, according to Charles, were in the finest classic style. And then

Chapter 1

her dressing gown, which finally she'd spotted, was silken, and all this luxury was, truth to tell, very appealing.

She walked into Charles' bedroom. He always slept with the windows shut and the nightstand lamp on, and no wind ever bothered him. His sleeping pills were carefully placed next to his pack of cigarettes, his lighter, his bottle of mineral water, and his alarm clock, which was set for eight o'clock sharp. Only *Le Monde* was lying around on the floor. She sat down at the foot of the bed and looked at him.

Charles was fifty years old and had pleasant features, slightly soft, and an unhappy look when he was asleep. This particular morning, he looked even sadder than usual. He had dealings in real estate, and thus a great deal of money, but his relationships with other people were rather uneasy, thanks to a certain blend of politeness and reserve that at times made him come across as remote, even cold. They had been living together now for two years — if "living together" was the proper term for occupying the same apartment, seeing the same people, and once in a while sleeping in the same bed.

He turned towards the wall and groaned a little. She thought yet one more time that she surely must make him unhappy, but her very next thought was that he would have been unhappy with *any* woman twenty years his junior who had a flair for independence. She took a cigarette from the nightstand, lit it noiselessly, and resumed her musing. Charles' hair was graying on top, the veins stood out on his graceful hands, and his mouth was losing a bit of its youthful color. She felt a sudden surge of tenderness for him. How could anyone be so kind, so intelligent, and so unhappy? Yet she could do nothing for him; you can't console someone for having been born and being doomed to die.

She started coughing — it was a mistake to smoke on an empty stomach in the morning. One should never smoke on an empty stomach, nor for that matter should one partake of alcohol, drive fast, make love too often, tax one's heart, spend one's money, or do anything else. She yawned. She was going to get in the car and follow that spring breeze a long way out into the countryside. She wouldn't work today any more than she did on other days. Thanks to Charles, she had gotten very accustomed to not working.

Half an hour later, she was spinning down the *autoroute* towards Nancy, with a piano concerto on her convertible's radio. But was it by Grieg, Schumann, or Rachmaninoff? Certainly some romantic, but which one? This uncertainty annoyed her and pleased her at the same time. The only cultural icons she liked were ones that she knew by heart, and to those she was very sensitive. "I remember hearing that piece of music twenty times and I know I was miserable in that period of my life, and it stuck to my suffering like a decal." Already, though, she had forgotten who had caused her this sadness; already she must be growing old. But that was of little import to her. It had been ages since she had thought of herself, seen herself, even defined herself in her own eyes; it had been ages since she had run alone, with only the present beside her, in such a fine fresh dawn wind.

CHAPTER 2

The noise of the car in the courtyard woke Charles up. He heard Lucile humming as she closed the garage door, and he wondered, in a daze, what time it could possibly be. His watch said it was nearly eight. It briefly crossed his mind that Lucile might be sick, but hearing her carefree voice down below reassured him. For a split second, he felt tempted to open the window and to yell down to her, "Stop!", but he refrained. He knew this euphoria of hers: it was the euphoria of being alone.

He shut his eyes for a moment. This was the first of a thousand impulses he would stifle today in order not to inhibit Lucile, not to get in her way. If he'd been fifteen years younger, he would doubtless have been able to open the window and shout down, "Lucile, come back up, I'm awake!" in a slightly bossy yet casual tone. And she would have come upstairs and had a cup of tea with him. She would have sat down on his bed and soon he'd have had her in stitches with silly off-the-cuff remarks. But he shrugged his shoulders at this fantasy. Even fifteen years ago, he wouldn't have made her laugh. He had, in truth, never been funny. He'd only discovered how to be light-hearted a year ago, thanks to Lucile, and it seemed to be one of the slowest and hardest traits to acquire, if one isn't born with it.

He sat up in bed, noting with surprise an ashtray beside him.

Part I: *Le printemps*

At its center was was an extinguished cigarette, and he wondered if he might have forgotten, last night, to dump it into the fireplace before retiring. Impossible. Lucile must have come in and smoked in his room. Also, there was a little hollow on his bed, indicating she'd been sitting there. He himself never disturbed anything while sleeping. The various cleaning women who had overseen his bachelor's existence had often praised him for this quality. It was, in fact, something people had always complimented him for: his calmness, whether he was awake or asleep; his composure; his good manners. Some people were always being praised for their charm, but that had never happened to him, or at least never in a truly disinterested fashion, which was a pity: he would have felt instantly endowed with a marvelous, sparkling, beautiful set of feathers.

Certain words always made him suffer, cruelly and quietly, like a blurry memory one can't quite retrieve: the words "charming", "easy-going", "casual", and also, God only knows why, "balcony". Once he'd told Lucile about this ineffable nostalgia. Not about the other words, of course, but just this last one. " 'Balcony'?", she'd said with astonishment. "Why 'balcony'?" She repeated it: "Balcony, balcony", then asked him if he thought of it in the plural. He said yes. Then she asked if there had been balconies in his childhood, and he said no. She looked at him with fascination and, just as occurred every time she looked at him with something other than mere friendliness, a crazy hope would start to flutter inside him. But then she mumbled something about Baudelaire's *balcons du ciel*, his balconies in the sky, and that's where things remained. Nowhere, as usual.

Chapter 2

And yet he loved her; he didn't dare let her know just how much he loved her. Not that she would ever have taken any advantage of it, but just that it would have upset her, saddened her. It was already quite unexpected that she hadn't yet left him. All he offered her, after all, was security, and he knew that that was the least of her concerns. Or at least maybe it was.

He rang the bell, scooped up *Le Monde* from the floor, and tried reading. Nothing doing. He could just see Lucile driving too quickly, as usual, in the convertible — a very safe one, but even so — that he'd given her for Christmas. He'd called up a friend at the *Auto-Journal* to find out what the best sports car was, the one that held the road best, the safest make, and so on. He'd told Lucile it had been the easiest one to find, even tried to make it seem as if he'd ordered it on a whim the night before, "just casually". She had been thrilled. But if this morning he were to get a phone call telling him that a dark blue convertible had been found by the road, flipped on top of the body of a young woman whose papers... He stood up. He was being an idiot.

Pauline walked in, carrying him his breakfast on a tray. He smiled. "What's the weather like?"

"A bit overcast. But it smells like spring," said Pauline. She was sixty years old and had taken care of him for ten years. Poetic reflections were not her forte, however.

"Spring?" he repeated mindlessly.

"Yes, so said Mademoiselle Lucile. She came down to the kitchen before me, and she took an orange and said she had to run, that it smelled like spring."

Pauline smiled. Charles had been very worried, at the outset, that she would hate Lucile, but after a trial period of two months or so, Pauline's moral judgment emerged very clearly: Mademoiselle was ten years old, emotionally, and Monsieur, who wasn't any better, was simply incapable of protecting her against the vagaries of life. It was thus incumbent upon herself, Pauline, to take charge. So she dictated to Lucile, with admirable energy, when to take naps, what to eat, and not to indulge in drinking, and Lucile, quite taken by it all, or so it would seem, did as she was told. This was one of the small mysteries of his household that both befuddled and delighted Charles.

"All she took was an orange?" asked Charles.

"That's all. And she told me to tell You* to take a deep breath when You go out, because it smells like spring." Pauline's tone of voice was flat. Didn't she realize he was begging her to tell him more about what Lucile had said?

Pauline occasionally turned away from his gaze. At such moments he felt it wasn't Lucile that she resented, but the nature of his passion for her, his starved anguish, of which only Pauline caught rare glimpses, and which, despite her common sense and her maternal, slightly condescending acceptance of Lucile's personality, she was still at a loss to understand. She could have taken pity on him if he'd fallen under the spell of "a nasty lady", as she would put it, rather than of "a sweet person". She didn't realize, though, that things might be quite a bit worse than that.

---

* In this translation, the singular pronoun "You", when capitalized, corresponds to the formal or respectful second-person pronoun *vous* of French, and when uncapitalized, to the informal or intimate pronoun *tu*. See pages 90–92 of *Translator, Trader* for more on this convention.

CHAPTER 3

Claire Santré's apartment had once been very lavish, when poor old Santré had lived there. It was a little less so nowadays and you could see this in tiny details, such as the relative sparseness of the furniture, the blue curtains that had been dyed and re-dyed twenty times, and the wild appearance of the caterers, who occasionally took just a bit too long to remember which of the main salon's five doors led to the butler's quarters. Even so, it remained one of the loveliest apartments in the Avenue Montaigne, and invitations to Claire Santré's soirées were highly coveted. Claire herself was tall, slender, and energetic — a blonde who could just as easily have been a brunette. She was a bit over fifty though she didn't look it, and she spoke of love flippantly, in the manner of a worldly woman who is no longer seeking it but who retains good memories of it. As a consequence, women were very fond of her and men pursued her lustily, laughing all the while. She was one of that small, hardy cohort of Parisian women in their fifties who make it alone, not just staying alive but staying in style — on occasion even setting it.

At her elegant dinners, Claire Santré would invariably have one or two Americans and one or two Venezuelans, about whom she warned her friends ahead of time that they weren't terribly fun people but that she was doing business with them. As for them, they would inevitably be seated next to some fashionable Parisienne whose banter they couldn't quite keep up with, consisting, as it so often did, of riddles, unfinished allusions, and incomprehensible jokes, all of which one could expect them to recount with great mirth on their return to Caracas. And in exchange for this, Claire received exclusive French rights to Venezuelan fabrics, or sometimes the reverse, and there was never a lack of whiskey at her parties. All in all, Claire was an adroit woman, and she only spoke ill of someone if it was an absolute necessity in order to avoid looking foolish.

For ten years now, Charles Blassans-Lignières had been a mainstay of Claire's soirées. He had loaned her a great deal of money but he never reminded her of it at all. He was wealthy, good-looking, a man of few but well-chosen words, and every so often he would give in and take on a mistress from Claire's stable of *protégées*. It would generally last a year, sometimes two. He'd take them to Italy in August and he'd send them to Saint-Tropez when they complained of the summer heat, or to Megève when they complained of fatigue in winter. Each time, it would wind down with a lovely gift that spelled the death knell for their liaison, although usually no one knew quite why, and then, six months later, Claire would once again "go on the lookout" for him.

But it had now been some two full years that this calm and pragmatic man had been beyond the reach of Claire's romantic schemes. He had taken a real shine to Lucile, and Lucile was somehow elusive. She was lively, polite, and often amusing, but she obstinately refused to speak of herself, of Charles, or of her plans in life. Before meeting Charles, she had worked at a modest little newspaper — one of those papers that claim to be leftist so as not to have to remunerate their contributors very lavishly and whose social commitment goes no further than that. She'd pretty much stopped working for it as of late, and in fact, no one had the slightest idea how she spent her days. If she had a lover on the side, he certainly wasn't in Claire's entourage, even though Claire had sent several of her most appealing musketeers Lucile's way. But without success. One day, running out of ideas, Claire had suggested to Lucile that she try one of those Balzac-style affairs that so many Parisian women engage in, and which would at the very least endow her with a mink stole and a check from Charles worth at least as much as a mink.

"I don't need money," protested Lucile, "and I hate that kind of playing-around on the side." Her tone was curt and she could not even look Claire straight in the face. The latter, after a moment of panic, had one of those bolts from the blue that justified her social reputation. Taking Lucile's hands in hers, she said, "Thank You, *mon petit.* Please understand — I love Charles as a brother and I don't know You well. Excuse my indiscretion. In fact, if You had accepted, I would have been concerned for his sake."

On hearing this, Lucile burst out laughing and Claire, who had been vaguely hoping for Lucile to melt forgivingly in her arms, became quite worried about what Lucile might tell Charles, until the next dinner where, to her relief, she saw he was still just the same old Charles. So Lucile knew how to keep quiet.

Part I: *Le printemps*

Or, perhaps, how to forget.

In any case, this spring had something troublesome up its sleeve. Claire was mumbling to herself while looking over the food the caterers had just brought, and Johnny, who by convention was always the first guest to arrive, was following her all about. He had gone for young men until he was forty-five, but now he no longer had the strength, after a hard day's work and a dinner in town, to go out on the prowl for a pretty boy at midnight. He settled for tailing them with a melancholy gaze at fancy receptions. High-society living kills everything, even vices. Even the pious will have to give it credit for this. Johnny had thus become Claire's devoted knight-at-arms. He accompanied her to premières and to dinners, and he played the host at her apartment a bit uneasily but with great aplomb. His name was actually Jean, but as everyone seemed to prefer the jauntier sound of "Johnny", he had bowed to popular demand, and over two decades he'd even managed to acquire a slight Anglo-Saxon accent.

"Who's on Your mind, my sweet?" asked Johnny. "You seem very nervous."

"I was thinking about Charles. I was also thinking about Diane. Tonight, you know, she's supposed to bring that stunning new beau of hers along. I've only seen him once, but I'm not counting on him to liven up the festivities. How can such a gorgeous thirty-year-old be so glum?"

"Diane's got the wrong idea, always falling for intellectuals. It's never worked for her."

"Oh, there are intellectuals who are perfectly fun," said

Claire tolerantly. "But Antoine in any case is no intellectual. All he does is put out a series of books at Renouard's. And what do they pay in publishing? Nothing. You know that as well as I do. And so Diane's money, luckily for her, has just what it takes to…"

"I don't think he cares so much about that," said Johnny in a quiet voice. He found Antoine very desirable.

"Well, he'll come around to it," said Claire with a world-weary tone that bespoke long experience. "Diane's in her forties and rolling in dough, while he's thirty and brings home only 200,000 francs* a month. Such a mismatch can't last forever."

Johnny started to laugh but then cut it off all at once. He had put on a cream to cover up his wrinkles — Pierre-André had suggested it — and he hadn't given it enough time to dry. He was supposed to keep a stony face until 8:30. But come to think of it, it *was* 8:30, so Johnny took up his laugh again, and Claire shot an astonished look at him. Johnny was an angel, but he'd been hit a few times by enemy fire back in '42 when he was playing the hero in the R.A.F., and something in his brain had surely been damaged. It was a… what do they call it?… a *lobe* — yes, a lobe must have been affected. She looked at him with amusement. When you thought that those slender white hands, now arranging the flowers on the table with such great care, had once

---

* In 1960, the French franc was reset to 100 old francs — *anciens francs* — but a large fraction of the French populace kept speaking for many years only in old francs, as does Claire here, and as do all the characters in *La Chamade*. 100 old francs were worth roughly 20 American cents, so Antoine's salary of 200,000 old francs was worth about $400.

grasped a machine gun and a joystick and had brought flaming airplanes safely home in the blackest of night… Human beings were really unpredictable. You could never know all there was to know about anyone. And that was in fact precisely why Claire was never bored. She gave a long sigh of satisfaction, which was suddenly cut off by the tight silk ribbon of her dress. Cardin was too much — he thought of her as a mere sylph!

•   •   •

Lucile tried to hide a yawn; all it took was inhaling on the side of her mouth and exhaling quietly in front, through her teeth. Maybe it looked a little rabbit-like, but at least that way one's eyes weren't full of tears afterwards. This dinner seemed like it would never end. She was seated between poor Johnny, who'd been nervously rubbing his cheeks during the entire meal, and a good-looking but very taciturn young man who she'd been told was Diane Mirbel's new lover. His quietness didn't bother her, though. She didn't have the slightest interest in being charming this evening. She'd gotten up too early. She tried to recall the scent of that damned breeze and closed her eyes for a moment. When she opened them, her gaze was met by Diane's, who was looking at her so sternly that she was bewildered. Was Diane that terribly in love with this young man, or was she jealous? Lucile glanced over at him: his hair was so blond as to look ashen, and he had a very determined chin. He was rolling up a little ball of dough. In fact, there was a whole lineup of little bread-balls around his plate.

The conversation had turned to the theater, and things were

getting lively because Claire was swooning over a play that Diane abhorred. Lucile made a stab at small talk by asking her neighbor, "Have You seen this play?"

"No. I never go to the theater. How about You?"

"Not often. Last time I went, I saw this English comedy, very delightful, at the Atelier, with that actress who later died in a car crash — what was her name?"

"Sarah," he said in a very subdued voice, slowly lowering his hands to the tablecloth.

On seeing the tension in his face, Lucile was petrified. Her instant reaction was, "Oh my God, what an unhappy fellow!"

"Forgive me," she said.

He turned towards her and asked, "What?" in a doleful voice. He didn't even seem to see her. She heard him breathing right next to her, very unevenly, the way someone does who's just been hit hard, and the thought that she'd been the one who'd hit him, even though unwittingly, was unbearable for her. She never derived any pleasure from teasing people, let alone from being cruel.

"What are You daydreaming about, Antoine?" The tone of Diane's voice had a peculiar quality to it, a little too light a lilt, and for a moment there was an awkward silence. Antoine didn't say a word in reply; he seemed blind and deaf.

"Oh, there's no doubt about it — he's daydreaming!" exclaimed Claire with a chuckle. "Antoine, Antoine…"

He still said nothing, and now silence reigned over the whole room. All the guests, their forks frozen in mid-air, were watching this pallid young man, who himself was staring with no particular interest at a carafe in the middle of the table. Out of the blue, Lucile put her hand on his shirtsleeve, and he seemed to wake up.

"You were saying…?"

"I was saying that You were daydreaming," said Diane in a curt fashion, "and we were wondering what about. Is it indiscreet to ask?"

"It's always indiscreet," interpolated Charles. He, like everyone else, was now looking very attentively at Antoine, who had arrived as Diane's latest lover, or perhaps her gigolo, but who all at once had become a Young Man Who Daydreamed. And a sudden flash of envy and nostalgia swept over the table.

There was also a flash of resentment in Claire's brain. After all, this was a dinner for a privileged class of people, well-known people, brilliant and witty people, people who were up on everything. This young lad should have been listening, laughing, lapping it all up with gratitude. If he was daydreaming about having a *croque-monsieur* with some young cutie in a Latin-quarter snack-bar, well then, let him just dump Diane, one of the most successful and charming women in all of Paris. And who, by the way, didn't look close to her age of forty-five… Except tonight; tonight she was very pale and edgy. If Claire didn't know her so well, she could easily have thought she was unhappy.

In any case, Claire went on: "I bet You were dreaming of a Ferrari! Carlos just bought the latest model, he took me for a spin in it the other day, and I thought my time had come. But by God, the fellow really knows how to drive!" she added with a touch of surprise, for Carlos was next in line for some royal something-or-other, and to Claire it seemed rather miraculous that he knew how to do anything at all other than just hang around in Paris's ritziest hotels while awaiting the return of the monarchy.

Antoine looked towards Lucile and smiled at her. He had light brown eyes, almost yellow, a strong nose, a wide and attractive mouth, and something very virile in his face that contrasted with the pallor and adolescent delicacy of his hair.

"Please forgive me," he said very softly. "You must think I'm very rude." He was looking straight at her, his gaze not sliding lazily down to the tablecloth or onto her shoulders, as so often happened, and he seemed to be focused on her completely, to the exclusion of the rest of the company.

"In just three sentences, we've already said 'Forgive me' twice," replied Lucile.

"We're doing things backwards," said Antoine jovially. "Couples always wind up saying, 'Forgive me', or at least one of the two does. 'Please forgive me — I just don't love you any more.'"

"At least that's still quite civil. What really gets me, personally, is the 'honest' style: 'Please forgive me, I thought I loved you, but I was wrong. It's my duty to tell you.'"

"Surely that hasn't happened to You very often," said Antoine.

"Thanks a *lot*!"

"What I meant is, You surely haven't given many men the chance to say such a thing to You. Your bags would have already been in the taxi!"

Part I: Le printemps

"Especially since all I carry around is a couple of sweaters and a toothbrush," said Lucile rather merrily.

After a puzzled moment Antoine replied, "Hm! And here I'd been thinking You were Blassans-Lignières' mistress."

"What a shame," thought Lucile to herself. "He'd seemed pretty bright till now." For her, there was no way that such crassness and intelligence could coexist in one person.

"It's true, You're quite right," she said. "And if I were to leave him now, it would actually be in my own car, and with plenty of dresses, to boot. Charles is very generous." She had been speaking in a calm voice. Antoine looked down.

"I'm sorry, but I just hate this dinner and this atmosphere."

"Well, don't come to such parties any more. After all, at Your age, it's dangerous."

"You know, *mon petit*," said Antoine, looking suddenly put upon, "I'm without any doubt older than You are."

She burst out laughing, and as she did so, both Diane and Charles looked over at the two of them. Diane and Charles had been placed next to each other, at the far end of the table, looking directly towards their *protégés* — the parents at one end, their children at the other — thirty-year-old children who refused to act like grown-ups. Lucile cut her laugh short: after all, she was making nothing of her life, and there was no one that she loved. What a joke! If she hadn't by nature been so full of *joie de vivre*, she would have killed herself.

Antoine was laughing, and Diane was suffering. She'd seen him burst out laughing, with some female. Antoine never laughed with her. She would much rather he'd kissed Lucile.

Chapter 3

She despised this laugh, and this sudden youthful glow that had come out of nowhere. What on earth were they laughing about? She glanced over at Charles, but he seemed touched by it all. Well, she knew he'd grown a little nutty over the past two years. This kid Lucile had a bit of charm and she behaved perfectly well, but she was no great beauty and she wasn't a great wit either. For that matter, neither was Antoine. She'd had men far better-looking than Antoine go head over heels for her. Yes, head over heels. It's just that, well, Antoine was the one that she loved now. She loved him, she yearned for him to love her, and one day she would surely have him all to herself. He would forget about that dead little actress, and he'd only think of her, Diane…

Sarah… How many times had she heard that name, "Sarah". He'd talked about her all the time at the outset, until one day when Diane, at her wits' end, had said to him that Sarah had been unfaithful to him and that moreover everyone knew it. He simply replied, "I knew it, too," in a flat voice, and after that her name never came up again between them. But he still muttered it at night, while sleeping. But soon, soon… when he would turn over in his sleep and stretch his arm out across her body in the dark, it would be *her* name that he'd murmur.

All at once Diane felt her eyes filling up with tears. She started to cough, and Charles kindly patted her on the back. This dinner seemed like it would never end. Claire Santré had drunk a little too much, which was happening more and more often these days. She was holding forth very insistently about painting, and at a level considerably above her knowledge, and

Johnny, whose passion was art, looked like he was being tortured.

"And so," Claire was saying exuberantly, "when the delivery guy turned up at my door with this package in his arms, and when I got the thing out in the open, I thought I was going blind, and so you know what I said to him?"

The assembled company boredly shook its collective head.

"Well, I said to him: 'My good man, I thought I had eyes to see with, but by God, I was wrong; I don't see a thing on this canvas, my man, not one blessed thing.'" And with an eloquent gesture, doubtless intended to convey the emptiness of the canvas, Claire emptied out her wineglass on the tablecloth. Everyone took this as a cue to rise from the table, but Lucile and Antoine did so looking at the floor, for they were both giggling like crazy.

CHAPTER 4

Enough cannot be said of the benefits, the dangers, and the power of shared laughter. It is no less central to love than are affection, desire, and despair. The shared laughter of Antoine and Lucile was the sudden mirth of schoolchildren. Both of them were desired, disrobed, and adored by serious persons, and knowing they would inevitably suffer the consequences in one way or another, they gave themselves over to their giggling in one corner of the salon. Parisian etiquette, although it requires lovers to be seated apart at dinner, offers in compensation a small respite after dinner, during which lover finds lover and the two exchange observations, words of tenderness, or possibly reproaches. Diane was thus waiting for Antoine to come join her, and Charles had taken a first step towards Lucile. But Lucile was determinedly looking out the window, with tears of laughter clouding her eyes, and the moment her gaze met that of Antoine, who was standing close by, she quickly turned away, while he hid his face in his handkerchief. For a little while, Claire did her best to ignore them, but it was undeniable that jealousy and even a slight resentment were taking over the salon. She dispatched Johnny, with a flip of her head that meant, "Tell those children to shape up fast or they will not be invited back" — but unfortunately her gesture was intercepted by Antoine, who quickly turned away to conceal his mirth. Johnny in the meanwhile played it lightly:

"For pity's sake, Lucile, clue me in — I'm dying of curiosity."

"Oh, it's nothing," she replied, "Nothing at all. In fact, that's what's so terrible!"

"Terrible," echoed Antoine, whose hair was all mussed up, and who suddenly looked even younger and more dazzling, and Johnny felt a sharp surge of raging desire.

But Diane was approaching. She was filled with wrath, and her wrath became her. Her celebrated regal carriage, her famous green eyes, and her extreme slenderness made a true warhorse of her.

"So what did you say to each other that you found so hilarious?" queried Diane in an even voice but in which one could detect both tolerance and insecurity, but mostly the latter.

"Oh — us? Nothing, really," replied Antoine very innocently. But that little word "us", a word she had never once squeezed out of him, neither for any shared hope nor for any shared memory, pushed Diane to the boiling point.

"Well, kindly stop acting in such a rude fashion," she intoned. "If the two of you can't be pleasant, then at least be polite."

There ensued a moment of silence. To Lucile it seemed understandable for Diane to snap at her lover, but issuing orders to the two of them struck her as a bit over the top.

"You've lost control of Yourself," said Lucile. "You have no right to tell me not to laugh."

"Nor me," said Antoine with deliberation.

"And now you must excuse me — I'm terribly tired," replied Diane. "Good night. Charles, would You mind taking me home?" she said to the unlucky gentleman who had just walked up. "I've got a splitting headache."

Charles bowed politely, and Lucile gave him a smile, adding, "I'll see You at home."

With Charles and Diane gone, a jolly pandemonium broke out, the kind that typically follows a big scene at a soirée, with everyone talking at cross-purposes for several minutes before settling down to gossip about the juicy event that had just taken place. Lucile and Antoine, however, stayed out of it. She leaned against the balcony railing and looked at him pensively, while he calmly puffed on a cigarette.

"I'm terribly sorry," she said. "I really shouldn't have flown off the handle like that."

"Just come along with me," replied Antoine. "I'll take You home before things get too dramatic."

Claire shook their hands with a knowing look. They were quite right to go home, but she knew all too well what being young was all about. And indeed, they did make quite an attractive couple. She could even help them out... but what was she thinking? What about her friend Charles Blassans-Lignières? Had she lost her mind tonight?

• • •

Paris was dark, glowing, and seductive, and so they decided to walk back home. The relief that they had initially felt as they watched the door close on their would-be co-conspirator Claire was now turning into a sudden yearning either to split up immediately or else to get to know each other, but in any case to do something that would put a completely different cap on this disjointed evening. Lucile had no desire whatsoever to play the role that all the guests' eyes had been urging on her when she'd bidden them all good night: that of the young woman who leaves her elderly protector in the lurch to go off with some dashing young blade. This was utterly out of the question. After all, she'd once said to Charles, "I may make You unhappy, but I'll never make You seem ridiculous." And in fact, the few times that she had been unfaithful to him, he would have had no reason to suspect anything at all. This soirée, though, *had* been ridiculous.

What was she doing, hanging around in the streets with this total stranger? She turned towards him and he smiled back at her. "Don't look so down in the mouth. We'll get a drink on the way home, all right?"

But in truth they had several. They went into five bars, while avoiding two others that clearly would have been unbearable for Antoine to set foot in with anyone other than Sarah, and the whole time they talked and talked. They crossed and recrossed the Seine while talking, then headed up the Rue de Rivoli as far as the Place de la Concorde, went into Harry's Bar, and left it just as fast. That morning's very same breeze had now picked up again, and Lucile was almost keeling over from a mixture of extreme drowsiness, too much whiskey, and all that attention.

Chapter 4

"She was being unfaithful to me, You understand," said Antoine. "The poor thing really believed that this was the thing to do — to sleep around with producers and journalists and the like. She lied to me day and night and I resented her, I acted proud, I acted ironic, and I judged her harshly. But by what right, my God — for she loved me — yes, there's no doubt, she did love me — it wasn't like she was mooching off of me... And then that evening, the day before she died, she practically begged me not to let her leave for Deauville. But all I said to her was: 'Go on, go on — it's what you've got your heart set on.' What a fool, what an arrogant fool I was!"

As they walked by a bridge, he inquired about Lucile's life.

"I've never understood anything at all about anything," said Lucile. "Life mostly made sense to me until I left my parents' home. I wanted to get a degree in Paris. But it was all a pipe dream. Ever since, I've been looking everywhere for parents, in my lovers, in my friends, and it's all right with me to have nothing of my own — not any plans and not any worries. I like this kind of life, it's terrible but true. I don't know why it is, but the moment I wake up something in me feels things are going right. I'll never be able to change. What could I do? Work? I don't have any great talents. Maybe I'd have to love someone, the way You do. Oh, Antoine, Antoine, why on earth are You involved with Diane?"

"She loves me," he replied. "And I go for thin, tall women like her. Sarah was short and stocky, and that brought tears of pity to my eyes. Do You know what I mean? But she also got on my nerves."

Part I: *Le printemps*

Tiredness suited him well. They were walking up the Rue du Bac, and decided on a whim to go into a rather ghastly smoke-shop café. Inside, they looked at each other without smiling but unjudgmentally. The jukebox was playing some familiar Strauss waltz to which a tipsy customer was trying to dance, teeteringly, at one end of the bar. "It's late, it's very late," whispered a little voice inside Lucile's head. "Charles must be going out of his mind with worry. You don't even like this fellow, so just go home."

And all at once, she found that her cheek was pressed tightly against Antoine's jacket. With one arm, he was holding her against himself, wordlessly, with his chin on her hair. She felt a strange calm settling over the two of them. The bartender, the tipsy dancer, the music, the lights all seemed to be eternal — or then again, maybe she herself had never existed. She couldn't figure anything out any more. They took a taxi and he left her at her door. They said good-bye to each other in a polite fashion, without even exchanging addresses or phone numbers.

CHAPTER 5

$\mathcal{B}ut$ the social whirl lost no time in reuniting them. Diane had made a scene and there was not one woman who'd been at that dinner who could possibly imagine inviting Diane back without inviting Charles, or more precisely, Antoine without Lucile. Diane had switched sides without warning: she had moved from the side of the executioners, where she had done very well for herself for twenty full years, over to the victims' side. She was jealous, she had let it be seen, and now she was lost. The distant blare of hunting horns could be heard in the sweet Parisian spring.

By one of those strange reversals that were so typical of this upper-crust crowd, everything that had once contributed to her prestige and power now became part of her vulnerability: her beauty was "no longer quite what it had been in her youth", her jewels were now "no longer adequate" (whereas a mere week earlier the tiniest one of them would have been just fine for any of her friends), and even her Rolls-Royce, "which wasn't going to leave her", seemed impotent. Poor Diane: her craving had turned inside out just like a glove and now everything was exposed; no matter how much makeup she caked on her face, no matter how heavily she loaded herself down with diamonds, the only companion she would now be able to take for a spin in her fancy car was her Pekingese pooch. At last, at last, Diane had become an object of pity.

Of course she knew all this. She was so familiar with her town, and she'd had the good luck, when she was thirty, to marry an intelligent writer who had given her a few lessons in the intricacies of Parisian high society but who then one day, completely turned off by it all, had simply flown the coop. Diane undeniably had pluck, which she owed in equal parts to an Irish background, a sadistic nanny she'd had when very little, and her personal fortune, which was sizable enough that she had never had to curry favor with anyone at all. But adversity, no matter what some might say, humiliates everyone, women in particular, and now Diane, who had essentially never succumbed to passion, who had only deigned to turn her gaze towards men who first eyed her with interest, all of a sudden found herself, to her horror, staring with longing at Antoine, who was looking in another direction altogether. And already she was calculating how to win him back without recourse to feminine wiles.

What did he covet? He didn't care at all for money. He earned a pathetic little salary from his publishing house and when he couldn't afford to invite her out, he simply refused to go to restaurants. And thus she was condemned to having frequent *tête-à-tête* dinners with him at her place, a situation that would have seemed ludicrous to her only six months ago. But luckily, there were premières galore, and an endless succession of society suppers and fancy banquets — all those delights that Paris offers with no strings attached to those who are sufficiently well-heeled.

From time to time Antoine said, in a vague tone of voice,

that all he cared about was books and that one of these days he would make it big in the publishing world. And it was true that at these dinners, he only grew lively if he ran into someone who was willing to chew the fat about literature at least a little bit with him.

That year, as it happened, sharing one's bed with an author was quite the fashion, which inspired Diane to suggest to Antoine, "Maybe you could win the Goncourt!" He, however, retorted that he was lousy at writing and that you had to be top-notch to tackle a book at all, let alone win a prize. She didn't give up, and urged him, "But I'm sure that if you tried...", or "Don't you remember old X, who...?" — but Antoine, never one to shout, just shouted back, "It's out of the question!" No, he would wind up as an editor at Renouard, pulling down 200,000 francs a month, and even fifty years down the road he'd still be dripping endless tears for Sarah. And yet, despite it all, Diane loved him.

•   •   •

After that terrible dinner, she had not slept a wink: Antoine had finally returned to his apartment at dawn, drunk without any doubt. She had phoned him every hour, poised to hang up the moment she heard his voice; all she wanted was to know where he was. At 6:30, he'd finally answered, whispering just "I'm very sleepy" in a childish voice, and without even asking who was calling. He must have hung out in those bars along Saint-Germain, and quite likely with Lucile. But she had better not mention Lucile to him — one should never name what one is afraid of. The next day, she called up Claire to apologize for her hasty exit; she'd had such a frightful headache all evening.

"It's true — You looked pretty awful," said Claire in a friendly and understanding manner.

"Well, I'm not getting any younger," said Diane bitterly. "And these young studs can be pretty demanding."

Claire gave a knowing laugh. She took great delight in hearing hints, or, more precisely, specific descriptions of lascivious activity, and there's no one on this earth who can be more specific and precise about the virility of her lover than one Parisian socialite talking to another. It was as if the constant use of passionate adjectives for their dress designers left them no choice but to use raw physical terms in describing their lovers. And thus, after a few rather favorable comments had been exchanged about Antoine, Claire was growing edgy while Diane was talking in circles. But then Claire took a daring plunge: "That little Lucile is quite annoying, with her stupid schoolgirl giggling. How old is she, anyway — thirty or so?"

"She's got lovely gray eyes," said Diane, "and if it's good enough for our fine friend Charles…"

"Two years with *her* has got to be a damn long stretch," sighed Claire.

"But it's with him as well, my treasure, and don't You forget it!" With that witticism, both women burst out laughing and hung up feeling delighted. Diane felt she'd somehow made up for the scene the night before. And Claire could say that Diane, who never had second thoughts about anything she did, had called up at noon to apologize. The thing was, Diane had

Chapter 5

forgotten a key principle of Parisian society, which is that one must never apologize for anything at all, and that whatever one does must be done with an insouciant air.

And so Johnny, following Claire's instructions, had Charles Blassans-Lignières invited to the première of a play where Diane too was supposed to show up. It was agreed that afterwards, they would all go out — "just us friends" — to dinner somewhere. Aside from the amusement that the Lucile–Antoine reunion would provide her, Claire had the assurance that Charles would cover the dinner all by himself. And this was most convenient, since Johnny, after all, was scraping the bottom of the barrel these days, and it was inconceivable to ask Diane to pay, and Claire couldn't remember if she'd had the sense to invite any other rich male — a precious species, by the way, that was rapidly growing endangered in this day and age when pretty much the only decently upkept people were men belonging to men. In any case, the play would certainly be most entertaining because it was by Bijou Dubois, and if anyone knew what good theater was, it was Bijou Dubois.

"What the hell, my darling," Claire was saying to Johnny as they rode together in a taxi to the Atelier, "I really can't take any more of Your modern theater. When I watch actors seated in big plush chairs droning on and on with platitudes about life, I'm bored to tears. And I won't hide it from You," she added with verve, "I far prefer the lighter fare on the boulevards... Johnny, are You listening?"

Johnny, who was hearing this same refrain of Claire's for the umpteenth time this season, nodded sagely. Claire was a dear but her intensity exhausted him, and suddenly he had a strong yearning to jump out of the taxi, saunter up the Boulevard de Clichy, swarming with people, buy himself a cone of sizzling *frites,* and, who knows, maybe even get beaten up by a mugger. The schemes Claire cooked up struck him as so simplistic, and he was always amazed when they actually worked.

At the Place Dancourt, all the guests were mingling nicely, saying hello and earnestly telling each other that this was without any doubt Paris's loveliest theater but that this little square where it was located was frightfully provincial. Out of the blue, Lucile appeared, emerging from a café with Charles, and she sat down on a bench to devour a huge sandwich. After a moment or two of tsk-tsking, a couple of hungry guests followed suit. Just then, Diane's car pulled up with its noiseless purr and parked more or less randomly very close to the bench. After Antoine got out, he opened the door for Diane and then turned around. He spotted Lucile with her mouth full of food and looking happy, and Charles as well, who was rising in embarrassment to greet Diane.

"My goodness — you're all having a picnic? What a splendid idea!" said Diane. She had already glanced about and noticed Edmée de Guilt, Doudou Wilson, and Madame Bert, who were all following Lucile's lead and eating at various benches.

"It's nine o'clock, and they won't start for at least a quarter of an hour. Antoine, be a good boy and trot over to that café for me, would You? I'm starving."

Antoine balked. Lucile watched him look at the café and at Diane, weighing things in his mind, and then make a resigned gesture and head off across the street. When he pushed open the café door, Lucile saw the owner rise immediately, walk around the counter, and shake his hand with a look of deep commiseration. Then the waiter came over as well. Lucile could only see Antoine's back, but she had the impression that he was recoiling, slowly collapsing almost as if under a hail of blows. And then all at once she recalled: Sarah. This same theater, the rehearsals, the café where Antoine must so often have waited for her. And to which he'd never returned.

"For Heaven's sake, is Antoine hoisting a few in there, or what?" said Diane. As she turned around, she saw Antoine trying to back out of the café door, as if apologizing, and without a single sandwich for anyone. Right then the owner's wife entered, nodding her head warmly and taking Antoine's hand in hers. How often he must have laughed with her, in the old days, while waiting for Sarah. It was always so merry in the cafés next to theaters during rehearsals.

"What's eating at him?" asked Diane.

"Sarah," replied Lucile, without looking at her.

That name troubled Diane but she knew that one shouldn't ask Antoine any questions about her, one shouldn't even talk to him about her. He came back to the group, his face white as a sheet. In a flash Diane understood, and she turned around so abruptly that Lucile had to jerk backwards to avoid being hit.

"So," thought Diane, "this girl knows the story, too — but by what right?" Antoine belonged to her, Diane, and so did his laugh and so did his grief. It was on *her* shoulder that he dreamed, late at night, of Sarah. It was over *her*, Diane, that he preferred the memory of Sarah. It...

But the theater bell was ringing. Diane took Antoine's arm and ushered him in. He let himself be led along, distractedly. After politely greeting a few critics — friends of Diane's — he helped her sit down. The traditional three knocks resounded in the hall, and, in the darkness, Diane leaned over him, saying, "Oh, my poor baby."

And he offered no resistance when she took his hand.

CHAPTER 6

At the intermission, they split into two smaller groups. Lucile and Antoine smiled at each other from afar, and, for the first time, each of them felt a little spark for the other. He watched her talking, absent-mindedly leaning on Charles' powerful shoulder, and the curve of her neck and the slightly amused flair of her mouth attracted him. He wished he could just cut his way through the crowd and kiss her. It had been ages since he'd felt desire, out of the blue, for a woman he didn't know. Just at this moment she turned around and her gaze met his and she froze, recognizing the meaning of his look, but then she forced an awkward little smile. She had never before paid any attention to Antoine's good looks; it had taken his desire for her to awaken in her a sensitivity to his attractiveness. The truth of the matter was that she had been this way her whole life, never taking any notice — whether by sheer luck or out of a nearly pathological fear of involvement — of anyone but men who took a fancy to her. But now, as she turned away from Antoine, imagining his sensual mouth and the golden light in his eyes, she wondered how it could possibly have happened that they had failed to kiss, the other evening.

Charles, feeling her pulling away from his shoulder, glanced at her and at once recognized that soft, pensive, nearly resigned look that came over her face whenever she was warming up to someone. On turning around, he saw it was Antoine.

At the play's end, the little group pulled back together. Claire was raving about the acting as well as the jewels of some maharani she'd spotted, and also about the weather's unusual mildness — all in all, she was in a quite euphoric mood. People were having trouble settling on a restaurant, but in the end they decided to go to a place out in Marnes, as it was clear to everyone that the greenery and the evening air would please Claire no end. Diane's driver was waiting patiently, when all of a sudden Charles walked up to Diane and said, "Would You mind taking me in Your car, Diane? We arrived in Lucile's convertible but this evening I'm feeling a bit decrepit, and I may be coming down with a cold. Let Antoine go with Lucile."

Diane didn't blink; instead, it was Claire who stared and then rolled her eyes in disbelief.

"Well, why not?", said Diane. "I'll see You in a bit, Antoine — just don't drive too fast." And so Charles and Diane joined Claire and Johnny in the Rolls, while Lucile and Antoine remained on the sidewalk, slightly stunned. Neither Charles nor Diane looked back at them, but Claire sent them a such a merry conspiratorial wink that they were shocked, and both pretended not to have seen it. Lucile was puzzled. It was perfectly in keeping with Charles' character to bring suffering upon himself, but how, she wondered, could he possibly have picked up on a desire in her that even she herself had only become aware of an hour earlier? This was quite annoying. The only times she'd ever been unfaithful to Charles were with young men she knew he would never run into anywhere. If there was anything she hated, it was when two lovers made secret little plots behind the back of a third, and the amused titterings that this gave rise to in observers such as Claire. Lucile did not want to be a party to anything of the sort. And so, when Antoine placed his hand on her shoulder, she shook her head. But on the other hand, life was simple, it was a lovely evening, and she was drawn to this new fellow. So, wait and see. The number of times she'd said "wait and see" to herself in her thirty years of existence was way beyond counting. She found herself chuckling.

"What's so funny?" asked Antoine.

"Oh, I was just amused at myself. The car's up the hill there. Let's see — where are my keys? Do You want to drive?"

And so he drove. They stayed silent at first, just taking in the fresh night air in the open convertible, both feeling ill at ease. Antoine was driving slowly. Only when they reached the Place de l'Étoile did he turn towards her and ask, "Why did Charles do that?"

"I don't know," replied Lucile. And as soon as they had exchanged these words, they both realized that they amounted to an admission, a confirmation of their furtively exchanged smiles at the intermission, and now it was undeniable that something was up between them and that there would be no going back. She was thinking, "Why didn't I just say, 'Oh, that?' and cast Charles' act as the very sensible decision of a man who's catching a cold?" But she'd been too slow on the uptake. Now all she wanted was to get to the restaurant quickly. Or else for Antoine to make some out-of-line remark or a crude pass at her, and she'd then quickly send him on his way. But Antoine was staying silent and driving calmly through the Bois de Boulogne. As they followed the twists of the Seine in their purring convertible, they must have looked for all the world like two golden lovers — she the daughter of the Dupont textile empire, he the son of the Dubois confectionery kingdom, with their wedding set for one week hence in the Palais de Chaillot, with both families in full accord. They would have two children.

"Just one more bridge now," announced Antoine as he made the turn toward Marnes. "How many bridges you and I have crossed together!" This was the first allusion to their recent escapade. All at once Lucile recalled how she'd stayed hidden behind his jacket in that little café, something she'd entirely forgotten about. Feeling flustered, she replied, "Yes, that's quite true — it's…"

And as she vaguely waved her hand in the air, Antoine caught it in his and squeezed it tenderly, not letting go. They were entering the Parc de Saint-Cloud. "Let's see," thought Lucile, "he'll hold my hand while we cross Saint-Cloud, it's springtime… Nothing to panic over — I'm not a sixteen-year-old girl, after all." But her heart was throbbing wildly and it felt as if all the blood was flowing out of her face and hands and was collecting in her throat and choking her.

When he pulled over to the side of the road, Lucile's head was spinning. He took her in his arms, kissed her passionately, and she could feel him trembling as much as she was. He sat back up, looked at her, and she returned his gaze without flinching at all, and then he reached for her again. This time he kissed her slowly, deliberately, kissed her temples, her cheeks, then back to her mouth, and as she looked at this calm, sensitive face hovering just above her own, she knew beyond a doubt that she would see it again many times just like this, and she knew that from this moment on, she would be like putty in his hands. She had totally forgotten that one can hunger for someone so deeply. She must have been in a long, deep sleep. For how long? Two, three years? But she couldn't think of any other face that had had such an impact.

"What's come over me?" whispered Antoine uneasily while nuzzling Lucile's hair, "What's come over me?"

As she smiled, Antoine felt her cheek rubbing against his, and he smiled back.

"We've got to rejoin the others," said Lucile softly.

"No," said Antoine, "No...", but a moment later he released her, and the sudden loss they both felt left no doubt as to the power of what was happening to them.

Antoine quickly started the car and Lucile crookedly put her makeup back on. When they pulled up at the restaurant, they saw the Rolls was already there, and they realized in a flash that they could have passed it in Paris, that it could have been behind them as they entered Saint-Cloud, and it could easily have come up behind them and surprised them in its headlights, like two birds in the night. This hadn't occurred to them for a second. But there it was now, reigning over the small square, a symbol of power and luxury and of their ties to the others, and the little blue convertible parked next to it seemed ridiculously childish and vulnerable.

•   •   •

Lucile was taking off her makeup. She felt totally exhausted and she was scrutinizing the tiny wrinkles that were beginning to appear at the corners of her eyes and mouth, wondering what meaning they had, and who or what had provoked them. These were not wrinkles due to passion or to hard work. There was no doubt that they were signs of her easy life, her idleness, her frivolity — and, for a brief moment, she revolted herself. She wiped her forehead with one hand, thinking to herself that in the past year she'd been having more and more of these flashes of self-loathing. She would have to go see her doctor soon. Surely it was just a matter of blood pressure. All she'd need to do was take some vitamins, and then she could once again start wasting her life (or dreaming it away) every bit as gaily as before. She heard herself saying, with a trace of rancor, "Charles... Why did You let me go off alone with Antoine?"

The moment she said it, she realized that she was seeking to provoke a scene, a drama — anything other than this calm self-loathing. And she knew Charles would be the one to pay the price, the one who would suffer. It was one thing for her to be drawn only to extremes, but it was quite another to demand that others indulge this peculiarity of hers. Anyway, the query had already been launched, and, like a javelin, it was now sailing across her bedroom and across the landing and was heading straight for Charles, who was unhurriedly undressing for the night in his own bedroom. He was so tired that for a brief moment he thought he might dodge her question and just say,

Chapter 6

"Oh, You know, Lucile — I was just worried I was catching a cold." She wouldn't have asked for more clarity; her quests for truth, her *moments russes,* were never terribly long-lived. But at this point he felt a need to know, perhaps to suffer, for he had long since lost his youthful craving for security, a craving once so deep that it had caused him to overlook, for twenty-some years, all the escapades of his various mistresses.

"I thought You'd taken a shine to him." He didn't turn around, but just stared at himself in the mirror, noting with surprise that he hadn't turned pale.

"So You're quite determined to throw me into the arms of any man I'm attracted to?"

"Don't be so harsh on me, Lucile. Things are looking too worrisome this time."

But in fact, she'd already crossed his bedroom and was now wrapping her arms around his neck while cooing, "I'm sorry, so sorry" in a soft, blurry voice. As he looked in the mirror, all he could see, spilling over her shoulder, was Lucile's dark hair — a long shock of it falling onto her arm — and he felt surging up in him a familiar constriction of the heart, a familiar anguish: "She's all in the world I care for, and she'll never truly be mine. She'll leave me. How could I ever have imagined loving any other shock of hair, or any other human being?" Clearly, he mused, love must derive its power solely from this impression of irreplaceability.

"I didn't really mean what I said," said Lucile. "It's just that I don't like it when —"

"You don't like it when I'm so damn obliging," said Charles, now turning to face her. "But I assure You that I wasn't trying to oblige You. I just wanted to see if I'd been right about something, that's all."

"If You'd been right about *what*?"

"About the look on Your face as the two of you arrived at the restaurant. About that way You had of not looking at him. I know You too well, Lucile. He's turned Your head."

Lucile dropped her arms to her sides. "Well, so what?" she said. "Is it set in stone somewhere that if you're attracted to one person then that means some other person has to suffer? Won't I ever be able to find inner peace? Is this some kind of law of nature? And what have *You* done with all *Your* free time when apart from me? And with... with..."

She was growing confused and starting to sputter, but at the same time she had the very clear sensation of having always, her whole life through, been misunderstood.

"I never took any advantage of my free time away from You," said Charles as a sad little smile crossed his face, "because I'm in love with You, as You know very well. And as for Your freedom, it seems to me that life is wide open to You. You're drawn to Antoine, and that's a fact. Either You'll follow up on it or You won't, and either I'll find out about it or I won't. But there's nothing I can do about it in any case."

He had stretched himself out on his bed, in his dressing gown, while Lucile was standing near him. He sat up on the edge of the bed.

"It's true," said Lucile dreamily, "It's true..: I'm very drawn to him."

Chapter 6

They looked at each other. "If something started up between us, would You suffer?" said Lucile unexpectedly.

"Yes," said Charles. "Why?"

"Because if You said no, I would leave You," she replied starkly, and then stretched out partly on Charles' bed, her head on her hand, her knees pulled up to her chin, and her face filled with relief. In but two minutes, she was fast asleep, and Charles Blassans-Lignières had a very rough time sharing the blankets equitably with her.

CHAPTER 7

He got her number from Johnny and called her the next morning. At four o'clock, they met up at his place, in the half-bohemian, half-conventional room that he lived in on the Rue de Poitiers. As she entered, she didn't even see the room — all she saw was Antoine who kissed her without saying anything, not even a simple greeting, as if they hadn't been apart for an instant since Saint-Cloud. What then took place is that which takes place between a man and a woman who are invaded by a mutual fire.

Within moments, they were both sure they had never before known so intense a pleasure. They lost track of the boundaries of their bodies, and soon it became utterly irrelevant how modest or how crude were the words they were exchanging with each other. The notion that in only an hour or two they would have to part struck them as obscene. They already knew that from now on, whatever the other one did would always be welcome, and as they whisperingly rediscovered the vulgar, awkward, and puerile words of physical love, and also the pride and the gratitude for pleasure given and pleasure received, they constantly tossed them back and forth. And they knew that this moment was truly rare and that life offers no higher reward than the discovery of one's long-sought missing half. Physical passion —

once unforeseeable but now unavoidable — was going to turn what might have been merely a fling into a full-blown love affair.

The sky was darkening but neither one of them was willing to look at the clock. They smoked side by side, staring up at the ceiling, retaining on their bodies the mingled scents of love and tussling and sweat, and together they breathed them in as if they were warriors exhausted from a long fight from which both had emerged victorious. The sheets were lying scattered on the floor, and Antoine's hand was resting on Lucile's hip.

"I'll never again be able to run into you without blushing," said Lucile, "nor watch you leave without it hurting, nor talk to you in front of someone else without looking away."

Turning sideways and propping her head up on her hand, she surveyed the messy room and the narrow window. Antoine moved his hand to her shoulder and observed how straight and smooth her back was; a gulf of fifteen years, indeed an entire lifetime, separated her from Diane. As she looked back towards him, he squeezed her shoulder and then reached over and touched her face, gripping her lower jaw almost fiercely. He clenched his fingers around her face, covering her mouth with his palm. They stared at each other and, without exchanging a word, promised each other that no matter what, they would somehow share a thousand more hours just like these last few.

CHAPTER 8

"Wipe that frown off Your face, old boy," said Johnny. "We're at a cocktail party, not a horror show!"

And he handed a glass of wine to Antoine, who smiled vacuously while focusing intently on the front door. They'd been there for an hour, it was already around nine o'clock, and there was still no sign of Lucile. What the hell was she doing? She'd promised him she would come. He clearly recalled how she'd said, "Tomorrow, tomorrow," as she was walking out of his apartment. He hadn't seen her since then. Could she be mocking him? After all, she was living off of Blassans-Lignières — she was his mistress — and she could surely find young and willing males like him anywhere she looked. Maybe he'd simply dreamed the whole *Rouge et Noir* afternoon of the day before, or maybe for her it had merely been one of countless similar casual flings. Or else maybe he was just a conceited fool.

Diane, meanwhile, was heading his way with their host tight in tow — an American who everyone had told him was "nuts about literature".

"William, of course You know Antoine," she chirped confidently, as if it were inconceivable that anyone could be unaware that Antoine was her lover.

"Why yes, to be sure!", replied William, casting an admiring glance at Antoine.

"So what's next — is he going to open my mouth and inspect my teeth?" thought Antoine to himself, trying to contain his annoyance.

"William's been telling me all sorts of racy anecdotes about Scott Fitzgerald," resumed Diane. "He was a close friend of William's father. Antoine simply adores Fitzgerald. You've got to tell him everything, William, and don't hold anything back…"

But whatever else she said was lost on Antoine, for Lucile had just come in. Her eyes darted rapidly all around the room, and all at once Antoine understood Johnny's earlier quip: her face radiated terror, exactly as his must have just five short minutes ago. She caught sight of him and stopped her scan, and right then, out of pure reflex, Antoine, overcome by a flash of desire, started to move towards her. "I'm going to go right up to her, take her in my arms, kiss her on the mouth, and the hell with everyone else." Even from afar, Lucile detected his urge and for a split second she almost let him go ahead and do it. The night and the day had just been too long for her to bear, and then Charles had been so late coming home from work that for two whole hours she'd been frightened sick that they'd get to the party too late. And so there they stood, motionlessly facing each other now like two cars idling at a red light, and then suddenly, without warning, Lucile turned away with a quick jerk reflecting her exasperated sense of helplessness. She couldn't let Antoine do this, and she tried to convince herself that her motivation was to spare Charles, but deep down she knew that she was really reacting out of fear.

Chapter 8

Johnny, standing nearby, gave her a smile and looked at her with a peculiar sense of concern. She returned his smile and he took her arm to lead her to the buffet.

"You gave me a fright," said Johnny.

"I did? How?" She looked him straight in the eye. Oh, no — was it already all starting, after just one day? Your coterie of confidants, and your friends (the ones who know and the ones who don't), and all the snickering behind your back...? For God's sake, please, no...

Johnny shrugged his shoulders. "I'm terribly fond of You," he said gently. "You don't give a damn, but I care a great deal for You."

Something in his voice touched Lucile. She looked at him. He must be terribly lonely. "Why wouldn't I give a damn?"

"Because all You really care about is the things You Yourself like. Everything else is just in Your way. Don't You agree? Anyway, the chance to be part of our little circle here is pretty nice. And it'll let You stay sane a bit longer than otherwise."

She heard his words but they didn't register. Antoine had disappeared in a jungle of heads somewhere at the other end of the salon. Where was he? "Where are you, my crazy fool, my lover, Antoine, where have you hidden that great big bony body of yours, what good do those beautiful yellow eyes do you if you don't see me here, just a few steps away from you, my fool, my darling fool?" A wave of tenderness washed over her. What was Johnny prattling on about, now? Well, yes — *obviously* she only cared about things she liked — and right now, what she liked was Antoine. It struck her that for the first time in many years, something in her life was dazzlingly clear.

Johnny pondered this sudden clarity with a mixture of envy and sadness. There was no doubt that he was genuinely fond of Lucile — he liked her reticence when in public, the way certain things bored her, the way she laughed. But now he was seeing her face afresh — a younger-seeming, rather girlish face, almost wild from longing — and unbidden, a memory from deep in his past bubbled up of how he, too, had once felt such a wild longing, more powerful than anything else in the world. It had been Roger. Yes, he too had waited anxiously for someone to appear at salon gatherings, and he too had bounced between feelings that life was ending and that it was beginning to blossom again. But how much truth was there, and how much fantasy was there, in all these love stories?

Anyway, this brash young Antoine certainly hadn't wasted a moment — wasn't it only yesterday morning that he'd called, asking for Lucile's phone number? And so calmly, too, as if it were merely a routine kind of man-to-man thing. It was odd, but there definitely was, in their connection, a sort of masculine camaraderie, and it had never once crossed Johnny's mind to tell Claire about that phone call, even though it would surely have given her a *frisson* of secret delight. No, there were still a few little things that Johnny wouldn't do for Claire, even though, God knows, he needed money terribly.

Diane hadn't noticed Antoine's spontaneous step towards Lucile, since her dress had miraculously gotten snagged on the corner of a low pedestal at the very moment when Lucile walked in, so that only William had been caught off guard by the young man's abortive attempt to dart off just as Scott Fitzgerald's name came up. But in any case, only a moment later Antoine had regained his composure and was helping unsnag Diane, although as he did so, a few bits of glitter fell from her dress to the floor.

"Antoine, your hands are trembling," said Diane a little too loudly. Generally, she addressed Antoine with *vous* when they were in public, the hidden intent being that she could then audibly drop a *tu* every so often, as if by accident — but lately, these little "accidents" had been taking place just a tiny bit too often, and Antoine despised her for that. In fact, for the past two days he'd despised most everything about her. He couldn't stand her sleepiness, her voice, her elegant style, her way of moving — in short, he resented her very existence and the fact that the only thing she represented now for him was an entrée into these glitzy salons where Lucile might show up. And on top of it all, he hated himself for not having been able to bring himself to touch her since yesterday. She'd soon notice it and would get very upset. In this arena, Antoine had always acted very properly and reliably, in that curious way that a blend of sensuality and insensitivity tends to bring about. He had no idea, though, that this very weakness of his was a source of hope for Diane, who at times was terrified of her very efficient, unexpressive, unromantic lover. Thus it is that human passion is fueled by the slightest scrap, even by signals that are diametrically opposed to one's hopes.

In the meantime, Antoine was again scanning the room for Lucile. He knew she was around, and now he was watching the door just as anxiously out of fear that she might leave as he had been watching it only minutes earlier in the hope that she would come in. The sudden voice of Blassans-Lignières, coming from behind him, startled him, and he spun about. There was Lucile and he shook her hand, and he did likewise with Charles, in a cordial manner. Then his gaze once again met Lucile's, and when he saw the sparkle in her eyes, such a powerful feeling of victory and overwhelming joy invaded him that he had to give a little cough in order to conceal the expression on his face.

"Diane," said Blassans-Lignières, "it's William who owns that Boldini that I was telling You about at dinner the other evening. William, You've simply got to show it to her."

For a brief instant, Antoine and Charles chanced to look each other straight in the eye before Charles moved off, flanked by William and Diane, and what Antoine saw there was a totally honest look, betraying fear and worry. Was Charles suffering? Did he suspect anything? Antoine hadn't previously asked himself such questions. He had been worried only about Diane, but even then, only slightly so. The truth was, ever since Sarah's death, he hadn't dared to ask any questions about anyone at all. But now here he was, alone, directly facing Lucile, and in his head he was asking her many questions: "Who are you? What do you want of me? What are you doing here? What am I to you?"

· · ·

"I thought I'd never make it," said Lucile. At the same time, she was thinking to herself, "I don't know a thing about him except for how he makes love. So why is this situation that

Chapter 8

we're in so intense? It's everyone else's fault. If we were free, not watched over, we would without any doubt be calmer, our blood would run cooler." For a moment, she wanted to spin on her heels and go join the little crew that had set sail for the Boldini. What future awaited her — how many lies, how many quick trysts? She took the cigarette that Antoine was offering her, placing her hand on his while he gave her a light. She instantly recognized that heat, the feel of that hand, and she closed her eyes, first once and then once more, as if secretly giving herself permission to indulge...

Out of the blue, Antoine asked her, "Will You come again tomorrow?", for some reason reverting from *tu* to *vous*. "At the same time?"

He was sure that he wouldn't feel at ease for even a moment until he knew exactly when he would once again press her tightly against himself. She said yes. And the sense of relief that came flooding into his soul was so powerful that for a brief moment he even questioned if their getting together the next day really mattered to him at all or not. But that doubt was quickly dispelled, for he had read enough literature to believe that anxiety, even more deeply than jealousy, is the great driving force of passion. Moreover, he was quite convinced that all he would need to do was reach out his hand, draw Lucile to his side, right in the middle of this salon, and a huge scandal would erupt, an irreversible act would have been carried out; and it was this very conviction that allowed him to refrain from reaching his hand out, and even allowed him to savor an ambiguous but intense pleasure that he had seldom felt before: that of dissimulation.

Part I: Le printemps

"Well, well — so here you are, my little ones! And what have we done with our friends?"

Claire Santré's throaty voice caught them both off guard. Draping herself with one hand over Lucile's shoulder, she stared at Antoine admiringly, looking as if she'd tried to see him through Lucile's eyes and had done a fine job of it. "So, the special issue on feminine complicity has just arrived," thought Lucile but, to her great surprise, it didn't upset her at all. Claire was right, Antoine was very handsome right now, looking somehow uneasy and self-confident at the same time. But he was too ill at ease to be able to keep up this façade for much longer — this was a man made to read books, to stride briskly, to speak softly, and to make sweet love; this was not a man made for the social whirl. Even less than she herself was, since her indifference and her devil-may-care attitude at least provided her with a protective diving suit that could withstand all the pressures in the fathomless depths of social relationships.

"It seems that there's a Boldini in this fellow William's apartment," said Antoine contemptuously. "And Diane and Charles are taking it in."

He realized this was the first time he'd referred to Blassans-Lignières by his first name. The act of deceiving someone forced you, without your quite knowing why, to accept a certain degree of intimacy.

Claire exclaimed, "A Boldini? Did he just get it? I wonder where he came across it! Nobody's told me about it…" This last was spoken in a certain peeved tone of voice that she always had whenever a lacuna turned up in her vast stock of knowledge.

Chapter 8

"Oh, poor William — I'm sure he was robbed blind again. Only an American would go out and buy a Boldini without consulting Santos."

Somewhat calmed down by thinking of poor William's naïve blunder, she turned her attention back to Lucile. It seemed about time, at last, to make this uppity girl pay for her cheekiness, her sullen silences, and her refusal to play the game. Lucile was looking up at Antoine with a calm and amused smile, a secure smile. That word, "secure", hit the nail on the head. It was a smile that only a woman who is intimately involved with a man can have.

"But when, for God's sake, *when*, could they have..." And Claire's mind abruptly spun into high gear. "Now let's see, the dinner in Marnes was three evenings back, and nothing had happened yet. It must have been some afternoon — nobody in Paris makes love at night any more, everybody's just too worn out by then, and of course these two, on top of it all, have their other mates. So... this afternoon?!" And, with piercing eyes and a quivering nose, she scrutinized the couple, doing her best to make out any telltale traces of love's pleasure left behind on their faces, seeking with that crazy intensity that curiosity gives to a certain type of woman.

Lucile picked up on what Claire was doing, and in spite of herself, burst out laughing. Claire backed off a little bit, letting her zealous hunting-hound stare melt into a gentler, more re-signed look that said, "Now I understand everything, I accept everything" — but unfortunately no one noticed it at all.

Antoine instead was focused on Lucile and now was laughing

comfortably with her, delighted to see her laughing, delighted to know that the next day she'd tell him all about it, lying beside him in his bed in that delicious, drowsy hour that always follows lovemaking. And so he didn't ask her, "Why are You laughing?" Many a secret liaison unintentionally gives itself away through just such silences, or through a conspicuous lack of questions, through a leading remark that one doesn't comment on, through the insertion of a secret phrase that had been deliberately chosen for its blandness but that is so exceedingly bland that it draws attention to itself. In any case, even the most casual observer who saw Lucile and Antoine laughing, who saw their faces glowing with happiness, could not have missed the signs.

They themselves vaguely realized this, and they took advantage, with a sort of pride, of the short truce that had been afforded them by the Boldini, these few moments when they could look at each other and enjoy doing so without setting off alarm bells in a certain pair of other guests. And although they would have denied it, the presence of Claire and the rest of the crowd doubled their pleasure. They felt like teen-agers, even children, who have been warned not to do something but who do it anyway, and who haven't yet been caught and punished.

Diane was now slicing her way back towards them, tacking agilely through the crowd, unable to dodge a doting friend who took her hand and kissed it, but from whom she instantly ripped it away, at the same time ignoring his well-meaning question about her health as well as someone else's warm words about how lovely she looked. Wading through a buzzing background of "How are you doing, Diane dear? How well You look, Diane!

Chapter 8

Do tell, where did you ever find that divine outfit, Diane?", she hastened to get back to that dark and hateful corner where she'd left her lover, her love, with that stupid girl he seemed so smitten with. She hated Charles for having dragged her out of the main room, she hated Boldini, she hated William for the insipid and interminable tale he'd told of how he'd made his purchase.

He'd gotten it for a song, naturally — it had been a unique chance, the dumb seller had completely fallen for his ploys. God, it was a drag, this obsession of the super-rich for doing nothing but swinging deal after deal. Wangling discounts from dressmakers, cousin prices at Cartier's, and being pleased as punch with themselves for these trivial accomplishments. At least *she*'d not fallen into this trap, thank the Lord — she wasn't one of those coy rich dames who finagle each and every seller into giving them sweeter deals when they don't in the least need to do so. It occurred to her she should tell this to Antoine — it would give him a good laugh. High society amused him; he was always quoting Proust on this topic and on a good many others, which somewhat rankled Diane, as she herself had practically no time at all to read. That little Lucile, though, had surely read all of Proust, you could just see it in her eyes — after all, living as she did off of Charles, she must have oodles of free time for reading.

All at once Diane cut these thoughts off. "My God," she thought, "I'm growing vulgar. Is it unavoidable, as one grows older, to become vulgar in this way?" And though she ached, she still flashed a smile at Coco de Balileul and winked back at Maxime who'd just winked at her for no clear reason, and then she tripped over another half-dozen friendly, beaming hurdles;

she was running a torturous steeplechase just to get back to Antoine, who was laughing over in that corner, laughing in that deep bass voice of his, and whose laugh she simply *had* to squelch. She took one more step and then shut her eyes with a sense of sweet relief: it was with Claire Santré that Antoine was laughing. Lucile had her back turned towards the two of them.

CHAPTER 9

"The party tonight was pretty wild," said Charles. "Everyone's drinking more and more, wouldn't You say?"

It was raining and the car was gliding smoothly along the banks of the Seine. Lucile had stuck her head out the window as was her wont, and little raindrops were pelting her face; she was drinking in the smell of Paris on this April night, and she was recalling the despairing look on Antoine's face when they'd had to say good-night politely to each other a half hour earlier, and she was filled with wonder at it all.

"Everyone seems more and more frightened these days," she observed rather cheerily. "Frightened of growing old, frightened of losing what they have, frightened they won't get what they want, frightened of getting bored, frightened of being boring — they all seem to be in a state of constant despair and yearning."

"Do You find that amusing?" asked Charles.

"Sometimes I find it funny, and other times it touches me. Don't You feel that way?"

"I don't think about it all that much, to tell the truth," said Charles. "I'm not much of a psychologist, as You know. All I know is that more and more often, people who I don't even recognize come up to me and give me big hugs, and also, more and more people seem to be getting tipsy in these salon parties."

Part I: *Le printemps*

What he couldn't say to Lucile was this: "All I care about is You. I spend hours and hours trying to fathom Your psyche. I'm hounded by one single idea. And I, too, am frightened, just as You were saying, frightened of losing what I have. I, too, live in that perpetual state of despair and yearning You described."

Lucile pulled her head back inside and looked at him. Out of the blue she felt an immense tenderness for him welling up inside of her — never had she felt so much love for him. She so badly wished she could share this wild joy coursing through her veins as she looked ahead to the next afternoon. "It's ten o'clock at night, and in just nineteen hours, I'll be in Antoine's arms once again. I just hope I can sleep late tomorrow morning, so I won't have to count the hours." She placed her hand on Charles' hand. His was an attractive hand, delicate and well cared for, though a few little brownish spots were starting to show.

"So how was that Boldini, anyway?"

"Oh, she's trying to make me feel good," thought Charles bitterly. "She knows that I'm not just a businessman but that I also love art. What she doesn't know is that I'm fifty years old and that I'm desperately unhappy."

"Quite lovely. From his best period. And William got it for a song!"

"He's always getting things for a song, that William," chirped Lucile with a little laugh.

"That's exactly what Diane said to me," said Charles.

There was an uneasy silence. "Well, I'm not going to let there be these awkward silences every time he brings up Diane or

Antoine," Lucile thought to herself. "That's stupid. If only I could just tell him the truth: that I'm crazy about Antoine, that I dream of laughing with him and being in his arms. But what more terrible thing could I say to this man who loves me? He might be able to accept my sleeping with Antoine, but not my laughing with him. I'm very aware that nothing brings on jealousy like laughter."

"Diane's acting a bit weird these days," said Lucile. "I was talking with Antoine and Claire when I saw her coming back into the salon. She had a kind of lost stare on her face... I was frightened to see her that way." She tried to laugh.

Charles turned towards her and said, "Frightened? Didn't You feel sorry for her?"

"Oh, yes," said Lucile calmly. "I felt sorry for her, too. It's no picnic for a woman to grow old."

"Nor for a man," said Charles emphatically. "Believe me."

The obviously artificial mirth that ensued made their blood run cold. "All right," said Lucile to herself, "so that's how things are. We'll dodge all the delicate areas, we'll crack little jokes, we'll do things his way. But come hell or high water, tomorrow afternoon at five I'm going to be in Antoine's arms." And this woman who had always despised love's irrationality was thrilled to find herself brimming over with it.

The fact was, there was nothing — no person, no plea of any sort — that would be able to keep her from rejoining Antoine the next day, from reveling in the union with his body, his breath, his voice. This she knew, and the ferocity of her desire — she who was forever postponing and procrastinating because of her capricious moods or changes in the weather — astonished her even more than that surge of sheer joy she'd felt when she'd caught sight of Antoine a couple of hours earlier.

Her only prior affair of passion, at age twenty, had been an unhappy one, and it had left her with a curious aftertaste in which caring blended with melancholy, a sensation not all that different from her residual feeling about religion: both were bright hopes that she'd let go of. But now, coming in a huge rush, love — joyous love — was revealing its full force to her, and it seemed to her that the very core of her being, far from limiting its focus to just one other person, was growing huge, unlimited, exultant. She, whose days had been casually slipping through her fingers, each one of them indistinguishable from all the others, was suddenly terrified to think how little of life now remained: she would never have enough time to love Antoine.

"By the way, Lucile, I'm going to have to go off to New York fairly soon. Will You come with me?"

Charles' voice was calm, as if he was expecting her to say yes; indeed, Lucile loved traveling and he knew it well. She didn't answer immediately.

"Why not? Would You be gone for a long time?"

"Not a chance," she was thinking. "Not a chance. What would I possibly do without Antoine for ten days? Charles is always giving me these big decisions to make, sometimes too early and sometimes too late, but in any case it's just too hard on me. I'd trade all the cities in the world just for Antoine's little room. The only voyages left for me now, the only discoveries I still hunger for, are those that he and I will make together, side by side in the darkness." And as a certain little image suddenly bubbled up from her memory, she got all flustered and quickly turned her gaze toward the street.

"I'd say ten or fifteen days," replied Charles. "New York in the springtime is really lovely. You only saw how it is in the dead of winter. I remember one evening when it was so bitterly cold that Your nose turned blue. Your eyes were bulging, Your hair was bristling out of indignation, and You were giving me these dirty looks that implied it was all my fault!"

The image made him come out with a tender and wistful little laugh. Lucile, too, vividly recalled the unbearable coldness of that winter, but for her there was no tender side to the memory. Mostly what she remembered was a mad dash in a taxi from their hotel to some restaurant. The one who cherished these melancholy and golden memories of the heart was Charles, not herself, and all at once this made her feel ashamed. Even in her emotional life, she was totally dependent on Charles, and that was what troubled her more than anything else. She didn't want to make him suffer, didn't want to lie to him, didn't want to tell him the truth — all she wanted was for him to figure it out on his own without her having to tell him anything. Yes, indeed — she really was a coward, through and through.

•   •   •

They got together two or three times a week. Antoine demonstrated tremendous imagination in concocting pretexts for leaving work early, and as for Lucile, she had never made a practice of accounting for her daylight activities to Charles.

Part I: *Le printemps*

They always met up, trembling, in that same small room, and sank swiftly into the darkness, with hardly any time at all for words. They knew nothing about each other, but their bodies meshed with such fervor, such piety, such a rush of power, that the intensity of their union would totally derail their memories; each time, after saying good-bye, they both would once again seek some tangible recollection, at least one word that had been whispered in the darkness, some gesture, but always in vain. Whenever they separated, they were like sleepwalkers, lost and disoriented, and only after a couple of hours had passed would they start once more to look forward to their next meeting, the sole source of meaning in their lives, the sole reality they knew. All else for them was dead. It was only through such anticipation that they had any awareness of the time, the weather, or other people, since their impatience turned all these things into obstacles.

Thus Lucile, before going off to her rendezvous with Antoine, would check her purse six times for her car keys, would mentally rehearse the route to his apartment ten times, would cast a dozen glances at the very alarm clock that for all her life she'd looked at with nothing but immense disdain. And Antoine would tell his secretary ten times that he had an important meeting at four o'clock, and each time he would leave the office at quarter of four, even though it took him just two short minutes to walk home from work. And every time they arrived, they were both a little pale — she because she'd thought she'd never escape from a horrible traffic jam, and he because he'd gotten tied up with one of the authors in their stable, who simply would not stop talking. They would embrace with a deep sigh, as if they had barely managed to escape some dire fate, when in fact that dire fate would, in the worst possible case, have been a delay of five minutes.

They said "Je t'aime" to each other at the height of passion, but never at any other time. Sometimes while Lucile, eyes closed, was regaining her breath, Antoine would bend down and caress her face and shoulder with his hand, tenderly murmuring, "You make me so happy, you know." And she would smile. He spoke to her about her smile, telling her how much it drove him crazy whenever, wide-eyed, she would flash it at someone else.

"Your smile is just too helpless-looking," he said. "It's upsetting to me."

"But usually my mind is on something else — smiling is just my way of being friendly. I don't look helpless, I just look dumb."

"God only knows what you're thinking about," he countered. "But at parties, you always seem like you're pondering some deep secret or reliving some stroke of bad luck."

"Actually, yes, there is a certain secret I have in mind..." she replied, pulling his head down to her shoulder and whispering, "Don't think so much, Antoine — let's just be happy together."

And then he would go quiet, not daring to tell her what was constantly eating at him, what was keeping him awake night after night in bed next to Diane, who also was having rough nights and who would pretend to be asleep. "It can't go on this way, can't go on this way... Why isn't *she* the one by my side?"

Lucile's devil-may-care way of being, her ability to shut her eyes to any problem in life, made him uneasy. She refused to speak of Charles, refused to make any plan of any sort. Maybe she was involved with Blassans-Lignières in order to gain something? But she seemed so free, she would so instinctively drop out of any conversation the instant it turned to money (and of course no one talks about money more than people who have too much of it...) that he couldn't imagine her ever deliberately trying to get something out of someone. She would say, "I always take the path of least resistance" or "I hate possessiveness" or "I missed you" — and he simply couldn't put all these things together in his head. He had an uneasy presentiment that something would happen, that they would be discovered, that fate would soon replace him with another lover, and he despised himself for such thoughts.

Antoine knew that he was easy-going — sensual but moral. He'd certainly never had as deep a feeling for any woman as he did for Lucile, but he had nonetheless had quite a few liaisons, and out of a feeling of guilt, he had come to see his affair with Sarah — which, in truth, had just been a bagatelle — as a tragic love story. He knew he was extremely prone to inner conflict. In fact, he was nearly as talented at being unhappy as at being happy, and Lucile threw him for a loop. He found it baffling that she had only had one prior love affair, ten years earlier, that for her it was water long since under the bridge, and that she looked upon this new love affair as a marvelous, unpredictable, unexpected, fragile gift, whose future course she did her best to avoid imagining, almost as if out of superstitious fear. She savored waiting for him, she savored the feeling of missing him, she savored the hiddenness of their affair, just as she would have savored living with him in the light of day. Every moment of happiness was a thing unto itself.

And if, over these past two months, she had occasionally caught herself getting mawkish over sappy love songs that she chanced to hear, she didn't feel in the least troubled by the songs' hackneyed themes of "you and only you" or "forever and ever". Since her only moral principle was not to lie to herself, she found herself being gradually but inexorably pulled into a state of involuntary but profound cynicism. It was almost as if her honest tracking of her emotions had this cynicism as an inevitable consequence, whereas cheaters and liars could preserve their unbridled romanticism over the entire course of their lives. She adored Antoine but she cared for Charles; Antoine made her happy, but she at least did not make Charles unhappy. Cherishing both at once, she didn't care enough about being of one mind to feel self-contempt for sharing herself between the two of them. Her utter lack of self-importance made her passionate. In a word, she was happy.

•　　•　　•

It was through a complete accident that she found out one day that she could suffer.

It had been three days since she'd seen Antoine, as the vicissitudes of Parisian life had carried the two of them to different sets of theaters and dinners. She was supposed to meet him at four o'clock, and she arrived on time, but to her surprise, he didn't open the door to let her in. For the first time ever, she made use of the key he'd given her. No one was there, the shutters were open, and for an instant she thought that she'd mistakenly entered someone else's apartment, since the room she had always come to was a dark room, in which Antoine would habitually turn on only a red floor lamp that lit up nothing but the bed and a little patch of ceiling. Intrigued, she walked around this room, at once so familiar and so unfamiliar to her, reading the titles of the books on the shelves, picking up a tie on the floor, scrutinizing a rather droll and charming turn-of-the-century painting that she'd never before even noticed. All at once she found herself looking at her lover as a young bachelor, occasionally hard-working, quite modest and simple. So who *was* this Antoine? Where did he come from? What were his parents like? What had his childhood been like?

She sat down on the bed, and then, suddenly feeling uneasy, stood back up and walked over to the window. She felt like an intruder in a stranger's home, she felt she shouldn't be there. And most of all, for the first time it hit her that Antoine was not like her, but was another — an other, a not her — and that all her intimacy with his hands, his mouth, his eyes, his body, did not mean he was her irrevocable soulmate. And where was he, anyway? It was 4:15, she hadn't seen him for three whole days, and the damn phone wasn't even ringing. She meandered about in the sad little room, from the door to the window and back, she pulled out a book at random, flipped it open, couldn't make sense of what she was reading, closed it and reshelved it. Time was passing. If he couldn't make it, he could at least have phoned her. She picked the phone up, hoping to find it was out

Chapter 9

of order, but no such luck. And what if he just didn't feel like coming? This thought suddenly made her freeze in the middle of the room, stock still but quiveringly alert, the way certain soldiers look in old engravings, just after having been struck by a fatal bullet. And out of nowhere, a host of memories started swirling before her eyes: the time when she thought she'd detected some anger in Antoine's eyes — maybe it had actually been boredom with her; that other time he'd hesitated when she'd asked what was troubling him — well, maybe it wasn't due to his fear of upsetting her, as she'd thought then, but to his fear of hurting her by confessing the truth: that he no longer loved her. And in a flash she mentally replayed a dozen scenes with Antoine, now reperceiving them all as revealing his loss of interest in her.

"All right, then," she said aloud, "so he doesn't love me any more." She said it softly and calmly, but instantly the words flew straight back at her, stinging her like the crack of a whip, and reflexively her hand rushed up to her neck to ward off the blow. "Oh, what am I going to do with myself if Antoine doesn't love me any more?" And a bleak future loomed before her, drained of lifeblood, warmth, and laughter, like that petrified cinder-covered plain in Peru that had recently appeared in a photograph in *Paris-Match* and that had aroused a somewhat morbid fascination on Antoine's part.

She remained standing, succumbing to an internal shaking that grew so violent that she had to consciously come to her own rescue. "Come on, come on," she repeated aloud, "Come on," addressing the words to her own body and her heart, as if to two frightened horses. She lay down on the bed, trying to make herself breathe very quietly. It didn't work. Hit by an attack of panic and despair, she curled up into a ball, wrapping her arms about her shoulders, burying her face in the pillow. She heard herself moaning "Antoine, Antoine…", and simultaneously with this unbearable pain, she was overcome by a sense of bewilderment. "You are out of your mind," she told herself, "out of your mind," yet some other alien voice inside her, for once much stronger, cried out, "But Antoine's yellow eyes, Antoine's voice — what will you ever do without Antoine, you idiot?" Five o'clock rang out from the steeple of a nearby church, and she felt as if some cruel and crazed god was ringing the bells just in order to taunt her.

The next moment, Antoine walked in. As soon as he saw the expression on her face, he stopped in his tracks, then dropped down beside her on the bed. He went wild with joy, though he had no idea why, covering her face and her hair with tender kisses, explaining his lateness, and lambasting his boss for having called him into his office and kept him there for an hour. Lucile clung to him, murmuring his name in a voice still very unsure of itself. Finally she sat up in the bed and turned away from him.

"You know, Antoine," she said, "I love you, and it's for keeps."

"Me too," he replied, "so it works out nicely."

For a while they remained wordless and meditative. Then Lucile gave a resigned little laugh, turned back to face him, and watched him intently as the face she adored slowly drew nearer to her own.

CHAPTER 10

As she was going out the door two hours later, she decided it had all been a crazy fluke. Exhausted from lovemaking, content with the world, and with her head clear, she found herself thinking that the roots of her half-hour of panic had more to do with nerves than with love, and she resolved to sleep more, drink less, and so on. She was far too used to living in her own private world to be able to accept the idea that anyone or anything could be indispensable to her. The very notion struck her as shocking rather than desirable.

As her car quietly glided along the bends of the Seine, she drove in a trance-like state, admiring the golden river ahead of her on one of the first beautiful spring evenings. A smile crossed her face. "What on earth got into me? At my age? With my lifestyle? After all, I'm someone's mistress, I'm supposed to be a cynical woman." This thought made her chuckle, and the driver of a nearby car, waiting for the light to change, gave her a friendly smile that she absent-mindedly returned, still buried in her musings. "So who am I?" How she might appear to others, or, for that matter, to herself, was of no import whatsoever to her. She paid no attention to how she acted; was this a sin? A sign of mental decay? When younger, she had read a great deal before realizing that she was fulfilled. And she had gone through a long period of soul-searching before turning into the well-fed and well-dressed pet that she now was, so adroit at sidestepping life's difficult situations. Where was she headed, what was she doing with her life?

Thanks to a peculiar lifeline in her palm, she had long since accepted the notion that she would die young — in fact, she took it for granted as her fate. But what if she were to grow old, instead? She tried to envision herself as poor, decrepit, abandoned by Charles, drearily toiling away in some completely unrewarding job. She did her best to give herself a good scare, but it didn't work. Rather, it crossed her mind that whatever happened, the Seine, as it flowed by the Grand Palais, would always be just as golden and luminous as today, and that that was all that really mattered. She had no need of this purring vehicle, nor of this silky Laroche coat, in order to live — of that she was quite sure. And Charles, too, was quite sure of it, and that made him miserable. And each time she left Antoine's apartment, she felt herself overcome by such a rush of tenderness for Blassans-Lignières, and such a great longing to bring him happiness.

She had no idea that right now, Charles, who always expected to find her waiting for him when he got back from work, was pacing back and forth in his bedroom, just as she had been doing three hours earlier, and that he was asking himself the very same question: "What if she never came back again?" But she didn't suspect any of this nor did she find out, because when she walked in, Charles was stretched out on his bed, placidly reading *Le Monde*. The sound of her car was always a dead giveaway. In a calm voice he asked her, "Did You have a good day?", and she tenderly kissed him. He often wore a cologne that she very much liked, and she thought to herself that she really ought to buy a bottle of it for Antoine.

"Pretty nice," she said. "I was just scared that…" But she caught herself. She felt like opening up to Charles, telling him everything — "I was scared I would lose Antoine, I was scared of loving him." But she couldn't do it. And so she had no one to tell about this weird afternoon, never having been one to confide in people, and it made her feel somehow sad.

"I was scared of the idea of living on the sidelines," she finished up in a flustered manner.

"On the sidelines of what?"

"Of life. Or at least what other people call life. Charles, does a person really have to love someone, or at least have an unhappy love affair, really have to work, make their own money, accomplish things, in order to live life truly?"

"It's not an absolute necessity," said Charles, lowering his gaze, "as long as one is happy."

"And You think that's enough?"

"Easily," he replied. And something in his voice, some unexpected little quaver that made him seem far away, lost in wistful thoughts, tore at Lucile's heart.

She sat down on the bed, reached over and caressed his weary face. Charles closed his eyes and smiled gently. She felt compassionate, generous, able to make him happy — and it didn't occur to her that all these warm feelings might merely be because Antoine had come back, and that if he hadn't, then she might well have despised Charles instead. When one is happy, one willingly shares the credit for one's happiness with others, and it's only when one is suffering that one realizes they were nothing but insignificant observers of one's joy.

"What are we doing tonight?" asked Lucile.

"We've got a dinner at Diane's," said Charles. "Had You forgotten about it?" His voice was disbelieving and delighted at the same time. She instantly guessed how come, and blushed. If she were to reply "Yes," although she'd be telling the truth, she would also be misleading him. And yet she surely couldn't say to him, "I'd forgotten about the dinner, but not about Antoine. In fact, I've just gotten back from his place. And we were so lost in our passion that when we said goodbye we thought we wouldn't see each other until tomorrow."

What she instead said was, "I hadn't forgotten about the dinner, but I didn't know it was at her place. Which dress do You want me to put on?"

Actually, she was surprised that she didn't feel more joy at the prospect of seeing Antoine again in just a few hours. Instead, she was vaguely annoyed at the thought. With Antoine, she had reached a paroxysm of euphoria that afternoon, and it struck her that her cup was pretty much full, if that metaphor could be applied to one's emotions. The fact was, she would much rather have shared a relaxed dinner with Charles. And she was just about to say this to him when she cut herself short: doing so would give him too much pleasure based on a lie, and she didn't want to lie to him.

"What were You about to say?"

"I don't remember."

Chapter 10

"Your metaphysical reflections make You look even more muddled than usual."

She gave a little laugh. "So I look muddled most of the time?"

"Completely! I wouldn't ever let You travel all alone, for example. If I did, I'd finally catch up with You a week later, in the transit lounge of some godforsaken little burg's railway station, surrounded by heaps of paperback novels and totally up on the lives of all the place's bartenders…"

He looked almost serious in describing this droll scenario, and she erupted in laughter. He must really think her incapable of dealing with life, and in a burst of clarity it hit her that this was what tied her to him, far more than any need for security. The point was, he fully accepted her lack of responsibility, he approved of the unconscious choice she'd made, fifteen years earlier, to remain an eternal adolescent. This was the very choice that without a doubt drove Antoine up a wall. And quite possibly, the perfect alignment between what she wanted to be and what Charles saw in her might just turn out to be stronger than any fiery affair that would require her to give up her way of being.

"While we're waiting, how about a whiskey?" suggested Charles. "I'm dead tired."

"Pauline doesn't want me drinking any more," said Lucile. "Why don't You ask her for an extra-large glass, and then I'll share it with You."

Charles smiled and rang for Pauline. Lucile thought to herself, "I'm starting to act like a little girl, without meaning to, and if I don't watch out, soon I'll have a bunch of stuffed animals on my bed." She stood up, stretched, and went into her own room, where, gazing at her bed, she wondered if someday she would wake up with Antoine right next to her.

CHAPTER 11

$\mathcal{D}iane's$ apartment, in the Rue Cambon, looked very lovely, with fresh flowers everywhere, and even though the evening breeze was very mild and she had left the French doors open, big fires were burning in the two fireplaces, one at each end of the salon. Lucile, charmed by it all, moved about the room, alternately taking in whiffs of air from the street, already presaging the hot and dusty summer soon to come, and the smell of the flaming logs, which brought back for her the previous autumn, such a harsh one, inextricably linked in her memory with the woods in Sologne where Charles took her on hunts.

"How elegant," said Lucile to Diane, "to have mixed two seasons in a single party."

"Yes," said Diane, "but You know, one always feels inappropriately dressed."

Lucile gave a laugh. She had a soft and communicative laugh, she was clearly feeling quite at ease, and Diane began to wonder if wasn't foolish to be jealous of her. Basically, Lucile was well-behaved; to be sure, she had that absent-minded way about her, a little out of it, which she shared with Antoine, but perhaps that was as far as it went between the two of them. Blassans-Lignières looked perfectly relaxed and Antoine had never been in a better mood... Surely her suspicions were groundless. And all at once she felt a burst of warmth, almost of gratitude, towards Lucile.

"Come with me and I'll show You the rest of the apartment. What do You say?"

Lucile earnestly examined the bathroom done in Italian tilework, admiringly commented on the fancy fixtures in a large closet in the hallway, and then followed Diane into her bedroom.

"Please don't mind the clutter in here," said Diane.

Antoine, who had arrived late, had changed in Diane's bedroom, and the shirt and tie he'd had on in the afternoon were lying on the floor. Diane quickly glanced over at Lucile, but saw merely the slightest sign of embarrassment, which anyone who was well brought up would have had. However, something was goading Diane, something she felt ashamed of but that she couldn't fight off. She picked up the clothes, placed them on a chair, turned to face Lucile, who hadn't moved, and gave a conspiratorial little smile. "Honestly, men are so messy..."

Lucile stared right back at her and agreeably said, "Charles is very neat." She could hardly keep herself from giggling. "So now," she was thinking, "is she also going to complain about how Antoine never puts the cap back on the toothpaste tube?" She didn't feel in the least bit jealous; in fact, seeing the tie there had felt like running into an old high-school friend, by some miracle, at the base of the Pyramids. All the while, Lucile had been thinking how truly lovely Diane was, and how baffling it was of Antoine to be abandoning Diane for her. Lucile felt objective and observant, and also very kind-hearted, just as she felt, in fact, every time that she drank a little too much.

Chapter 11

"We really should be getting back to the guests," said Diane. "Goodness knows why I take it on myself every so often to throw one of these parties. For me as the hostess, it's so exhausting. And on top of it all, I don't get the feeling that people have all that great a time, anyway."

"It looks pretty lively to me," said Lucile with conviction. "And also, Claire's acting a bit snooty, which is always a good sign…"

"Ah, so You noticed it too?", said Diane with a smile. "I didn't think — I mean, You always look a bit, uh…"

"Muddled," said Lucile.

"That's it precisely."

"Just this evening, Charles called me that once again. I'll probably wind up believing it."

The two of them broke out in a simultaneous laugh, and all of a sudden Lucile felt a twinge of fondness for Diane. At least in this little circle, Diane had to be one of the only women with a bit of moral backbone, and she'd never heard her say anything trite or vulgar. Even Charles had kind words for her, and Charles was extremely critical of a certain type of vulgarity that Lucile had noticed was quite common. It was such a shame that she couldn't make friends with Diane. Or maybe one day, if Diane were truly intelligent, everything might work out for the best. This extravagantly optimistic thought struck Lucile as yet another sign of her own wisdom, and if it hadn't been for Antoine's arrival in the room right then, she would've launched into an explanation to Diane that could only have ended up in a catastrophe.

Part I: *Le printemps*

"Destret is looking for You everywhere," said Antoine. "He's furious." He seemed confused to see Diane and Lucile together.

"He must think that I'm jealous and that I was trying to find traces of evidence," thought Diane, reassured by Lucile's conspicuous good humor. "Poor Antoine…"

"Don't worry about us, I was just showing Lucile around the apartment. She'd never seen the place before."

And Lucile, highly amused by Antoine's look of bewilderment, started laughing with Diane. With his two women ganging up on him, Antoine felt his masculine hackles starting to rise. "What is this? I jump out of the arms of one of them, go off and sleep with the other one, and the next thing I know, the two of them are getting together and laughing at me. If that doesn't take the cake!"

"Did I say something funny?" he asked.

"Oh no, not at all," replied Diane. "It's just that You seem overly concerned with Destret's little tantrums, when You know as well as I do that the man is perpetually in a pique. It just amused us, that's all." With that, she walked out of the bedroom, and Lucile, following in her wake, made a face at Antoine, expressing scorn and outrage. For a moment he was thrown, but then he smiled. After all, it had only been two hours since she'd said to him, "I love you, and it's for keeps," and he could still hear her voice as she'd said it. So let her act smug right now — it didn't matter.

Lucile, back in the salon, bumped into Johnny, who, clearly quite bored, rushed up to her, handed her a glass, and pulled her aside near a window. "I think You're terrific, Lucile," he said. "At least with You I can feel comfortable. I know You're not going to regale me with Your comments on the play that just opened, or on the quirky manners of various guests."

"That's what You say to me at every party."

"Well, I just wanted to tell You that You should watch out," said Johnny abruptly. "You're wearing a suspicious-seeming happiness."

Reflexively, she ran her hand across her face almost as if to wipe off her happiness, like a mask she'd forgotten to remove. But it was true: that very day, she'd said "I love you" to someone who had replied, "Me too." Was this so obvious to everyone present? All at once she felt she was the focal point of the assembled group, she thought she saw eyes turning her way, and she started blushing. In one quick gulp she downed the glass of nearly unadulterated scotch that Johnny had given her.

"I'm just in a good mood," she softly protested, "and I find all these people quite charming."

And all of a sudden, though generally she was very retiring at these affairs, Lucile took it into her head to distract attention from her euphoric glow by following the ploy of certain unattractive ladies who never seem to stop jabbering away, hoping thereby to deflect attention from their misfortune. And so she glided from group to group, acting pleasant, ditzy, and sweet, even going so far as to compliment an astounded Claire Santré on the loveliness of her gown. Charles followed her with his eyes, most intrigued, and he was just about to spirit her off when Diane took his arm and said, "Charles, this is the first beautiful spring evening we've had, and we're going dancing. Nobody feels like sleeping, and I'd bet that Lucile feels less like it than anyone else in the room."

She watched Lucile with a sense of friendly amusement, and Charles, who was aware of her jealousy and who had also seen her take Lucile aside a few minutes earlier, suddenly felt reassured by it all. Lucile had apparently gotten over Antoine. And between the lines, Diane was proposing to him a little party, a celebration in honor of this new state of tranquillity that they both craved. He accepted.

•   •   •

They all agreed to meet up in a nightclub. Charles and Lucile were the first to arrive, and they danced and chatted gaily, since Lucile, feeling in her element, just couldn't stop talking. But then she fell abruptly silent. She'd spotted a tall man at the door, a little taller than anyone near him, in a dark blue suit, and his eyes were yellow. This man's face she knew by heart; she knew every mark on the skin under that dark blue suit, she knew intimately the shape of his shoulders. He walked in their direction and found himself a seat. As Diane was downstairs putting on her makeup, he invited Lucile to dance. The touch of his hand on her shoulder, the way his palm pressed against hers, and that curious distance, just a trace too far, that he kept between his cheek and hers, a distance that she knew so well from the heights of their passion, churned her up so much that she deliberately put on a faintly bored expression aimed at pulling the wool over the eyes of an audience that didn't even see her. It was the first time she had danced with Antoine, and they were playing one of those lilting romantic ballads that you could hear everywhere that spring.

He walked her back to their table. Diane, now with her makeup in place, was dancing with Charles. Lucile and Antoine sat down on the *banquette*, suitably far apart.

"So you enjoyed that?" He looked furious.

"Well, sure — didn't you?" replied Lucile, caught off guard.

"Not one bit," said Antoine. "I don't get any kick at all out of this kind of get-together. Also, unlike you, I detest playing the hypocrite." And the truth was, he hadn't been able to talk with Lucile all evening long, and he very much desired her. The thought that in but a few minutes she would be leaving with Charles was eating at him terribly. He was suffering from a crisis of possessiveness of the type that so often results from frustrated desire.

"You're just cut out for this kind of life," he added.

"And you?"

"I'm not. Some men base their masculine pride on their ability to juggle two women. But as for me, my masculine pride would never allow me to take pleasure from making two women suffer."

"If only you could have seen yourself in Diane's bedroom," exclaimed Lucile. "You had such a guilty look..." And at this little jab, she burst out in laughter.

"Don't laugh," said Antoine, clearly restraining himself. "In ten minutes, you'll be in Charles' arms, or else alone, but whatever, you'll be far away from me..."

Part I: *Le printemps*

"But tomorrow…"

"I've had it up to here with your tomorrows," said Antoine angrily. "You've got to get that through your pretty little head."

Lucile didn't reply. She tried to look very serious but it didn't work at all. The alcohol was going to her head. Some random young man came up and invited her to dance, but Antoine shooed him off without mincing any words, and for a brief moment, Lucile couldn't stand him. She would gladly have danced, talked, or even absconded with a third party — she no longer felt herself obligated in any way, except to keep herself happy.

"I've had a teensy bit too much to drink," she said in a sad little voice.

"You can say *that* again," replied Antoine.

"Maybe you should have done the same," she said. "You're no fun tonight." This was the first time they had ever had an argument. But when she looked over at his obstinate, childlike face, she melted. "Antoine, you know that…"

"Yeah, yeah — that you love me, and for keeps." At this he abruptly stood up. Diane was headed back towards their table along with Charles, who looked very tired. He shot an imploring glance toward Lucile, at the same time asking Diane to excuse them: he had to get up early the next morning, and this club was really just too loud for him. Lucile made no protests, and simply followed him out. But in the car, for the first time ever since she'd met him, she felt like a prisoner.

CHAPTER 12

$\mathcal{D}$iane was in the bathroom, taking off her makeup. Antoine had turned on the record player and, seated on the floor, was listening to, though not really hearing, a concerto by Beethoven. Diane could see him in the mirror, and the sight made her smile. Antoine was always sitting down right in front of the turntable as if it were a campfire or a pagan statue; it did no good whatsoever to explain to him that the sound came from those two fancy loudspeakers at the far ends of the bedroom, and that they shot each note straight toward the center of her room right where her bed was — he still just plunked himself down by the turntable itself, as if spellbound by the spinning of the glowing black disk.

Having carefully removed her daytime makeup, Diane put on her nighttime makeup, so well calculated to conceal wrinkles without deepening them. Letting her skin breathe without makeup at night (as all the women's magazines recommended) was no more an option for her than letting her heart breathe. Those days were long gone. She considered her looks crucial for holding onto Antoine, so she wasn't going to compromise one bit of her current beauty in the hopes of stretching it out into some blurry, uncertain future. Certain temperaments — in fact, the most generous ones — harvest only the short-term pleasures and burn all the rest. This was Diane's philosophy.

Antoine was nervously listening to the soft noises emanating from the bathroom. The tearing-out of pieces of Kleenex and the rustling of Diane's hairbrush largely drowned out the violins and the brasses of the orchestra. In five minutes, he was going to have to get up, undress, and slide in between these wonderfully luxurious sheets, right beside this exquisitely groomed woman, in this incomparably elegant bedroom. And yet it was Lucile he craved — Lucile, who always would fly into his flat, flop down on his landlady's flimsy bed, flick her clothes off in a flash, and later flee in just the same way. Lucile was his ever-elusive, ever-fugitive, ever-welcomed one. She never settled down, she never would settle down, he never would wake up at her side, she would forever be just a fleeting presence in his life. What's more, he had wrecked her evening and now he felt his throat tightening up, in the intense despair of a teen-ager.

Diane emerged from the bathroom in her blue negligee and gazed briefly at Antoine's back and the nape of his neck, blond and straight, not letting herself read the least trace of hostility into either of them. She was tired, she'd had a bit to drink, which was unusual for her, and she was in a good mood. Without any seductive intentions, she was just hoping that Antoine would talk to her, laugh with her, tell her of his childhood. She had no way of knowing that his mind was racing, obsessed with his presumed moral obligation to make love to her, nor did she expect that he, quite unfairly, believed her incapable of wanting anything but his physical self. And so, when she sat down near him and looped her arm through his in a friendly fashion, his unspoken reaction was, "All right, all right — give me a second" — a boorish thought, and one quite distant from his usual style. After all, even in the dreariest of his prior affairs, he had always treated lovemaking with a certain respect, had always preceded physical contact by a short period of meditation.

"I adore this concerto," said Diane.

"Yes, lovely, isn't it," replied Antoine, with that politely disdainful lilt of someone lying on the beach to whom it has just been pointed out how blue the Mediterranean is.

"The party worked out pretty well, wouldn't you say?"

"Real fireworks," said Antoine, and he stretched out on his back on the carpet, eyes closed. In this position he seemed huge, and eternally alone. The tone of his own words echoed in his brain, sarcastic and nasty, and he couldn't stand himself. Diane was sitting there immobile, "old and handsome, and painted and fine". Now where had he just read that phrase? Oh, yes — in the diary of Samuel Pepys.

"Were you very bored?" She had stood up again and now was walking around the room, righting a drooping flower in a vase, running her fingers over a fine piece of woodwork. He could see her through his eyelashes. She loved objects, she loved these damned objects, and he was one of them — he was a masterpiece in her museum, he was her young gigolo. Oh, not really, of course — and yet he was always dining with *her* friends, sleeping in *her* apartment, living *her* life. Yes, he was a fine one to judge Lucile! She at least had the excuse of being a woman.

"Aren't you going to answer? Were you that extremely bored?"

Part I: *Le printemps*

Oh, her voice. Her questions. Her negligee. Her perfume. He couldn't take it any longer. He flopped over onto his stomach, putting his arms over his head. She kneeled down next to him. "Antoine... Antoine..." There was such desperation, such tenderness in her voice that he turned over once again, to face her. Her eyes were a little too bright. They stared at each other and then he turned his head, beckoning her towards him. She made an awkward and timid little motion towards lying down beside him, as if she feared she'd crack, as if she'd been hit by a spasm of rheumatism. And he, precisely because he didn't love her, felt desire for her.

•　•　•

Charles had departed for New York, alone, and his trip had shrunk down to just four days. Lucile, in her topless car, roamed the ever-bluer streets of Paris, waiting for the arrival of summer. She could already feel it in every fragrance in the air, in every glint of light on the Seine; she could already sense that familiar old smell of dust, trees, and soil that would soon engulf the Boulevard Saint-Germain at night, with its tall chestnut trees silhouetted against the pink sky, almost totally blotting it out; and those streetlamps, always lit too soon, annually made to lose face when, switching over from their wintertime role of cherished guides, they would become semi-parasites in the summer — caught between one day's night, which never would quite grow dark, and the next day's dawn, already champing at the bit to spread itself out all over the sky.

The first of her free evenings, Lucile hung around Saint-

Chapter 12

Germain-des-Prés, and there by chance she bumped into some friends from her university days and the first couple of years thereafter. They excitedly hailed her like a ghost from the past, and she rapidly started to feel the part. Once they'd gotten beyond a few jokes and shared memories, though, she saw that they were all caught up in their jobs, their material belongings, and their girlfriends, and that her carefree existence annoyed them more than it entertained them. It showed that you could break the money barrier just like the sound barrier. Once you'd crossed it, every word uttered would only reach you after a delay, coming to you a few seconds too late.

She declined their invitation to have dinner at their old hangout, the bistrot on Rue Cujas, and instead went home at 8:30, somewhat depressed. Pauline, glad to see her, cooked her a steak in the kitchen, after which Lucile lay down on her bed, with her window wide open. The evening light on the rug was fast receding, the street noise was growing fainter, and she recalled how, two months earlier, she'd been awakened by the wind. Not a languorous and heavy wind like this evening's, but a cheeky, quick, eager breeze, which had insisted that she wake up, much as this wind was urging her to drift off to sleep. Between the two, there had been Antoine — and so much life had been lived.

She was supposed to have dinner with him the next day — alone together, the first time ever. And that worried her. For once, she was more frightened that someone would find her boring than the reverse. But then again, she felt so richly fulfilled by life, she was experiencing such a sweet sensation, lying on this bed and sinking gradually further into the shadows, she was so taken with the idea that the earth was round and life complex, that she had the feeling that nothing could harm her in any way.

There are certain moments of perfect happiness — often moments of utter solitude — which, when recalled in life's bitterer periods, can save one from despair, even more so than the memory of times spent with friends, for one knows that one was happy all alone, for no clear reason. One knows that it is possible. And thus happiness, which can seem so tightly linked to someone who has made you suffer — someone on whom you were once profoundly, almost physically dependent — reveals a very different face, now looking like a smooth, round, solid object, no longer tied to anything specific, now floating within reach (far off, to be sure, but definitely reachable). And this memory is more comforting than the memory of any happiness shared with a former lover, for now you look back on that affair as a blunder you made, and now the happiness it gave you seems to have been based on nothing at all.

She was supposed to show up at Antoine's place at six the next day. They would take her car and would go off for a dinner somewhere in the countryside. They would have the whole night to themselves. She fell asleep with a smile.

•   •   •

The gravel was crunching under the waiters' feet, some bats were swooping around the lights on the terrace, and at the next table, a couple with very pink faces was wordlessly gulping down an *omelette flambée*. They were fifteen kilometers outside of Paris, it was a bit chilly, and the lady who ran the place had solicitously wrapped a shawl around Lucile's shoulders. This was one of a thousand similar small inns that offer adulterous or simply weary Parisians an almost failsafe privacy as well as fresh country air. The wind had done a good job of messing up Antoine's hair, and he was laughing. Lucile was telling him about her childhood, a happy childhood.

"… My father was a lawyer. He was just crazy about La Fontaine. He would walk along the banks of the Indre river reciting his fables by heart — and some years later, he himself took to writing fables — while adapting the roles, of course. I must be one of the very few women in France who can recite word for word a fable called *L'Agneau et le Corbeau.* Don't you feel lucky?"

"I'm very lucky," replied Antoine. "I know it. But go on."

"He died when I was twelve, and just at that time my brother was stricken by polio. He's still confined to a wheelchair. My mother dedicated herself to him with an all-consuming passion, as you might expect. She won't leave his side. I think she's sort of forgotten about me."

Lucile abruptly went silent. When she'd first come to Paris, she had sent some money each month to her mother, with great difficulty. But for the past two years, Charles had taken over this burden, without ever so much as mentioning a word about it to Lucile.

"Well, *my* parents hated each other," said Antoine. "They stayed married only because they wanted me to have a home. But believe me, I'd much rather have had two homes." He smiled, reached out across the table, and squeezed Lucile's hand.

"Do you realize — we have the whole evening ahead of us, and the whole night!"

"We'll take it easy going back to Paris. The top will be down, and you'll drive slowly because it's chilly. I'll light your cigarettes for you so you don't have to let go of the wheel."

"We'll go slowly because that's what you like. And we'll go dancing. Then, we'll go home to our little bed, and tomorrow morning, you'll finally find out if I drink coffee or tea, and how much sugar I take."

"We're going to dance? But we'll run into people we know!"

"Well, come on, now," replied Antoine curtly. "Do you really think I'm planning on spending the rest of my life hiding away?"

She didn't reply, just looked down.

"You're going to have to make a decision," said Antoine gently, "but not tonight — don't worry."

She looked back up, so visibly relieved that he couldn't help laughing. "I know very well that the slightest reprieve lets you breathe easy. You really live for the moment, don't you?"

She didn't answer. She felt totally at ease with him, totally natural; he made her feel like laughing, talking, making love — he gave her all she wanted, and that very fact frightened her somewhat.

●　　●　　●

She woke up early the next morning, and for a brief moment she felt disoriented when she first opened her eyes onto a messy room and a long arm speckled with blond hair, which kept her from moving. She quickly closed her eyes, flipped over onto her stomach, and smiled. She was next to Antoine, and now she knew the meaning of the phrase "a night of love". They'd gone dancing and hadn't run into anyone they knew. They'd come home to his apartment and they'd talked, made love, smoked, talked some more, and made love again, until at last daybreak found them on the bed, drunk on words and caresses, in that wondrous, exhausted period of grace that often follows over-indulgence. Their ardor had been so intense that night that they'd almost felt they were dying, and so sleep had arrived like a miraculous raft onto which they'd hoisted themselves before fainting away, still holding each other's hand in one last act of defiant togetherness. She gazed at Antoine's profile, at his neck, at the little hairs that were sprouting on his cheeks, at the blue circles under his eyes, and it seemed inconceivable to her that she had ever been able to wake up anywhere but right beside him. She loved his way of being so nonchalant and dreamy during the day, and so powerful and precise at night. It was as if love-making awoke in him a joyous pagan that knew only one law — the irrepressible drive of sensual pleasure.

He turned his head towards her, opened his eyes, and gazed at her with the slightly hesitant, slightly baffled look of a baby, which so many men have when they wake up. He recognized her, smiled, and turned his body to face her. He drooped his heavy head, still warm from sleep, onto her shoulder, and she looked with amusement at his large feet that stuck out from the tangle of sheets at the far end of the bed. He sighed and mumbled something in a plaintive little voice.

Part I: *Le printemps*

"It's amazing — in the morning your eyes are light yellow," she said. "They look like beer."

"What a poet you are," he replied, and then, without warning, he sat straight up, grabbed her face, and turned it towards the light. "Yours are nearly blue."

"No, they're gray. Green–gray."

"Braggart."

They were now facing each other, both sitting up in bed, naked. He was still holding her face, looking very intensely at her, and they were smiling at each other. His shoulders were very wide and bony, and she slipped out of his grasp, pressing her cheek against his torso.

She could hear his heart throbbing wildly, every bit as wildly as her own. "Your heart's beating like mad," she said. "Is it fatigue?"

"No," said Antoine. "It's a mad ache they call *la chamade.*"

"What exactly is *la chamade?*"

"You can go look it up in the dictionary. I don't have the time to explain it to you now." And so saying, he lazily sprawled himself out all across the bed. Outside, it was broad daylight.

At noon, Antoine phoned his office, explaining that he had a fever but that he would be coming in later in the afternoon.

"I know I must sound like a schoolboy, giving such a lame excuse," said Antoine, "but there's no way I'm going to let myself get tossed out on my ass. It's how I earn my bread, as they say."

"Do you make a lot of money?" asked Lucile nonchalantly.

"Very little," he replied equally nonchalantly. "Is that a big deal to you?"

Chapter 12

She broke out in a laugh. "No, it's just that I find money convenient, that's all."

"Convenient to the point of being a big deal?"

Taken aback, Lucile stared at him. "Why the sudden third degree?"

"Because I'm planning on living with you, which means supporting your lifestyle…"

"I beg your pardon," said Lucile, abruptly cutting him off. "I'm perfectly capable of supporting myself. I worked for a year at *L'Appel*, a paper that went under a while back. It was actually quite fun, except that everyone was so depressingly serious and preachy, and also…"

Antoine reached over and covered her mouth with his hand. "You heard what I said. I want to live with you, or else not to see you at all any more. I live in this little hovel, I don't earn much money, and there's no way in the world I could afford to have you lead the life you're leading these days. Do you hear me?"

"But… what about Charles?" blurted Lucile in a feeble voice.

"It's Charles or me," said Antoine. "He gets back tomorrow, right? So tomorrow evening, you come here — and for keeps — or else we won't be seeing each other any more. That's it. *Voilà.*"

He stood up and strode into the bathroom. Lucile started biting her nails and struggled to make sense of all this, but made little headway. She stretched her arms and closed her eyes. This had been bound to happen, she'd known it was in the cards —

after all, men were all so horribly tiring. But now she had a day and a half to make up her mind — and *prendre une décision* was among the most terrifying phrases in the entire French language to her.

CHAPTER 13

The airport at Orly was flooded with a cold sunlight that reflected off the high windows, off the silver fuselages of the airplanes, off the puddles on the runway, and sparkled in a thousand shining gray bursts that dazzled the eye. Charles' flight was already two hours late, and Lucile was pacing nervously in the large hall. If something should happen to him, she wouldn't be able to bear it; it would be her fault, for she'd refused to take this trip with him, and instead she'd cheated on him. As for that sad and resolute look that she'd been rehearsing two hours earlier, a look intended to warn Charles, even before she said a thing to him, that something was very wrong, it was now drifting over, without her suspecting it, into a look exuding anguish and compassion. And that was the look he saw as he emerged from customs.

He flashed her a warm and reassuring smile that made her eyes brim with tears, then headed straight towards her, kissed her tenderly, held her for a moment against himself, and right then Lucile's eye glimpsed a young woman shooting a nasty look of pure envy straight at her. Lucile was always forgetting how good-looking a man Charles was, since his tenderness was so totally hers. He loved her for what she was, didn't make her account for herself in any way, didn't ask a thing of her, and suddenly she felt a rush of resentment towards Antoine. It was easy enough for him to give her an ultimatum to make a choice and break things off with Charles — but one can hardly live two years with another human being without becoming deeply attached. She reached for Charles' hand and held it, not letting go of it. She felt as if she now had to protect him, not quite remembering that it would be from her own self that she'd be protecting him.

"I felt so lonely without You," said Charles. He smiled, tipped the porter, showed the chauffeur his suitcases, all with his usual aplomb. It had been a good while since she'd noticed how simple and effortless everything was with him. He opened the door for her, walked around the car, sat down next to her, took her hand again, almost shyly, and said to the chauffeur, "To the apartment," with the voice of a man who is overjoyed to be returning home again. But Lucile felt caught in a trap.

"Why did You miss me, what do You see in me still?" Her voice was despairing, but Charles smiled as if she were merely teasing him.

"You're everything to me — You know that."

"I don't deserve such feelings," she protested.

"Oh, that notion of 'deserving', You know, when it comes to love, well… Say, I brought You a lovely gift from New York."

"What is it?"

But he didn't want to tell her, and they gently argued all the way home. When Pauline spied them, she whimpered in great relief, since to her any airplane trip at all was a life-threatening risk; then, together, they all unpacked Charles' suitcases. He'd brought Lucile a light-colored mink coat, the same gray color as her eyes, silky and soft, and as she tried it on, he laughed as merrily as a little boy. Later that afternoon, she telephoned Antoine to tell him that she had to see him, that she hadn't had the courage to break the bad news to Charles.

"Well, I won't see you until you do," said Antoine in a very peculiar voice, and abruptly hung up on her.

For four whole days, she didn't see or hear from him and, still reeling from her anger, did not suffer from it. She deeply resented his having hung up on her so crudely. She hated any type of rudeness. But the truth was, she was very nearly certain that he would call her back. They had become too entangled that night, they had gone too far together into love's mysteries, they had become two disciples of one single cult, and now their cult had taken on a life of its own, independently of the whims of either of them. Antoine's mind might well be hostile to her, but his body was now her body's friend, it needed hers to feel whole, it missed hers. Their bodies were like two horses that were great companions, separated temporarily by a tiff between their owners, but that would wind up galloping off together into sun-drenched climes of pure pleasure. Any other ending struck her as impossible. She couldn't imagine how people could hold their own passions at bay; she had never understood any need or reason for doing so. And in the self-indulgent climate of post-Louis-Philippe France, she had a hard time conceiving of any superior moral principle to that of heeding the call of one's own hot, churning blood.

Most of all, she resented Antoine for not having let her

explain herself. She would have told him about the plane's delay and her anguish while waiting for it, she would have proven to him that she had acted in good faith. She would certainly have been able to stick to her resolve and to inform Charles of her decision that evening. But she'd found it so difficult to make up her mind, she'd struggled so hard to bring herself to the point where she could make the dramatic cutoff, that the failure of her attempt to do so now seemed to her a cabalistic omen. Insincere acts often bring out superstition in their wake. In the meantime, Antoine still hadn't called and she was growing bored.

•　　•　　•

Summer was drawing nigh and soirées were starting to be held outdoors, and so one evening, Charles took her to some nondescript dinner party at the Pré-Catelan. In the middle of a very lively group standing underneath a tree were Antoine and Diane, and Lucile recognized his laugh even before she saw him. She couldn't help thinking, "Oh my, he's laughing without me," but nonetheless a joyful impulse drew her towards him. With a smile, she extended her hand, but he didn't return her smile, merely bowing in the most perfunctory manner, and looking away. All at once the Pré-Catelan, so bright and verdant, took on a melancholy cast, and Lucile could see the futility of all these people's lives, their impoverishment, the desperate ennui that pervaded this restaurant, this crowd, and her own life. If it weren't for Antoine and his yellow eyes, his little den of iniquity, and the few moments of truth that she knew three times a week in his arms, every last detail of this troubled and falsely jolly social set would feel like it was the pathetic creation of some third-rate set designer. Claire Santré looked utterly hideous this evening, Johnny looked ridiculous, and Diane half-dead. Lucile recoiled from her in shock.

"Don't go running off, Lucile," intoned Diane in an imperious voice. "That's a lovely dress You have on."

Lately, Diane had taken to lavishing little compliments like this on Lucile, thinking that doing so would demonstrate her total self-confidence. But it just made Johnny smile, and even more so Claire, to whom Johnny had finally "confessed" all that he knew. Naturally, their little circle had all been let in on the news, and so now, at the exact moment when Lucile and Antoine were standing there next to each other, confused, ashen-faced, and greatly upset, people were looking at them in that half-envious, half-ironic way that is generally reserved for new lovers. Lucile, stepping back towards Diane, said, in a lackluster voice, "I just got this dress yesterday, but I think it might be a little too chilly this evening."

"It would be harder to catch cold with Your dress than with Coco Dourede's dress," Johnny observed wryly. "Never seen so little cloth for such a big surface area. And she even told me that it washes as easily as a handkerchief. But I'd bet it takes less time."

Lucile glanced over at Coco Dourede who, it was quite true, was meandering about half-naked under the dangling garlands of light bulbs. A deep, delicious smell of damp earth was rising up from the Bois de Boulogne.

"My little Lucile, You don't look too chipper," said Claire.

Part I: *Le printemps*

Her eyes were sparkling, and her hand was draped over Johnny's arm. He, too, was keenly observing Lucile. And Diane, as well, intrigued by her silence, was watching her. "My God, these people are all wolves," thought Lucile. "Wolves — and they would tear me to shreds with their curiosity, if they could." And with a sheepish smile, she said, "I'm really cold. I'm going to go ask Charles for my coat."

"Allow me," said Johnny. "The guy in the cloakroom is very good-looking."

He came back very quickly. After that first brush with Antoine as she arrived, Lucile hadn't looked straight at him even once, but she was keeping an eye on him from the side, the way certain birds do.

"Oh, it's a new coat!" exclaimed Claire. "That pastel gray is divine — I've never seen You in that color before."

"Charles brought it back for me from New York," said Lucile. And just then her gaze met Antoine's, and what she read in it made her want to give him a slap. She turned away abruptly and walked off.

"Minks used to make me look radiant, in my younger days," said Claire cheerfully. But Diane was frowning. Antoine, right next to her, had put on what she called his "blind façade" — he had gone immobile, and had a blank look on his face.

"Go get me a whiskey," said Diane to him. Since she didn't dare ask him any questions, now she was giving him orders instead. At least that comforted her a little bit.

Lucile and Antoine made no moves at all in each other's direction all evening long. But towards midnight, they wound up

Chapter 13

accidentally seated at the opposite ends of a table, each one alone, as everyone else had gone off to dance. Without seeming extremely rude, he could hardly avoid joining her, and anyway, he didn't want to alienate her yet further. What he had suffered over these past several days was crushing him. He had imagined her in Charles' arms, kissing him, whispering things to Charles that she'd only said to him, Antoine. Worst of all, he'd imagined her face with a certain special expression on it, open but somehow also concealing a powerful secret. He'd seen her face with that special expression, and to see it again was now his sole aim. He was mortally jealous of this woman's attention. And he walked around the table and sat down next to her.

She didn't even look at him, and without warning he cracked, leaned forward. This was impossible, this was unbearable, this aloof stranger who only a few days earlier had been stark naked in the sunlight, right by his side.

"Lucile," he said, "why are you doing this to us?"

"*Me*!? What about *you*?" she snapped. "Just because you have a tantrum, I'm supposed to cut things off within twenty-four hours? That was just too much." She felt totally desperate and totally calm. Drained.

"This isn't... it's... this is no tantrum," he said, his words tumbling over each other. "I'm possessive, and I can't help it. I can't stand lying any more, it's killing me. Believe me. The idea that... that..." He paused, drew his hand across his face, and then went on. "Tell me — since Charles got back, have you... have the two of you..."

She looked daggers at him, and spat out, "Have I slept with

him? Well, what do you think? He brought me back a mink coat, didn't he?"

"You're not thinking about what you're saying," retorted Antoine.

"No. But you — you were imagining us together. I saw it in your face a few minutes ago. And I hate you for that."

A couple was coming back from the dance floor, and Antoine rose swiftly to his feet. "Come dance with me," he said. "I've got to talk with you."

"No," she replied. "What I just said is true, isn't it?"

"Perhaps... Sometimes one has stupid reflexes."

"But not vulgar ones," said Lucile, and she looked away from him.

"She's making out that I'm in the wrong," he thought. "First she cheats on me, and then she makes out that *I'm* in the wrong." A wave of anger swept over him, and he seized her by the wrist, pulling her towards him with such a sharp tug that several heads turned. "Come on and dance."

But she resisted, with tears of anger and hurt welling up in her eyes. "I don't feel like dancing."

Antoine felt trapped inside himself, no more capable of letting go of her than of dragging her off by force. And at the same time, he was fascinated by her tears, and a strange thought flashed through his mind. "I've never seen her cry... How I wish that some night, she would cry on my shoulder over some childhood sorrow — I'd so love to console her."

"Let go of me, Antoine!" she said quietly.

Things were becoming grotesque. He was far stronger than

she was, and he'd pulled her halfway to her feet; at this point, she was no longer capable of smiling in a silly, casual manner, as if he were merely kidding around with her. No — people were watching them. He was crazy — crazy and mean — he frightened her — yet he appealed to her still.

"Now that's what they call the hesitation waltz…" chimed in Charles quite unexpectedly, standing right behind Antoine. In a flash, Antoine let go of her and spun around, fully intending to punch this old man in the face and then to hightail it out of there, leaving this crowd behind forever. But standing right by Charles, there was Diane — smiling, elegant as always, and a little intrigued, or so it seemed, and remote.

"So You're trying to get Lucile to dance with You by force?" she asked.

"That's right," replied Antoine with a glare, and suddenly he knew that he was going to break off with her that very evening, and a great sense of calm surged through him. Yet there was also great pity, for she mattered so little in this affair; he'd never cared one whit about her.

"But You're no rocker-boy," sneered Diane. "You're too old for that." And she was already starting to sit down.

Charles, too, was already leaning towards Lucile and was asking her, with a smile that belied the tension on his face, what had just taken place. And Lucile smiled right back at him. She knew she should just make up some random answer — she had no lack of imagination. In fact, every person here was overflowing with clever ploys for worming their way out of a *faux pas*, clever ways to be phony, clever tricks to nourish and maintain their petty secrets. That is, every person here except for him — Antoine. For a moment he teetered in indecision, then abruptly swiveled about, almost making an *entrechat,* and rapidly strode off into the night.

CHAPTER 14

$\mathcal{I}t$ was raining outside. She heard the drops splattering on the sidewalk in one of those summer showers, melancholy and gentle, that seem more like the whim of some gardener at loose ends than the fury of the elements. Thin slivers of dawnlight were already creeping onto the carpet, and she was lying in her bed, unable to fall asleep. She could feel her heart beating hard, growing more agitated, sending her blood in powerful bursts to all the furthest reaches of her body. She felt the tips of her fingers becoming heavier, and the blue vein that crossed her left temple like an arrow was throbbing. For almost two hours now, she hadn't been able to calm this wild heart of hers, but had just accepted its frenzy with a *mélange* of irony and despair. This had been going on ever since they'd returned from the Pré-Catelan, shortly after she'd spun about and become aware of Antoine's disappearance, Diane's sudden pallor, and the collective *frisson* of delight among all present at the sight of this little scandal.

She no longer felt any anger, and even wondered what had provoked it in the first place. That look on Antoine's face when the coat had been mentioned had seemed insulting to her, essentially implying that she was a venal woman. But in a sense, what else was she, if not that? She was living off of Charles and was very responsive to the gifts he gave her — surely responding more to the feelings behind them than to how much they had cost — but in any case accepting them all. That she couldn't deny, and in fact she had never even thought about it, so natural did it feel to her to be the mistress of a man who could afford it and whom, moreover, she valued highly. In a word, Antoine had made a huge error of judgment: he had concluded that she was dropping him and sticking with Charles for material reasons alone. He had thought her capable of such crass calculations, had judged her for it, and without any doubt had found her contemptible. She knew well that jealousy almost inevitably leads to ugly thoughts, acts, and judgments, but she couldn't tolerate this in Antoine, no matter how jealous he might be. She believed in him, in some sort of blood bond between them, believed in their spiritual intertwinedness, and she felt as if she had been dealt, through no fault of her own, a low blow.

What else could she have said to him? "Sure, Charles brought me back this coat, and sure, it made me happy. Sure, I've shared his bed since he got back, as will happen from time to time between us. But of course none of that has the least to do with what happens between you and me in the physical arena, because what you and I have is pure passion, and passion is unlike anything else on earth. Only when it's with yours does my body come alive and act creative and insightful, and by now you should realize that." But even then, he wouldn't have understood. It was a commonplace, a thousand times repeated and a thousand times confirmed, that men simply didn't get this quintessentially feminine type of message. She felt herself falling more and more deeply into an anti-male frame of mind, and this troubled her greatly.

"So should I bring up his physical relationship with Diane, and tell him that I'm not jealous? Does that make me some kind of monster? And even if I *am* a monster, what can I do about it? Nothing." But if she wasn't going to do anything, she would lose Antoine, and this thought made her tremble, made her toss and turn in her bed like a fish thrashing about on the grass. It was four in the morning.

Charles came into her bedroom. He sat down gently on her bed, his face drawn. In this harsh dawnlight, he really looked fifty, and the casual, almost sporting way he had thrown his dressing gown around himself didn't help at all. He placed his hand on Lucile's shoulder and sat there motionless for a short while.

"Weren't You able to sleep either?"

She made a feeble gesture of denial, tried to smile, to blame the food from the Pré-Catelan. But she just didn't have the will power any longer. She closed her eyes again.

"Maybe we should…", Charles started to say, but then he stopped and started again in a firmer tone. "Would You be able to take a trip? Either alone or with me, to the Côte d'Azur? You always told me that being at the seaside cured You of all ills."

She didn't ask him what kind of ill or cure he was alluding to — something in his way of questioning made it obvious that there was no point in asking.

"The Riviera," she repeated dreamily, "the Riviera…?" And behind her stubbornly closed eyelids, she could see the sea rushing up onto the beach, she could see the color of the sand in

the evening when the sun abandons it. Just what she loved —
just what she needed, surely.

"I'll leave with You as soon as You can arrange it," she said,
reopening her eyes to look at him, but he turned his face away
from her. She was astonished for a moment, but then she felt,
with a type of horror, the wet warmth of her *own* tears on her
cheek.

•   •   •

In early May, the Côte d'Azur is rather sparsely populated,
and the only restaurant that was open was theirs for the taking,
as was the hotel, as was the beach. After a week had gone by,
Charles was beginning to regain some hope. Lucile was
spending long hours in the sun and the sea, was reading avidly,
was discussing her books with him, was gulping down one grilled
fish after another, was playing cards with the few couples that
they ran into on the beach — in a word, was seeming happy. Or
at least content. It was just that she was also drinking a lot in the
evenings, and one night she'd made love in a violent, almost
aggressive fashion that he'd never seen in her before. He didn't
realize that all these acts were rooted in a hidden hope — that of
seeing Antoine again. She was tanning to please him, eating a
lot so as not to look scrawny to him, reading books published by
his company so they could talk about them together; and she was
drinking in order to forget him, and also in order to sleep.

To be sure, she didn't admit to herself that she was nour-
ishing any such hope; she was simply living like an animal
resigned to being slaughtered any day now, but once in a while,

in a moment of distraction, when she would momentarily let go of her clinging dependence on the elements, briefly forgetting the sun's warmth, the sea's freshness, and the sand's softness, then the memory of Antoine would come crashing down on her like a boulder, and she would submit to it in a weird blur of joy and desperation, stretching herself out to form a cross on the beach, feeling herself being crucified — not by nails piercing her hands, but by terrible sharp spears of memory plunging straight through her heart.

At such times, reeling in shock, she was astounded to feel her heart tip over and her emotions drain out, leaving it empty yet still unbearably heavy. What did she care about this sun, this sea, even her body's physical well-being, what did she care about those things that once had been all she needed to be happy, if Antoine wasn't there to share them all with her? She could have swum with him, could have tugged his blond hair, sopping wet and made even blonder by the Mediterranean waters, could have kissed him between one wave and the next, could have made love to him in the dunes right over there behind those still-deserted huts, could have lain motionless right next to him as dusk fell, and together with him watched the swallows swooping and gliding over the pink roofs. And time would then have been something not merely to kill — time would have been something to hold onto dearly, to cherish, not to let slip by.

Whenever she reached her wits' end, she would get up from the sand, looking a bit dazed, and head for the bar, for its most remote part, where Charles, lying in his *chaise longue,* couldn't see her. There she would order a cocktail or two and drink them under the vaguely sarcastic gaze of the bartender, who assumed she was an alcoholic cringing in shame, but she couldn't care less. In any case she'd most likely turn into one. Then she would walk back down to the beach, stretch out at Charles' feet, and close her eyes. The sun would become a white spot, and she could no longer tell its warmth weighing down on her skin from the alcohol's warmth coursing through her veins, and all she could see beneath her eyelids was a vague, blurry distortion of Antoine, no longer capable of hurting her. For a few hours then she'd regain a very primitive sense of autonomy from him, almost a vegetative state, thanks to which she could at least breathe a little.

Charles seemed happy, which was already quite something for him, and whenever she watched him walking towards her in his flannel pants, his dark blue blazer, and his loafers, with his scarf so precisely tucked into his shirt collar, she would powerfully fight off the image of Antoine, with his bare feet, his hair in his eyes, his shirt open to show his chest, and his narrow hips and long legs stuffed into an old pair of cotton pants. She'd known young men aplenty in her day, and there was no question that what she loved in Antoine was not his youth. She would have loved him if he'd been old. But in fact, she loved him for being just as old as he was, just as she loved him for being blond, loved him for being so very moralistic, loved him for being sensual, loved him for having loved her, and even loved him for not, it now was clear, loving her any longer. Thus it was. Her love was there, solid, standing there like a wall separating her from the sun and from life's comfort, even from the desire to live at all. And of all this she was quite ashamed. The pursuit of happiness had always been her guiding light, and unhappiness, if you brought it upon yourself, had always seemed inexcusable to her (a philosophy that had, incidentally, always earned for her, from her fellow human beings, a complete lack of understanding, and indeed, a nearly perpetual sense of being resented).

"So now I'm paying the price," she thought to herself with disgust — a disgust that was all the more intense since she'd never believed in the fairy-tale notion of moral debts, and since cultural and social taboos had always infuriated her, and since the fear she'd seen in a thousand other people of wrecking their own lives had always caused in her a shudder of revulsion, as if from a shameful illness. But now, she herself had caught this illness, she was suffering from it, and was suffering without any solace provided by telling herself so, which is doubtless one of the most unpleasant ways of suffering.

Charles had to go back to Paris. She took him to the station, promised she'd behave herself, was tender with him. He would be back in six days, and in the meantime he'd call her every evening, which he indeed did. But on the fifth day, around four in the afternoon, when Lucile absent-mindedly picked up the receiver, it was Antoine's voice that she heard. It had been exactly two weeks since she'd seen him.

CHAPTER 15

After having stormed out of the Pré-Catelan, Antoine had crossed the Bois de Boulogne on foot, talking to himself all the while, like someone crazed. Diane's driver had dashed off after him, offering his services, but to the fellow's great astonishment, Antoine had shoved 5,000 francs his way while muttering, "Here, take this for all the things You've done — it's not a lot, but it's all I've got on me." It seemed that Antoine, so ardent was his desire for things with Diane to be over and done with, figured that he had to spill the news to everyone. After that, he had rapidly covered the whole length of the Avenue de la Grande Armée, explaining along the way to some eager prostitute that he knew plenty of women of her type, then spinning about to go back and apologize to her. But by then she had disappeared, probably having instantly forgotten his remark, and he spent a full half-hour vainly trying to find her. Next, he had stepped into a bar somewhere along the Champs-Élysées, tried to get plastered, and eventually wound up sloppily locking horns with another drunk customer — on the face of it over some murky political issue, but in actual fact because the unfortunate fellow had stubbornly decided to block access to the jukebox, whereas Antoine, for his part, was adamantly determined to put on, as many times as possible, some song that he'd danced to, listened to, and hummed with Lucile.

"Oh, I'm so miserable," he thought, "so let's do it up right." Having emerged as the victor of the drunken brawl, he played his song eight times in a row, to the general consternation of nearly everyone present, and then had to hand over his identity card to the bartender, as he was at that point completely stripped of cash. He staggered back to his apartment at three in the morning, arriving exhausted but sobered up by the brisk morning air. In a word, he was being a typical young male. At times, anguish can elicit just as much strength, vivacity, and *élan* as can euphoria.

Waiting in front of the stairs to his building was Diane, sitting in her Rolls. He had already recognized it from afar, and had nearly done an about-face. But what changed his mind was the thought of her driver, reeling from sleepiness, having had to sit there for hours, waiting for Madame's boyfriend to come traipsing home whenever he felt like it. So Antoine walked up, opened the door for her, and Diane stepped wordlessly out. She had put her makeup back on in the car, and the rays of dawn not only made her mouth too red but also gave her face, with its well calculated look of indifference, an unintended appearance of immaturity, disorientation, and confusion. And indeed, even in her own eyes she was making a grievous error in coming in the wee hours to try to rekindle her lover's ardor, just as, two years earlier, she had made a grievous error by falling in love with him. It was simply that whereas this error had so far merely echoed in her life like background music in a movie, persistent but discreet, now it was turning into a cruel and inexorable drumroll.

Chapter 15

She could just see herself as she got out of the car, as she took the hand that Antoine extended her, as she made a last-ditch attempt to savor, for just a few more moments, playing the role of Woman Who Is Loved, before being suddenly plunged into the unknown and terrifying role of Woman Who Has Been Spurned. And just as she was releasing her driver to go home to sleep, she cast a weirdly palsy wink in his direction, almost as if to convey her desperate knowledge that he was about to be the cherished witness of these closing moments of her happiness.

"Am I disturbing You?", she asked as they climbed the stairs. Antoine shook his head, opened the door of his room for her, and stepped aside. This was only the second time that she had ever been here. The first time was when they had just met and Diane had found it amusing to spend their first night together in the apartment of this awkward and rather shabbily dressed young man. After that, though, she had offered him the *grand lit* in Rue Cambon, with all its luxury and pomposity, for this little room, after all, was pretty dingy and uninviting. But right now, she would have given anything in the world to be able to sleep in this rickety bed, with her clothes draped over the hideous chair that matched it. Antoine closed the shutters, switched on the red lamp, and ran his hand across his face. He was unshaven, he seemed to have lost weight in just those few hours, and overall, he had that scruffy look that grief so often brings out in men. And Diane no longer knew what she wanted to say to him.

Ever since he had precipitously bolted off, she had been turning one phrase over and over in her mind: "He owes me an explanation." But when you really came down to it, what *did* he

owe her? What could anyone really owe anyone else? She sat
down very erectly on the bed, despite feeling terribly tempted to
lie down on it and to say, "Antoine, I just felt the need to see you,
I was worried, but I'm so sleepy now, come to bed with me."
But Antoine kept on standing in the middle of the room, waiting,
and everything about his stance suggested that he wanted to
clarify this situation as soon as possible, which is to say, to bring
it to a crashing halt, and in so doing, to wound her terribly.

"That was a rather abrupt exit You made," said Diane.

"I'm sorry about that."

They were speaking like two actors, and he felt it. He was
waiting to summon up enough inner strength, enough resolve, to
say to her — uttering the poorly written but crucial line in his
script — "It's all over between us." He was vaguely hoping that
she would have some harsh words for him, that she would bring
up Lucile, and that her anger would give him enough strength to
be brutal. But instead, she seemed gentle, resigned, almost
fearful, and for a moment he thought to himself in horror that he
really didn't know this woman at all — and worse yet, that he
hadn't ever really tried to know her. Maybe her devotion to him
was for entirely different reasons than he had ever thought.
Maybe she saw more in him than just an elusive free spirit who
was good in bed. He'd always taken it for granted that she clung
to him solely because of her sensual needs and her wounded
pride (after all, she'd never managed to squeeze him under her
thumb, as she had all her other lovers) — but what if there were
other hidden factors behind the scenes? What if, all of a sudden,
out of the blue, Diane were to explode in tears? But that would

Chapter 15

be inconceivable. Diane's myth, the legend of her invulnerability and of her unflappability, was too solidly anchored in Paris, and he'd heard it repeated so very many times. For a few seconds, these two human beings nearly peered into each other's core — but then Diane opened her purse, took out her gold compact, and started daubing on more makeup. Although this was a desperate act by a woman in panic, he saw it as a crass act by a woman without feelings.

"What's more, Lucile doesn't love me, so I must simply be unlovable," he concluded in his mind, in a momentary burst of insincere self-loathing of a sort that unhappiness often brings on, and he lit up a cigarette.

He flicked his match into the fireplace — an annoyed and impatient gesture, which she assumed was due to boredom, and which aroused her anger. She forgot about Antoine and her passion for him, and her only concern became herself, Diane Mirbel, and the cruel fashion in which a man, her lover, had abandoned her for no apparent reason at the high point of a soirée, and in front of all her friends. She, too, reached for a cigarette with a trembling hand, and he offered her a match. The smoke had an unpleasant acrid taste. She had smoked too much and she suddenly realized that the chaotic and polyphonic racket that for the last few minutes had been driving her up a wall without her having even consciously noticed it was simply the chirping of birds in the street. They were awakening with the dawn and were greeting, delirious with joy, the first rays of sunlight to reach Paris.

She looked at Antoine and said, "Might I be told the reason

for Your rushing off that way? Or is that none of my business?"

"I can tell You," replied Antoine, directly returning her gaze, and just then a strange little expression that she'd never before seen distorted his mouth. "I'm in love with Lucile." "Lucile Saint-Léger," he then stupidly added, as if there could possibly have been the slightest doubt about who it was.

Diane's gaze fell. This evening's purse had a little scratch on top. This was unacceptable. She stared very intensely at the rip, seeing nothing other than it, and trying with all her might to focus her thoughts uniquely on it. "Now where in the world could I have done *that*?" She kept on waiting for her heart to start up again, for a sudden flash of daybreak, for anything at all — a phone ringing, a bomb dropping, a voice screaming in the street — to come and drown out the silent shouting inside her head. But nothing came, and the birds outside the window kept right on idiotically twittering, and this frenzy, this hubbub, was simply hateful.

"Well, well…", said Diane. "You might have told me about this a little earlier."

"I didn't really know it," replied Antoine. "I wasn't sure, I thought I was just jealous. But the point is, she doesn't love me — that's clear enough now — and I'm going to be miserable for good…"

He could have gone on. This was actually the first time he'd ever spoken to anyone about Lucile, and it gave him a bitter-sweet kind of pleasure that made him forget, with typically masculine obliviousness, that it was Diane that he was telling all this to. She, on the other hand, retained but a single word of

Chapter 15

what he had said: "jealous".

"What would You be jealous about? One can only be jealous about what is one's own, as You've told me a dozen times... So, were You her lover?"

Antoine did not reply. Anger began to surge into Diane, and to liberate her.

"Are You jealous of Blassans-Lignières? Or does his little cutie have another two or three lovers on the side? In any case, my poor Antoine, You'd be hard put to maintain that girl's lifestyle on Your salary, if that's of any consolation to You."

"That's hardly the point," he snapped back. And all at once he hated Diane for judging Lucile in just the same way as he himself had done four hours earlier. He wouldn't permit her to cast aspersions on Lucile. He'd told her the truth and now she should simply go away, should leave him alone to commune with his memory of Lucile at the Pré-Catelan, her eyes brimming with tears. Had she cried solely because he was hurting her wrists, or was it because she cared about him?

"Where did You meet up with her?" asked Diane's voice, floating in the distance. "Here?"

"Yes," he replied. "Afternoons." And he remembered how Lucile's face looked at the height of their passion, and her body, her voice, everything that now he'd lost through his stupidity and stubbornness, and he felt like kicking himself. There would be no more footfalls of Lucile in the stairwell, no more lazy languishing in the brilliant afternoon sun, no more *Rouge et Noir* scenes... Nothing was left at all. And the look he gave Diane was so wistful and so full of yearning that she recoiled from him.

"Although I never really thought that You loved me," she said, "I did give You credit for at least a certain degree of respect for me. But now, I fear..."

He looked at her without a drop of empathy and all at once in his eyes she detected an implacably hard male world, a world where a man was unable to respect a mistress whom he didn't love. Perhaps she was even giving him too much credit. Most likely, Antoine did respect her in some vague sense, but deep down she must be, in his eyes, the cheapest of whores, for she had shared her bed with him for two years without insisting that he love her nor that he tell her he did, and she had never even said it to him herself. And now, too late, she began to see in Antoine's yellow eyes the harsh childhood he had suffered — brutal, austere, and utterly devoid of, and therefore starved for, words of love, scenes of affection, exclamations of tenderness. Reserve and elegance such as hers would mean nothing to someone with such a background. And she instinctively knew that if she were to flop herself down on this bed as she so wished to do now, and were to beg him to join her, he would be taken aback and vaguely disgusted. After all, he was used to her socialite persona, to the face that she had been showing him now for two full years, and he wouldn't be interested in seeing another one.

There was no doubt that her haughty demeanor was now costing her dearly. But she was now also discovering that this pride that was holding her erectly seated on Antoine's bed at dawn, this pride that was so central to and so inseparable from her aristocratic persona that she had almost forgotten it existed, was her clearest, most intimate, most precious ally. Like a born

Chapter 15

horseman who unexpectedly discovers that his thirty years of riding have just allowed him to dodge the wheels of an onrushing bus, Diane, astonished, was witnessing this pride, this neglected or at best seldom exploited gift of hers, as it spared her from the worst fate possible — namely, coming to despise herself as a result of Antoine's withdrawal of his love.

"Why tell me this today," she asked softly, "when You probably could have continued in the same way for a long time? I didn't suspect anything much was going on between the two of you. Or rather, I had stopped thinking it was."

"I guess I'm just too miserable to be able to lie," replied Antoine. And he realized, to his surprise, that it was true — he would easily have been able to lie all night to Diane, consoling her and regaining her confidence, if only he'd been sure of seeing Lucile again the next day, or if he'd been sure of her love for him. Such bliss would allow him to do anything and, for a brief moment, he understood Lucile — her glibness and her ability to cover up, for which he had so severely rebuked her in these past few weeks. But now it was too late, too late — he had mortally wounded her, and now she wouldn't ever want to have anything more to do with him. But then what on earth was this *other* woman doing here in his apartment?

Diane, sensing the drift of his thoughts, blindly struck out at him, lacing her acid words with honey. "And so what becomes of Your dear Sarah in all of this? Has she finally died — for keeps, this time?"

Antoine said nothing in reply, but simply stared at her in pure rage — a look that she far preferred to that vaguely friendly but ever so distant look that he had been giving her only moments earlier. She was homing in on the very worst in him — his lack of empathy, his nastiness, his unforgivable qualities — and this afforded her some slight relief.

"I think it would be best if You left now," he said, after a long silence. "I wouldn't want us to part in some ugly scene, for You've always been so kind to me."

"I have never been kind to anyone," said Diane as she rose to her feet. "It's just that in certain circumstances, I found You to be quite good company. That's all."

She was holding herself perfectly erect in front of him, looking directly at him, and he had no way of knowing that it would have taken only the tiniest trace of a fond memory or of pity to cross his face for her to suddenly collapse in tears in his arms. But he felt no nostalgia for what he was leaving behind, and so she merely offered him her hand and watched him mechanically bend over to kiss it — and the expression of unbearable pain that crossed her face as for the final time she glimpsed that blond nape of his neck had already totally vanished as he raised his head. She whispered "Au revoir," bumped herself a little as she passed through the door frame, and then slipped into the stairwell.

Antoine lived three floors up, and it was only after descending two flights of stairs that she stopped, turning for a moment towards the moist and dirty wall of the landing, and pressed against it her celebrated face and her elegant, slender hands, now no longer of the slightest use to her.

CHAPTER 16

Antoine spent two weeks all alone. He walked a great deal, not speaking to anyone, and wasn't even surprised when he would run into someone he knew, some lady in Diane's coterie of friends, and was completely snubbed by her. He knew the rules of the game: having been brought by Diane into a small social set that was not his own, he was automatically expelled therefrom the moment that he left her. This was the protocol, and the perfunctory friendliness that Claire extended to him one evening when he encountered her by chance struck him as quite exceptional. In any case, she mentioned that Lucile and Charles were vacationing in Saint-Tropez, and she didn't seem in the least surprised to find out that Antoine knew nothing of it. It seemed perfectly natural that in casting out one woman, he should have irreparably lost the other one, too, forever. This realization actually made Antoine chuckle a little bit, although these days he felt less and less inclined toward laughter.

A snatch of a poem by Apollinaire kept running through his head: "Though ambling through *mon beau Paris,* I have no heart to perish here. The herds of buses, bellowing..." He didn't recall how it went on, and made no effort to track it down. And it was quite true that Paris was taking on a beauty ever more heartbreaking, blue, blonde, and languid, and it was also true that he no more had the heart to die here than to live here. When he thought about it, in fact, everything was for the best. Lucile was on the coast of the Mediterranean, which she'd told him she adored, so she was doubtless very happy once again, for that was the kind of life she was made for, and perhaps she was even sleeping with some handsome local lad behind Charles' back. As for Diane, she was going around in public with a young Cuban diplomat; he'd seen a charming snapshot of the couple at the opening performance of some ballet in some newspaper. Antoine himself was reading, not drinking at all, and once in a while he would get all twisted up in pangs of rage in the middle of the night when thinking about Lucile. All of this struck him as being clearly inevitable.

Hope had fled, for his memory gave him no reason to have any. The only images he could recall any longer were Lucile's passion in bed, and his own as well, but these recollections tore him apart rather than comforting him, for one can never be totally sure of how intense one's partner's pleasure is — nor, more troublingly, can one ever be sure that some stranger won't one day come along and bring an equal or even greater pleasure to one's former lover. Although he was convinced that he would never again know such carnal bliss as he'd known with Lucile, he had a hard time believing that she felt that way about him.

Sometimes he would once again see her haunted face that day when he had come home so late, and he would once again hear her saying, "You know, Antoine, I love you — and it's for keeps." And each time this happened, he would feel that he'd blown his chances that day, that he should have focused a little

more on her mind and a little less on her body, and he kept
thinking that although he had obviously possessed Lucile totally
on the physical level, he had completely overlooked her essence
as a human being. To be sure, they had laughed uproariously
together, and shared laughter was a *sine qua non* for true love —
but that in itself was not enough. All he needed to convince
himself of this was to replay in his mind the strange sense of
wistfulness that had suddenly overcome him right in the middle
of his fury that last evening at the Pré-Catelan when he had
spotted tears filling Lucile's eyes. For a man and a woman to
really love each other fully, it wasn't enough for them to have
given each other moments of ecstasy, or for them to have made
each other laugh uproariously — they also had to have made
each other suffer. Of course, Lucile might well disagree with
this. Actually, at this point, she wouldn't agree or disagree with
anything he said, for she was no longer part of his life. And he
would then suddenly cut off this internal dialogue, this pointless
rehashing of things with her, which he went through twenty
times a day, and he would abruptly rise from the spot where he
had abruptly sat down while walking through Paris. There was
no end in sight to this torment.

•　　•　　•

Two weeks passed and one day he ran into Johnny, who was
on vacation and on the make at the Café Flore, and who seemed
delighted to see Antoine once again. The two of them sat down
together and had a whiskey as Antoine watched, with amusement, Johnny's smug way of reacting when friends came up to

greet him and noticed Antoine. Just as he knew he was blond, Antoine was aware of being rather good-looking, but neither fact held great interest for him.

"So how's our friend Lucile doing?", said Johnny blithely, after a while.

"I wouldn't have the foggiest idea."

Johnny couldn't help laughing. "That's what I figured. You were quite right to split with her. She's a charming soul, but risky. I expect she'll wind up alcoholic, and pampered by old Charles, to boot."

"What makes You say that?" Antoine was monitoring his own voice, carefully calculating the degree of indifference it conveyed.

"Oh, she's already started her descent. One of my chums saw her on the beach, tipsy as hell. But surely this is no news to You..." And seeing Antoine's reaction, he chuckled. "Come now — You couldn't have failed to pick up on how crazy she was about You — anyone could see it a mile off, even without knowing her... Say — what's so funny?"

Antoine had started laughing and couldn't stop — he was wildly happy and wildly ashamed. He was so dumb — yes, he had been so, so dumb. Of course she loved him, of course she was thinking about him... How could he ever have thought that she wouldn't love him after those two months of ecstasy they'd shared? How could he have been so pessimistic, so self-centered, so imperceptive? She loved him and she missed him, and that's why she was guzzling in secret. Maybe she even thought that he'd forgotten her, when the truth was that she was all he'd been thinking about for two weeks. Maybe her unhappiness now was all due to his incredible stupidity. And in a burst of clarity, Antoine realized that he had to go track her down at once. He'd explain everything, he'd do anything she asked him to do, but most of all he would sweep her up in his arms, beg for her forgiveness, and they would kiss and kiss for hours on end. So where the hell was Saint-Tropez?

He had risen from his chair. "Come on now, calm down, my friend," said Johnny. "You're acting like someone who's gone off the deep end, old boy."

"Excuse me, please," said Antoine, "but I've got to go make a telephone call." And he ran all the way home, picked up the phone, got into an argument with some operator who took her sweet time explaining how to make long-distance calls to towns in the Var, then called three hotels and finally found out, at the fourth hotel, that Mademoiselle Saint-Léger was down at the beach but that she would be returning later, requested that they notify him as soon as she was back in her room, and at last plunked himself down on his bed, his hand glued to the telephone receiver, much as Sir Lancelot had clung to the hilt of his sword, ready to wait two hours, six hours, or his whole life, and thinking to himself that at this moment he was happier than he had ever been.

At four o'clock, the phone rang and he picked it up. A desk clerk told him to wait just one moment, and then he heard her say hello.

"Lucile? It's Antoine."

"Antoine," she repeated, as if in a dream.

Part I: *Le printemps*

"I've got... I really want to see you. Can I come?"

"Yes," she replied. "When?" And although her voice was calm, he could hear in her terseness the retreat and the final defeat of that horrible, cruel memory that for two full weeks had twisted her, shaken her, plagued her, made her toss and turn both night and day, just as it had him. He glanced down at his hand resting on the bed and was amazed to see that it wasn't quivering.

"Surely there's a plane this evening," he said. "I'll leave right now. Will you come and pick me up at Nice?"

"Yes," said Lucile, then hesitated for a moment before adding, "Are you at home?"

He didn't answer immediately, but just murmured, "Lucile, Lucile, Lucile...", then added, "Yes, I am."

"Oh, please hurry," she said, and hung up. Only then did it occur to him that she might well be in Charles' company, and moreover that he could ill afford a plane ticket. But these were just flickering background thoughts. He could easily mug someone on the street, bump off Charles, and even pilot a Boeing. And in fact, at exactly 7:30, had he felt like following the stewardess's suggestion, he could have admired, on the left side of the aircraft, the city of Lyon, had he had the slightest desire to do so.

After hanging up, Lucile closed her book, got a sweater from the closet, found the keys to the car that Charles had rented, and went downstairs. She caught a glimpse of herself in the mirror that crowded the entrance to the hotel, and she flashed herself a quick little smile, the kind of ambiguous smile you might give to someone who's gravely ill, certain to die soon, but who's just been released, seemingly in great shape, from the hospital. She made sure that she was extremely careful as she drove, since the road was very twisty and in bad condition. She couldn't let any kind of physical accident — an oblivious dog, a sloppy driver — come between her and Antoine. This thought obsessed her, rendering her numb and lost to herself, all the way to the airport.

There was a plane coming in from Paris at six, and although there wasn't the slightest chance that Antoine would be on it, she still went to the gate and waited for it. The next plane wasn't due in until eight, so she bought a cheap mystery and sat down in the upstairs bar, trying in vain to relate to the chain of events that were befalling a certain private detective — a very sharp one, at that — but for all his sharpness, he was unable to seduce her at this time. She had heard the phrase "overwhelmed with joy", but she had never personally tested its veracity; indeed, she was baffled by the fact that she felt crushed, broken, and exhausted — so much so that she wondered if she wasn't going to faint or fall asleep in her chair before eight o'clock.

She hailed the waiter and told him she was expecting someone on the eight o'clock flight — a piece of news that seemed of only minor interest to that gentleman. But in any case, she would greatly appreciate it, should something happen to her, if he would let Antoine know. How he might accomplish this she couldn't quite figure out, but she wanted to take every possible measure to protect this new being, this astounding and fragile new being, this happy being, most of all, that she had become. She even went so far as to switch tables because she couldn't easily see the big clock in the bar, and moreover, she had the impression that the loudspeakers could barely be heard from where she was sitting. When, at last, she had conscientiously absorbed every single black mark on the pages of her book, it was still only seven o'clock, a weeping woman was kissing the wounded but triumphant detective in the Miami hospital — and Lucile herself was very upset.

An hour passed, then two months, then thirty years, and finally Antoine appeared, the first to disembark, since he had no luggage to pick up at the end of the concourse. And for those first few moments as he approached her, all she could think was how thin and wan he looked, how poorly dressed he was, and how little she knew him, all the while admitting, in that same detached fashion, that she loved him. He walked up to her awkwardly and they shook hands almost without looking at each other. Then, after hesitating for just an instant, they headed towards the exit. He whispered that she was tan, and she expressed her hope, in a rather loud voice, that he had had a good trip. Once outside, they got into the car with Antoine at the wheel, and Lucile pointed out to him where the ignition was. The night was warm, the smells of the sea and the gasoline mingled together in the air, and the palm trees lining the road out of the airport were gently swaying in the breeze. They drove several kilometers without saying very much, without even knowing where they were going, and then Antoine stopped the car on the side of the road and put his arms around her. He didn't kiss her but simply held her tightly against himself, pressing his cheek against hers, and she almost burst into tears of relief. When he at last spoke to her, it was in a very gentle, soft voice, as if he were speaking to a small child.

"Where is Charles? He's got to be told what is happening, at this point."

"Yes," she said. "He's in Paris."

"Then we'll take the train to Paris tonight. There *is* a night train, isn't there? We'll catch it at Cannes."

She quietly accepted this decision, and slid over a little on the seat so she could look at him, finally really seeing those same eyes and that familiar mouth, and then he leaned over and kissed her.

At Cannes, they were able to get a berth in the sleeping car. All night long, they heard the grinding screams of the train on the tracks, their faces were momentarily lit up by flashes of light, and every so often, when they had peacefully stopped in some station, they would hear the metallic tap-tap-tapping of the railway inspector's steel bar assuring the state of the wheels, assuring their return to Paris, assuring their fate. And when they made love, it felt as if the train was going faster and faster, was going wild, and that the horrendous moans piercing the sleepy hamlets were coming only from themselves.

•   •   •

"I knew it," said Charles.

He was looking away, his forehead pressed against the windowpane. She was sitting on her bed, dizzy with exhaustion. She could still hear the clackety-clack of the train echoing in her ears. When they had pulled into the Gare de Lyon, very early, it was raining. And then she had telephoned Charles from his own apartment, from their apartment, and had awaited him. He had come very quickly and she had told him right away that she loved Antoine, and that she had no choice but to leave him. And so now he was pretending to be looking out the window, and she was quite surprised to notice that the nape of his neck, even in this situation so unbent, did not move her whatsoever, whereas Antoine's neck, with all its coarse and tangled hair, touched her so. There were some men who simply would never make you imagine them as little boys.

"I'd thought it would just blow over quickly," said Charles once more. "I mean, I was hoping..."

All at once he stopped and turned towards her. "It is crucial that You should understand that I love You. Don't think that I'm going to get over You, or that I'll forget You or replace You. I'm way beyond the age to make such substitutions." With a faint smile, he added, "I'm telling You, Lucile — You'll come back to me. I love You for what You are. Antoine loves You for what the two of you are together. He wants to be happy with You, which is how one is, at his age. But as for me, I want You to be happy independently of me. I'll just have to be patient."

She attempted a gesture of protest, but he quickly motioned her to wait, he hadn't finished. "Moreover, he'll resent You, or maybe he even resents You already, for what You are: hedonistic, carefree, and rather weak-willed. He won't be able keep from criticizing You for what he'll call Your 'foibles' or Your 'defects'. What he does not yet understand is that whatever makes a woman strong is the reason that certain men will love her, even if behind her strengths there hide great weaknesses. This he will

Chapter 16

learn from You. He will learn that You are bubbly, funny, and sweet only because You have all Your weaknesses. But by then it will be too late. At least this is what I believe. And You'll come back to me — because You know that I know these things."

And he chuckled for a moment. "I guess You aren't used to such long speeches from me, are You? In any case, when You go to him, tell him for me that if he hurts You, if he doesn't return You to me, either a month down the road or three years from now, intact and every bit as happy as You are today, I will smash him, just like that."

His voice was tinged with anger and she looked at him with wonder. He radiated a sense of strength, almost of violence, something alien to her in him. "I won't make any effort to hold You back now — there's no point, is there? But remember this very clearly: I will wait for You, however long it might take. And anything that You might want from me, of any sort whatever, You will have. So... are You leaving immediately?"

She nodded in confirmation.

"Everything that belongs to You will have to go." Then, since she was shaking her head, he said, in a more resolute tone, "It's tough — but I wouldn't be able to stand seeing Your coats lying around in Your closet or Your car in the garage. After all, You might be gone for a long time...", he added, smiling ever so slightly.

She stared at him blankly. She had foreseen that it would be this way — horrible — and that he would act this way — impeccably. Everything was unfolding exactly as she'd been expecting for such a long time, and mixed in with her despair at making him suffer there was a vague kind of pride at having been loved by him. This wasn't possible — she couldn't leave him like this, all alone in this huge apartment. She rose to her feet and said, "Charles, I..."

"No," he cut in. "You've been waiting long enough. Off with You, now." He stood there motionless, facing her, for a moment, and stared at her so intensely that he seemed lost in a dream. Then he leaned over, stroked her hair, and quickly turned away, saying, "Please leave now. I'll have Your suitcases driven over to the Rue de Poitiers very shortly."

She wasn't particularly surprised that he knew where Antoine lived. She just felt such deep shame at what she was doing that all she saw was a slightly curved back and a head of gray hair and it felt like this was all her doing. She whispered "Charles...", but could not figure out if she wanted to say "Thank You", "I'm sorry", or some other foolish banality, especially when he made a nervous and hopeless little gesture, without turning away — a gesture that meant that he just couldn't take much more of this, and so she walked backwards out of the room. In the staircase she realized she was crying, and she went back into the kitchen in great sobs, and fell on Pauline's shoulder, heaving in grief. Pauline consoled her, saying that men were such nuisances, and that one should never cry on their account.

She found Antoine outside, waiting for her in a café, in the bright sunlight.

PART TWO

L'Été

CHAPTER 17

She felt as if she had been stricken with a marvelous, weird malady that she recognized as happiness, but she balked at calling it that. In a way, she found it astonishing that two intelligent beings, so nervous and so edgy, could have come to be so totally drained of yearning, so tightly merged with each other that they merely needed to say "I love you" with a slight crack in their voice, for that said it all and there was really nothing to add to it. She knew that there was nothing to add, and in fact that there was nothing further to hope for — she knew that this, at last, was what people call "bliss" — but she could not help wondering how she would manage, on some far-off day in the future, to survive the memory of this bliss. She was happy; she was frightened.

They told each other everything about their childhoods and their pasts, but most of all, most of all, they kept on coming back to the last few months, never tiring of it, endlessly rehashing, in the way of all lovers, their very first meetings, all the tiniest details of their romance. With a genuine but rather naïve amazement that actually was very typical, they marveled at the fact that for such a long time they hadn't trusted their own feelings. But no matter how much they wallowed in their shared past, which had been troubled and frustrated, they were not dreaming of a shared future that held the promise of lasting tranquillity. Lucile, even more than Antoine, was scared of plans and of a simple life. And so, in the meantime, they were watching the present with fascination as it unfolded, with each day as it first broke finding them tightly joined in their little bed, never getting enough of one another, and with each evening as it fell finding them walking side by side in the mild, sweet, magical Parisian air. And there were certain moments when they were so happy that it seemed as if they no longer loved each other.

At such times, all it took was for Antoine to fail to show up for an hour after work, and then Lucile — who in the morning had seen him off with such calm — in fact, with an indifference so nearly total that she couldn't imagine she had ever been the way she was in Saint-Tropez: like a sickly, ravaged, voiceless animal — then Lucile would start to tremble, start to imagine Antoine's body crushed by a bus, and at such times she would finally give in and admit to herself that his presence indeed was bliss, since his absence was clearly despair. And at such times, all it took was for Lucile to smile by chance at some other man, and then Antoine (for whom the constant physical possession of her body, of which he never tired, served as a perfect tranquilizer) would start to feel weak, and he would instantly start lavishing on her all the affection that is required to sustain a fragile and flickering bond that has never fully gelled. Between the two of them there was something uneasy, nearly explosive, even in the moments of their greatest tenderness. And although at times this tension grew intensely painful, they also knew, albeit blurrily, that its disappearance from either of their lives would spell, then and there, the end of their love.

In fact, their relationship had in large part been determined by two emotional shocks of roughly equal importance: for her, it had been Antoine's delayed return that famous afternoon, while for him it had been Lucile's refusal to move into his apartment on the day Charles came back from New York. And Lucile, who did not have a great deal of self-confidence, as is true of many carefree-seeming people, had the confused belief that one day, Antoine would not return, whereas Antoine, for his part, had the confused belief that one night, Lucile would betray him. And almost as if with forethought, they kept these two wounds open, though their happiness should have healed them, much as the survivor of some terrible accident takes pleasure, after six months of painful healing, in reopening with a fingernail the very last scab in order to be able to keep on savoring the perfect smoothness of the rest of their body. Each of them needed, in their own way, a thorn in their side — he, simply because that was his deepest nature, and she, because this shared bliss was too alien for her.

Antoine woke up early each morning, and his body sensed, before his mind did, the presence of Lucile's body in the bed, and desired it, even before he had opened his eyes. Half asleep yet smiling, he would slide over to her, and often it took her moaning or the clenching of her hands against his back to finally strip away the last vestiges of his dreams from his mind. Like certain men and many children, Antoine slept deeply and soundly, and there was nothing he loved more than these slow and voluptuous awakenings. As for Lucile, her first awareness of the world each morning was the sensation of being made love to, and she would find herself drifting into consciousness with a mixture of surprise, pleasure, and a vague anger at this half-rape, which deprived her of all of her traditional rituals of waking up — opening her eyes, closing them again, rejecting the new day or else welcoming it — all the confused and deliciously private little conflicts in her soul. Sometimes she'd try to cheat by waking up first and thereby outwitting him, but since Antoine never slept longer than six hours, he always beat her to the punch, and he would just laugh at the annoyed expression on her face, taking enormous pleasure in ripping this woman from the deepest recesses of sleep and plunging her so swiftly into the deepest recesses of love. Most of all, he savored that moment when she would open her eyes, looking lost and uncertain, and then, on recognizing him, would reclose them almost as if under duress, at the very same time as she was tightly winding her arms around his neck.

Lucile's suitcases were perched on top of the wardrobe, and inside it, near his two suits, were hanging only those two or three dresses that Antoine liked best. In the bathroom, by contrast, there was plenty of evidence of a woman's presence, in the form of a plethora of little jars — most of them never even opened — that Lucile had stashed away. While he was shaving, Antoine would let fly one wisecrack after another about the uselessness of herbal face masks to stave off wrinkles, or jabs along those lines. Lucile would counter, saying that one day he would be glad to have such things, that he was aging before her eyes, and that he was in fact terribly ugly. He would kiss her. She would laugh. Paris that summer was extraordinarily beautiful.

Chapter 17

Each morning he would set off for work at 9:30, and she would stay in his room, quite content although hankering for a cup of tea, and yet unable, in her drowsy state, to go down and order one at the corner café. Instead, she would just pull out some book from any of the teetering stacks all over the room, and would read. The church bells that once had driven such a spike into her heart rang out every half hour, and now she was very fond of their sound. Sometimes, when she heard them start to ring, she would even put down her book and just smile out into space, as if she had recovered her childhood. Around 11:30 or so, Antoine would call her up, often with an easy-going tone, but sometimes with the rapid and impatient tone of The Man Who Is Swamped With Work. Each time this happened, Lucile would put on a terribly earnest voice in her replies, but inwardly she would be chuckling away, for she knew how dreamy and lazy he truly was, and she was just at that stage of being in love with someone when you are just as taken with the acts that they put on as you are with their most genuine traits. In fact, in their façades, which you effortlessly strip off, you perceive signs of their deepest trust in you.

At noon, she would meet up with him at the swimming pool at the Place de la Concorde, and they would sunbathe together and eat sandwiches side by side. Then he would head back to work — unless the sun, their talk, and the brushing of their bare skins, lightly tanned, had stirred up a mad ache in their loins, in which case he would lead her back, in great haste, to his little apartment, to their little apartment, and he would be late for work in the afternoon.

Part II: L'été

Those afternoons were the occasions when Lucile would take long leisurely strolls through Paris, bumping into friends or at least vague acquaintances, sipping on tomato juice in various sidewalk cafés. And, of course, since she radiated happiness, everyone talked to her. In the evenings, there were all the movies, the inviting drives one could take through the outskirts of town, all the half-empty cabarets where she would teach him to dance, all those unknown and easy-going faces teeming in the summer streets of Paris — and all the things they wanted to whisper to each other and all the ways they wanted to caress each other.

At the end of July, they bumped into Johnny at the Café Flore. He had just gotten back from a whirlwind weekend jaunt to Monte Carlo, and he had in tow a curly-headed young lad named Bruno. Johnny expressed delight on seeing them looking so happy together and asked them why they didn't get married. At this suggestion they erupted in laughter and pointed out to him that they weren't the type to be concerned about the future, but that even if they had been, marriage was a nutty idea. Johnny admitted that this was probably the case, and joined them in chuckling. But after they had walked off, he muttered, "What a shame" with a tone that intrigued his friend Bruno. Johnny, however, met Bruno's queries with an oddly wistful expression that the youth had never seen on him before, and to close matters, Johnny bluntly declared, "You wouldn't understand — it was just bad timing," an answer that seemed to satisfy the curiosity of his companion, whose role, to tell the truth, had nothing whatsoever to do with understanding anything.

Chapter 17

• • •

August rolled around and although Antoine had a month of vacation time, he was out of money, so he and Lucile had to stay at home.

Without any warning, it abruptly turned exceedingly hot that month, and all of Paris felt overwhelmed by the oppressive atmosphere of frequent thunderstorms with short but very violent downpours that left the streets exhausted yet renewed, like recuperating patients or young mothers who have just given birth. Lucile spent almost three weeks just sitting on the bed in her dressing gown. Her summer wardrobe consisted solely of bathing suits and cotton slacks, which she had bought for the beautiful warm days on the beaches of Monte-Carlo or Capri, where she had expected to go with Blassans-Lignières as in previous summers, and changing it was out of the question. So she read voraciously, smoked, went out and bought tomatoes for her lunch, made love with Antoine, talked about literature with him, and fell asleep. Whenever there was a thunderstorm, she felt terrified and would rush to snuggle up tightly against him, and he, touched by her fear, would explain in scientific terms all the murky goings-on between cumulus clouds, but she only half-believed it all, and he would call her "my little pagan" in a churned-up voice, but he never managed to churn her up in return until the last thunderclap had long since faded into the distance.

Sometimes he would cast a furtive, questioning glance at her. Her laziness, her incredible ability to do nothing at all and never to think about the future, her remarkable capacity for finding happiness in a long series of empty, inactive, indistinguishable days — all this struck him at times as outrageous, even verging on the repulsive. He knew very well that she loved him and that, for that reason, she wasn't going to grow tired of him any sooner than he would of her, but his intuition told him that what he was now seeing of her lifestyle was representative of her deepest essence, and he realized that it was only thanks to their mutual physical passion that he was able to put up with her perpetual stagnation. He often felt as if he had discovered a mysterious beast, an unheard-of plant, a mandrake. But whenever he felt this way, he would draw near to her on the bed, slide in between the sheets, never growing tired of their wild abandon, of their mingled sweat, of their torrid exhaustion, and in this way he would rediscover for himself, and in the clearest possible manner, that she was, after all, not a beast but a woman.

Over time, each of them had become completely familiar with the other one's body, had even made it a sort of scientific inquiry, although this science was not fully reliable since it was based on trying to give the other one pleasure, and so it was often utterly forgotten in the white heat of their lovemaking. At such moments it seemed inconceivable that they hadn't ever met in the first thirty years of their lives. And no day was allowed to come to an end until each had declared to the other, several times over, that apart from the moment they were experiencing right then, nothing else was real or had the slightest meaning.

And so August rolled by in a dreamlike fashion. On the eve of September first, towards midnight, they were lying side by side, and Antoine's alarm clock, which had sat there for a full month without once making a single tick, resumed its relentless march. It was set for eight in the morning. Antoine was lying motionless on his back, and his hand, which was holding a cigarette, was dangling down toward the floor. Rain began to fall lightly on the pavement, making gentle, slow splashes, and he guessed that the drops were warm, even suspected that they were salty, just like the tears he felt against his cheek, tears that had just started to roll, very quietly, out of Lucile's open eyes. There was no need for him to ask either her or the clouds what the reasons were for these salty drops. He knew very well that the summer was over, and though it was over, no doubt it had been the most beautiful time of their lives.

PART THREE

L'Automne

Je vis que tous les êtres ont une fatalité
du bonheur. L'action n'est pas
la vie mais une façon de
gâcher quelque force,
un énervement.

— Arthur Rimbaud

I saw that all beings drift inexorably
towards happiness. Being active
isn't life, but merely a way
of wasting strength —
just an annoyance.

CHAPTER 18

Lucile was waiting for the bus at the Place de l'Alma and was getting very annoyed. It was unusually cold and rainy this November, and the little booth at the bus stop was jammed with shivering people, sullen and nearly hostile. She had therefore chosen to stand outside of it, and her wet hair was plastered on her face. To make matters worse, she'd forgotten to take a number when she'd walked up, and six minutes later, when she finally remembered and took one, some woman chortled nastily at her. All at once, she felt a terrible pang of longing for her car, the sound of raindrops pelting its roof, and the timid turns she made on slick cobblestone streets. The only real charm of money, she reflected, was that it let you avoid all these hassles: waiting, annoyances, other people. She had just been at the Cinémathèque du Palais de Chaillot, where Antoine, exasperated by her lethargy, had suggested — in a tone verging on the imperious — that she go see a masterwork by the classic German director Pabst. The alleged masterwork had indeed turned out to be one, but she'd had to wait in line for a half hour surrounded by a horde of bratty, loudmouthed students, and the whole while she found herself wondering why she hadn't stayed comfortably at home in Antoine's little room and finished a thriller by Simenon, in which she was deeply engrossed.

Part III: L'automne

It was already after 6:30, she would get home after Antoine did, and just maybe, that might cure him of his recent deplorable obsession, which consisted in trying to drag Lucile into the outside world. He kept on telling her that it was abnormal and unhealthy, after having led a lively high-society life for three years, including what he referred to as "human relations", for her now to remain totally insulated in some tiny room with nothing at all to do. She would never have dared to tell him that she was just coming to realize that any city, even Paris, once you had gotten used to living well in it, turned terrifying when you had to deal with taking numbers for buses and had only 200 francs on your person, for it would humiliate him to hear such a thing almost as much as it humiliated her. After all, she clearly recalled getting by on little at twenty, and it troubled her to think that at thirty she was unable to take up such a lifestyle again.

Just then a bus pulled up, and the driver called for the first set of numbers, far lower than hers, and the unfortunate higher numbers all retreated into their glorified glassy rabbit-hutch. A sort of animal despair began to overwhelm Lucile. Within a half hour, if she wasn't unlucky, she'd be climbing onto a bus that would carry her to within 300 meters of Antoine's room — 300 meters that she'd have to negotiate through sheets of rain — and then she'd arrive tired, unkempt, and disheveled, only to encounter her equally exhausted companion. And if he were to inquire enthusiastically as to her reaction to the Pabst film, she'd feel like telling him instead about the unsavory throngs, the buses, and the horrid rat race that working people were subjected to, and he would be very disappointed.

Chapter 18

Another bus passed by, this one without even stopping. Out of the blue, she decided to walk home instead. Just then, an elderly lady wandered up and reached out to take a number from the machine. On a whim, Lucile proffered her her ticket: "Here, take mine — I'm going to hoof it."

The woman looked back at her quizzically, almost hostilely. Perhaps she thought Lucile was making this gesture out of charity, on account of her age or God knows what. It seemed that people were growing more and more suspicious all the time. They were so constantly overwhelmed by frustrations, worries, idiotic TV shows, and trashy newspapers that there was no room left to believe in disinterested benevolence.

Lucile practically apologized for her action, saying, "I live just a stone's throw away, I'm already running late, and anyway, the rain's letting up a bit, isn't it?"

This last little question verged on begging — and she felt like a total hypocrite as she turned her eyes towards the sky, since it was actually raining harder than ever. All the while, she was ruminating, "But what earthly difference should the approval of this old lady make to me? So what if she doesn't want my ticket and throws it away? I couldn't care less if she has to wait a half hour longer."

Her distress kept on mounting: "What ever came over me? I should have done what anyone else would do: toss the ticket in the garbage. Where did I get this dumb idea of wanting to be nice, wanting to radiate generosity on the Place de l'Alma at 6:30 in the evening at some random bus stop, wanting to get everybody to like me? These warm feelings, these spontaneous spurts of affection for total strangers, that kind of thing happens in the homes of well-heeled gentry over a couple of whiskeys, or else in some plush bar, or in a revolution." But even as she was thinking these thoughts, she was desperately hoping to prove to herself that she was wrong. The woman extended her hand to Lucile and took the number from her. "It's very kind of you," she said, and smiled.

Lucile flashed a shaky smile back at her, and walked off. Her plan was to follow the *quais* along the river as far as the Place de la Concorde, then cross it and take the Rue de Lille. And suddenly it struck her that she had followed exactly this same route on foot one evening — the very evening she'd met Antoine. But that had been in early spring when the fellow was still a stranger to her, and they'd set off on foot of their own free will in the warmth of that lonely night, spurning all the passing taxis for reasons very different from those keeping her from hailing one today. "I've got to stop this moaning and groaning," she said to herself. And what were their plans for the evening, anyway?

They were scheduled to have dinner at the home of Lucas Solder, a friend of Antoine's. He was a frustrated journalist who loved to talk and was prone to getting carried away by high abstractions. Antoine always enjoyed his company, and Lucile would have, too, were it not for his wife, who, each time she was left in the dark by the men's abstractions, would try to engage Lucile in conversations on topics as far-ranging as the latest sales at the Galeries Lafayette, or various female afflictions. To make matters worse, Nicole, who loved to "just throw things together", always cooked up the cheapest and the most inedible of meals.

Chapter 18

"I would so happily have eaten at the Relais Plaza," mused Lucile as she trudged along. "I would have ordered a daiquiri with ice, chatted with the bartender, and then gotten myself a hamburger and a salad — instead of having to face that heavy soup, that foul stew, those dried-out cheeses, and the lousy fruits that await me tonight. Who says that only the rich have the right to eat sparsely?" And for a few moments, she indulged herself by imagining the half-empty bar at the Relais Plaza, the ever-present gladiolas down at the far end of the counter, the friendly waiters she knew, and herself sitting alone at a little table, casually reading a newspaper while watching American ladies strolling along in their mink coats. But with a sudden pang she realized that this rêverie of hers didn't involve Antoine at all, that she'd imagined herself without him in her life. It had been a good long while since she'd dined alone, to be sure, but she nonetheless felt stricken with guilt.

As she approached the Rue de Poitiers, she started to trot, and when she reached the staircase, she ran up it. She found Antoine stretched out on the bed engrossed in *Le Monde* — it seemed she was fated to be with men who read *Le Monde* — and when he sat up, she threw herself into his arms. He was so warm, he smelled like cigarette smoke, he was so big and strong like this, lying on this bed... She would never tire of this big-boned body, these bright eyes, these rough hands now running through her drenched hair. He mumbled something or other about crazy women wandering around in the rain.

"So," he said at last, "how was that film?"

"It was terrific!" she replied.

Part III: L'automne

"You'll have to admit that I sent you off to see it with good reason."

"I admit it," she said. As she made this confession, she was standing in the bathroom with a towel in her right hand, and all at once she caught a glimpse of herself in the mirror as a strange little smile flickered across her face. She stood there speechlessly for a moment, then wiped the mirror with the towel, almost as if to erase the vestiges of a secret confidante who shouldn't have been there at all.

CHAPTER 19

She was waiting for Antoine in the little bar in the Rue de Lille where they had fallen into the habit of meeting up each evening at around 6:30. She was talking horses with the waiter, a quite good-looking and very chatty fellow named Étienne, whom Antoine suspected of harboring less than innocent feelings for Lucile. More than once she had taken a racing tip from him and it had always turned out disastrously, for which reason Antoine, every time he walked in, would cast a dubious glance in their direction, not out of jealousy but out of fear of being hit hard in the pocketbook.

This particular day, Lucile was in an excellent mood. They'd gone to sleep very late, having spent much of the night making elaborate and soaring plans that now she couldn't recall very clearly, but which saw them smoothly sailing to some beautiful beach in Africa, or else moving into a lovely country manor somewhere near Paris. Meanwhile, Étienne, with a gleam in his eye, was telling her all about his favorite, a horse named Ambroisie II, who was listed at ten to one but who was a sure bet to win the next day at Saint-Cloud. And the thousand-franc note that was pleasantly dreaming away in Lucile's pocket would surely have swiftly changed hands had Antoine not arrived just then, looking quite excited. He gave Lucile a peck, sat down, and ordered two whiskeys, which, in view of the fact that this was the twenty-sixth of the month, was a sign of celebration.

'What's up?" asked Lucile.

"I spoke with Sirer today," said Antoine to an obviously perplexed Lucile. "You know, the director of the paper *Le Réveil*... He's got a job for you in their archives department."

"In their archives?"

"Yes. It's pretty interesting work, there's not a whole lot to do, and he'll give you 100,000 francs a month as a starting salary."

Lucile looked at him with consternation. Now it all was coming back to her, what they had talked about the night before. Together, they had concluded that Lucile's life was no life at all, and that she had to find something to do. With great gusto she had welcomed the idea of working, and she'd even painted a rosy picture of herself at some newspaper, scrambling slowly but steadily toward the top, becoming one of those brilliant female journalists who were the talk of the town in Paris; undoubtedly she would have a lot of work and a lot of worries, but deep down she felt sure she had enough tenacity, humor, and ambition to make it. They would have a very swanky apartment paid for by the newspaper, since they would have to throw so many parties, but every year they would escape for at least a month, sailing on the balmy Mediterranean.

She had enthusiastically spun out this glowing image before Antoine last night, who at first had been skeptical but then had gradually warmed up to it, for after all, no one was more persuasive than Lucile when she got to talking about her plans,

Chapter 19

especially when they were as hare-brained and as unlike herself as this one was. What in the world had she drunk or read last night that had gotten her spinning such a crazy tale? The fact was, she had no more ambition than she had tenacity, and no greater interest in having a career than in killing herself.

"You know, this is a very good salary for this type of paper," said Antoine. He seemed very pleased with himself. She looked at him with tenderness: he was still under the influence of their nocturnal flight of fancy and must have been replaying it in his mind all day long, and then turned over every stone in Paris to find this job. Such positions were enormously coveted by droves of society women who, suddenly hit by a wave of depression resulting from their state of midlife torpor, would gladly pay for the chance to sweep floors, as long as they were the floors of a publishing house, a fashion house, or a newspaper. And here this nutcase Sirer was all set to pay *her*, Lucile — she who cared only for doing nothing. Life was so incredibly stupid. She smiled half-heartedly at Antoine.

"You don't seem too thrilled," he observed.

"Well, it's almost too good to be true," she replied morosely.

He looked at her with amusement. He knew very well that she was now regretting her fantasies of the previous night, and he also knew that she didn't dare admit it to him. But he truly thought that she couldn't possibly not be bored living this kind of life, and that she would wind up growing tired not only of her life but also of him, unless things changed. And more softly, he said to himself that those 100,000 francs, when added to his own salary, would allow Lucile to indulge in a far more cushy lifestyle.

Part III: *L'automne*

With that boyish optimism that many men have, he could just picture Lucile happily buying herself a couple of cute new dresses each month. Of course they wouldn't bear the signature of any famous designer, but they'd fit her to a tee because her figure was so ideal. She'd take taxis, she'd have friends to see, she'd think a bit about politics and about the world around her — in short, about other people.

There was no doubt that when he came home in the evenings, he would miss seeing her ensconced like some wild animal in its little den, and no doubt that he would miss the woman who lived only for the sake of reading and lovemaking, but on the other hand, it would somehow vaguely reassure him. After all, in her sedentary life, there was a fixation on the present and a disdain for the future that frightened him, that even offended him in some obscure fashion, as if he were only a piece on some movie set that was destined to be burned, without any possible chance of reprieve, as soon as the last scene had been filmed.

"So when would I start?" asked Lucile. And now she was genuinely smiling. At least she could give it a try. She'd actually held down jobs once or twice, when she'd been younger. Of course this line of work would bore her a little, but she'd hide that from Antoine.

"December first — in five or six days. Are you happy?"

She sent a wary glance his way. Could he really believe that she was happy at this prospect? She had already noticed a slight sadistic streak in him, but this time he looked innocent and quite convinced of what he was saying. She nodded gravely. "Yes,

I'm happy — very happy. You were right in thinking that things couldn't go on this way forever."

He leaned over and gave her a kiss across the table in such an impulsive and tender fashion that she felt sure that he understood her. She smiled against his cheek and together they chuckled indulgently at her trepidations. And she was greatly relieved at his having read her mind, for she was always uncomfortable when he construed her wrongly — but all the same, she felt slightly resentful at having been tricked.

That evening in their little room, Antoine, with pencil in hand, set about making some financial calculations that he found most encouraging. Of course, he said, he would take care of the rent and the phone bill — all those mundane matters. And then Lucile, with her own 100,000 francs, would be able to cover her dresses, her transportation, her lunches — in fact, there was an excellent canteen, actually quite delightful, at *Le Réveil,* where he could come join her for lunch sometimes.

Sitting on the bed, Lucile listened to these figures with great shock. Part of her wanted to tell him that any dress from Dior bore a price tag of at least 300,000 francs, that she hated the Métro (even when she didn't have to change lines), and that merely hearing the word "canteen" made her want to flee. She felt like an elitist — a dreadful, dyed-in-the-wool elitist. And yet, when he had finally stopped his pacing back and forth and when he turned towards her with a sweet, uncertain smile, as if he didn't quite believe his own figures, she couldn't help smiling herself. He was like a kid, figuring the grocery bill the way kids do, working out his budget the way cabinet ministers do, juggling his numbers the way grown men do. What did it matter, after all, that her lifestyle would have to flex a little in order to match these chimerical calculations, given that he was the one, in the end, who would carry them out?

CHAPTER 20

She felt as if she'd been there for years, although it was actually only two weeks since she'd taken up work at the office of *Le Réveil*. It was one big gray room, cluttered with desks, chests, and filing cabinets, and its sole window looked out onto a narrow alley in Les Halles, the ancient market district. She worked together with a young woman named Marianne, who was three months pregnant, very likable and efficient, and who spoke in equally tender and concerned tones about the future of the newspaper she worked for and that of the child she was carrying. Indeed, Lucile often had to wonder, when her colleague would come out with some corny cliché like "Paris is going to go crazy over this one!" or "*This* baby will knock 'em dead!", whether Marianne was speaking of the next issue of *Le Réveil* or of her imminent offspring Jérôme.

The two women sorted, side by side, various newspaper clippings, and tracked down, depending on the requests that came in, dossiers on India, penicillin, or Gary Cooper, and when such dossiers were handed to them in a scrambled state, they would neatly tidy them up and then re-file them where they belonged. This was all fine, but what drove Lucile batty was the incessant overarching tone of urgency and seriousness that reigned throughout the place, and the sinister theme of "efficiency", which was drummed into them day and night.

A week after her arrival, she had attended a general meeting of the editorial staff — truly a hive of honeybees, all busily buzzing about, exchanging pre-chewed platitudes — and to which the directors, aiming to ward off any accusations of elitism, had condescended to invite the ants from the ground floor, as well as those from Archives. And so for two full hours, a dumbfounded Lucile had witnessed a rapid-fire human comedy in which arrogance, bootlicking, pomposity, and mediocrity all vied with each other to do the best possible job in increasing the circulation of little Jérôme's rival. There were only three men there who didn't spout nonsense — the first because he was constantly sulking, the second because he was the paper's (hopefully appalled) director, and the third simply because he seemed to be a little bit more on the ball.

After it was over, she gave Antoine a blow-by-blow account of the proceedings, whereupon he, having gotten over his initial laughter, told her she was exaggerating and chided her for seeing everything in such bleak terms. To add insult to injury, he said she was getting too scrawny. And it was true, she was so bored that she wasn't even able to finish the sandwiches that — avoiding the canteen, to which she'd given one and only one try — she would go get herself at a nearby *brasserie*, where she would sit and read a novel. At 6:30, or sometimes even eight in the evening ("Lucile, my sweet, a thousand apologies for keeping You here so late, but You know we've got to put this baby to bed the day after tomorrow"), she'd try in vain to catch a taxi, eventually giving up and taking the Métro, almost always standing as she rode because she was loath to battle for a seat. She would look at the tired, preoccupied, glazed-over faces of her fellow riders and feel an intense yearning to rebel, far more on their account than on her own, for it seemed obvious to her that in her case, this whole rat race was merely a bad dream from which she was bound to wake up at any moment. And then, once she was back home, she'd find Antoine waiting for her, and as soon as he enfolded her in his arms, a sense of life's meaning would come rushing back to her.

That day, she had had it, and when she arrived at her usual *brasserie* at one o'clock, she ordered a cocktail from the surprised waiter (she never ordered drinks), and then another. She had a dossier to study and she riffled through it for a couple of minutes before closing it with a yawn. She was quite aware that they had suggested that she should write a few lines on the topic and that if they liked what she wrote, it might well be published. All well and good, but today wasn't the day for it. Nor was today the day for obediently trotting back to that gray office right after lunch and returning to the cute little rôle she'd been playing of Active Young Woman in front of other people who would be playing their grandiose little rôles of Thinkers, or else Men of Action. They were all lousy rôles, or at the very least it was a lousy play. Or then again, if Antoine was right and this play that she was acting in was a perfectly respectable and useful play, well then, her rôle in it was poorly written, or else it had been written for somebody else. Antoine was simply wrong — this was now crystal-clear to her in the glaring light of her two cocktails, for alcohol at times shines pitiless sharp spotlights on life, and right now it was revealing to her the thousands of little lies that she had been telling herself day after day in an effort to convince herself that she was happy. But in fact she was unhappy, and life was unfair.

Suddenly a wave of intense self-pity flooded over her. She ordered yet another cocktail, which prompted the waiter to ask her what was the matter. She replied "Everything" with a mournful expression, with which he commiserated, saying that some days were like that, and that she really ought to order her usual sandwich and, for once, eat it all, because otherwise she might well wind up like his cousin who was soon going to be coming up on six months in a high-altitude tuberculosis clinic. So… this young man had actually noticed she never ate a bite, so he felt some pity for her, even though all she ever said to him was "hello" and "good-bye", and so — bottom line — there was somebody who truly cared. And out of nowhere, tears started filling her eyes. Alcohol can just as easily make you maudlin as it can bring you insight, she now remembered. And so she ordered her sandwich and, putting on a serious look, opened the book she'd borrowed from Antoine's collection that morning. It was *The Wild Palms* by Faulkner, and fate was such that she quickly hit upon this monologue by Harry:

"… Respectability. That was what did it. I found out some time back that it's idleness breeds all our virtues, our most bearable qualities — contemplation, equableness, laziness, letting other people alone; good digestion mental and physical: the wisdom to concentrate on fleshly pleasures — eating and evacuating and fornication and sitting in the sun — than which there is nothing better, nothing to match, nothing else in all this world but to live for the short time you are loaned breath, to be alive and know it…"

Lucile stopped right there, shut her book, paid the waiter, and walked out. She headed straight back to the newspaper, told Sirer that she was quitting, and asked him not to say a thing to Antoine about it, all without offering a word of explanation. She stood there before him, straight, stubborn, and smiling, and he simply looked at her with bewilderment. She took off immediately, hailed a taxi, told the driver to take her to the Place Vendôme, and got out at a jeweler's where she promptly sold, at half-price, the pearl necklace that Charles had bought her that year for Christmas. She ordered a replica to be made of it in fake pearls, snubbed the knowing smile that the saleslady flashed at her, and walked out feeling a free woman. She spent a half hour looking at the impressionist paintings in the Jeu de Paume, another two hours watching a movie, and then, when she got home, she breezily announced to Antoine that she was coming to feel quite at home at *Le Réveil.* This way, he wouldn't be worried any more, and she'd feel at ease for a while. All in all, she felt far better lying to him than lying to herself.

• • •

And thus she spent a marvelous two weeks. Paris had been given back to her, along with her status of loafer — and also the money she needed to enjoy that status. She quickly returned to the lifestyle she'd gotten so used to, but now as an impostor — and naturally, the feeling of playing hooky greatly enhanced her pleasure, even in simple things.

One day, upstairs in a restaurant on the *rive gauche,* she discovered a kind of café-cum-library, and from then on she spent her afternoons there, reading books or chatting with various strange characters at loose ends, mostly alcoholics, who haunted the place. One of them, an aristocratic-looking old fellow who went around proclaiming he was a prince, asked her if she would care to join him for lunch one day at the Ritz Hotel, and the morning of that grand event she spent an hour getting dressed, trying to figure out which of the many cute suits that Charles had bought her had the most fashionable colors. And thus she had an exquisitely unreal lunch at the Espadon, sitting across from this eccentric gentleman who most gravely lied through his teeth to her, recounting his life in a fashion inspired a little by Tolstoy and a little by Malraux — and she, to be sure, returned the favor and lied right back at this eccentric gentleman, inventing a story in her best Scott Fitzgerald style.

He, in a word, was not only a Russian prince but also a historian, while she was an American heiress with a dollop more culture than usual. Both of them were dreadfully adored and dreadfully wealthy, and as the various *maîtres d'hôtel* fluttered solicitously about their table, they casually dropped Marcel Proust's name, for it turned out that her lunch companion had been on intimate terms with the great writer. At the end, he sprang for the bill, which certainly had to put a sizable dent in his upcoming month's budget, and they took leave of one another at four o'clock, each of them utterly enchanted by the other.

Chapter 20

When she got home, she told Antoine a thousand anecdotes about all the little goings-on at *Le Réveil*, and he was clearly amused. She took particular pleasure in lying to him because she loved him so much, and because she was so happy, and because she so truly wanted him to share in her happiness. One day, of course, he would find out; some day, even though she'd told Marianne not to do so, the office phone would ring and Marianne would answer it and blurt out that Lucile had been "away" for a month — but rather perversely, this sword of Damocles hanging over Lucile's head simply added an unexpected little twinge of excitement to each day that went by. She bought a series of ties for Antoine, as well as numerous art books and records for him, and whenever they talked, she would go on and on about all her advances, her free-lance assignments, and whatever else came to mind. She was brimming with joy and Antoine was thrilled with her joyousness. Selling that necklace had guaranteed her two solid months of goldbricking, self-indulgence, and confabulation — in other words, two months of sheer happiness.

There ensued a string of indistinguishable, unfocused days, full because they were so totally empty, tumultuous because they were so serene, with her spirit essentially drifting in an interval of time without start or finish, without landmarks, without purpose. She found herself reliving her old student days, when she had regularly cut classes at the Sorbonne, tasting once again that flavor of flaunting the law that for so long had been forgotten. There was simply no way to compare the free time that Charles had given her and the free time that she was stealing from

Antoine. And what better souvenir could one hope to retain from one's adolescence than that of an endless little white lie foisted on others, on the future, and often on oneself?

To what extent was Lucile fooling herself in courting disaster so blatantly, in flirting so dangerously with the chances of infuriating Antoine, of jeopardizing his trust in her, of sparking a showdown in which they would both be forced to face the truth: that she would never, in fact, be able to live that normal, balanced, and comfortable life that he was offering her? She knew very well that in sweeping this whole mess under the rug right now, she was not committing herself to dealing with it seriously in the long term. Something inside her was terribly determined, but she couldn't figure out what it was all about. The truth was, she was determined to do precisely what she enjoyed, and nothing else, but this is a difficult thing to admit to oneself when one supposedly loves someone else. Night after night she came back to Antoine's warmth, his laughter, and his body — and there was not one moment when she had the feeling that she was deceiving him. Life without Antoine was no more imaginable for her than life in an office. And the latter was seeming, with each passing day, less and less plausible.

As it grew colder, she slowly fell back into her sedentary lifestyle. Each morning she would rise with Antoine, go downstairs to have a coffee with him, and then, on occasion, would accompany him over to his publishing house, from which she would take off — ostensibly to rejoin the salt mines of *Le Réveil,* but in actual fact to retreat to their little den. There she would undress, crawl back under the covers, and doze till noon. In the afternoon, she would read, listen to records, smoke a lot, and then, six bells having struck, she would remake the bed, remove all traces of her presence, and sally forth, heading for the little bar in the Rue de Lille to meet up with Antoine, or else, twisting irony's knife just a bit more, she'd go to the bar near the Pont-Royal and wait there until eight o'clock, at which point she would return, looking frazzled, to the Rue de Poitiers where Antoine was waiting for her, full of sympathy for her overworked plight. When he kissed her, she would melt in the tenderness of his embrace, his compassion, and his *douceur* — all without the slightest sense of remorse. After all, she did deserve sympathy — sympathy for her willingness to so radically complicate her life, all for the sake of this very inflexible man. It would have been so simple to tell him, "I've quit my job," and thereby to free herself up from the burden of her daily charades. But since the charades made Antoine happy, might as well keep them up — and truth to tell, at times she considered herself a saint.

And thus, the day when Antoine stumbled upon the truth, Lucile was completely thrown.

• • •

"I called you three times this afternoon," he told her. He'd flung down his raincoat onto the chair without kissing her, and now was just standing there facing her, motionless. She smiled at him and said, "I had to go out for a good two hours. I guess Marianne didn't tell you."

"Indeed she did. And what time was it that you left the office?"

"By now it must be at least an hour ago."

"Oh?"

There was something in that little "Oh?" that made Lucile uneasy. She looked up but Antoine wasn't looking at her.

"I had to meet someone right by the *Réveil* office," he said very quickly. "I called to tell you that I'd come by and say hi. You weren't in at the time, so I went there right after my meeting, at 5:30. *Voilà.*"

"*Voilà,*" she echoed, her mind somewhere else.

"It's been *three weeks* since you last showed your nose there, Lucile. And they never paid you one red cent. I…" Up till that moment he'd been almost whispering, but now, without warning, his voice grew louder. In one brusque gesture he ripped his tie off and threw it at her. "Where in the hell did this new tie come from? And all those records? Where did you have lunch today?"

"Please," said Lucile, "don't yell at me… I mean, you don't think I went out and walked the streets, do you? Don't be ridiculous…"

The slap caught her so much off guard that she didn't budge, and for a second or two that reassuring little smile that she'd grown so used to putting on remained frozen on her face. But then she felt her cheek growing hot, and reflexively she lifted her hand to touch it. This childish gesture only infuriated Antoine even more. Being an easy-going type, he suffered from long and painful bouts of anger, far more painful for the punisher than for the victim.

"I don't have any idea what you've been doing, but I do know that you've been lying to me nonstop for three weeks now.

That's all I know."

A silence ensued. Lucile was thinking about the slap, and wondering with a mixture of anger and amusement what one does in such circumstances. Antoine's fury still struck her as all out of proportion to the situation.

"It's Charles," said Antoine.

She looked at him in confusion: "Charles?"

"Yes, Charles. All these ties and records, all your new jumpers — your lifestyle…"

At last she was catching his drift. For a split second she felt like laughing, but then she caught sight of his haunted face, so ghostly pale, and in a flash she was overcome by a terrible fear of losing him.

"It's got nothing to do with Charles," she blurted out. "It's Faulkner. No, listen — I'll explain it all to you. The money came from the pearls — I sold them."

"But you had them on just yesterday…"

"They're fake — take a closer look. All you need to do is bite them, and…" This just wasn't the moment, though, to suggest to Antoine that he should sample her pearls with his teeth, and she felt it clearly — nor was it the time to bring up Faulkner. She was turning out to be far more skilled at lying than at telling the truth. Her cheek felt like it was burning now.

"I just couldn't take that job any more…"

"After all of two weeks…"

"Yes, after all of two weeks. So I went to this jeweler's named Doris in Place Vendôme, and I sold them my pearls and I got a cheap copy of the necklace made for me — that's all."

Part III: L'automne

"And so what did you do all day long all this time?"

"I went for walks, I stayed at home — it was just like in the old days."

He was staring intently at her and it made her want to look away, but everybody knows that looking away in this kind of situation is a surefire sign of prevarication, and so she forced herself to stare back at Antoine. His yellow-eyed gaze had turned somehow darker, and in the midst of all her turmoil it occurred to her that anger made him more handsome, which was a very unusual quality.

"Why should I believe you? You've been telling me nothing but a pack of lies for three weeks straight."

"Because I have nothing more to confess," she said wearily, at last daring to look away. She leaned her forehead against the windowpane, absent-mindedly following a cat as it sauntered down the sidewalk in a nonchalant fashion that belied the biting cold outside. She went on, in a calm voice: "I had warned you that I wasn't cut out for... for anything of that sort. Either I'd have died of boredom or I'd have gone out of my mind. I was really unhappy, Antoine. That's the only possible thing to hold against me."

"Why didn't you tell me about any of this before?"

"Oh, you were just so pleased to see me working, to see me caught up in 'real life'. And also, I was a pretty good actress!"

Antoine stretched out on the bed. He had spent two hours in profound despair and jealousy, and now he felt exhausted as a result of his impetuous fit of pique. He believed her, he knew that she was telling the truth, and this truth struck him as being

Chapter 20

simultaneously reassuring and yet also indescribably bitter. She was alone, and she would always be alone; for a moment he even wondered if he mightn't have preferred it if she'd been unfaithful to him instead of lying to him. He uttered her name in a faraway voice: "Lucile... Don't you trust me at all?"

No sooner had he said this than she bent down and kissed him first on the cheek, then the forehead, then the eyes, mumbling that she loved him, that she loved no one but him, that he was crazy and silly and cruel. He let her say all this, and he even smiled at it a little; he was totally desperate.

PART FOUR

L'Hiver

CHAPTER 21

One month went by. With Antoine's blessing, Lucile had returned to her old ways, but even so she felt uneasy replying "Nothing" — always just "Nothing" — when Antoine got home from work and asked her what she'd done. The truth was, he asked the question reflexively, without any resentment, but he did ask it every single evening. And every so often, she could make out in his eyes a sense of confused sadness, and a certain distrust of her. He made love to her in an intensely focused frenzy and wildness, but afterwards, when he was lying on his back and she was hunched over him, she had the distinct feeling that he was looking at her without seeing her, that he even saw, instead of her, a boat bobbing on the ocean, or a cloud at the mercy of the wind — something moving, in any case, something that was slowly drifting towards oblivion. And yet he had never loved her so strongly, and he told her so. At such moments she would lie down tightly against him, close her eyes, and fall silent.

It's often said that people forget the power of language, but people also forget how powerfully silence can convey craziness, outrageousness, and absurdity. Lucile watched as shards of her childhood floated by behind her closed eyelids, and she saw the faces of certain men appear and disappear, the most salient one being that of Charles; sometimes, for no clear reason, she would see, in her mind's eye, Antoine's tie on Diane's rug, and other times the tree at the Pré-Catelan would loom up before her, for no reason. And all these memories, rather than pulling together coherently into a pleasantly vague unity that she had once so gaily called "my life", now remained just a scattered and troubling jumble of images, in her new and less happy state. Antoine was quite right, after all, to ask: What was going to become of them? Where were they headed, what was their destination? And this small bed, which once had been the most magical boat in all of Paris, was now turning into an endlessly drifting raft, and this small room, once so familiar to her, was turning into a remote and abstract background. By forcing her attention onto the specter of the future, he had, it seemed to her, closed the door to any future between them.

One morning in January she woke up with a violent bout of nausea. Antoine had already left without waking her, as he often did these days, as if she were recovering from some illness. She went into the bathroom and, not to her great surprise, threw up. The stockings that she had had to wash the night before were drying on the radiator, and it was while she was idly gazing at them and thinking to herself that there wasn't a single other pair in her chest of drawers and that their bedroom was just as cramped as this tiny bathroom was — in short, that she simply couldn't afford it — that she decided not to keep Antoine's baby.

•　　•　　•

She had but 40,000 francs left, and she was pregnant. After a long fight, life had finally caught up with her, and now she was in a fix. Life was becoming for Lucile what it was for her Métro-riding companions, and what writers so often depicted it as being: a world in which irresponsibility does not go unpunished. Antoine loved her and he would be only too willing to don the expectant-father hat, were she to tilt her portrayal of the situation in that way. If she were to say to him, "Something sweet is coming our way," he would take the unborn infant as a joy, of that much she was sure. But she didn't have the right to say any such thing. This child would strip her forever of her freedom and would not bring her happiness. Moreover, she knew she had deeply let Antoine down, and she had brought him to that point in an affair of the heart where every tiny act arouses suspicions of some sort. And so he would most likely believe that this accident was premeditated, although it certainly hadn't been. She loved him too much, or perhaps not enough — but whatever, she didn't want this child, she wanted only Antoine, joyful, blond, yellow-eyed, free to leave her. The only thing that could be said to be truly honest in her attitude was that, in totally abdicating all responsibility, she also refused to saddle anyone else with it.

This was hardly the moment to start daydreaming about Antoine Junior, three years old, scampering about on some beach, nor about Antoine Senior sternly correcting his son's homework. Rather, it was the moment to open one's eyes and to compare the size of this little room to the size of a crib, or the wages of a nanny to what Antoine brought home. It just didn't add up. Sure, there were plenty of women who would have made it all work out, but Lucile wasn't one of those. Nor was this the moment to get all distracted in thoughts about herself.

Part IV: *L'hiver*

And so, when Antoine got home, she explained to him that she was "in a certain way". His face went momentarily ashen, but quickly he enfolded her in his arms, murmuring in a dreamy voice, and she felt her jaw tightly clenching in an idiotic fashion.

"Are you positive that you don't want to keep it?"

"All I want is you," she replied. She didn't even broach the topic of money, fearing she could easily humiliate him. But he, on the other hand, while tenderly stroking her hair, was thinking that, were she so inclined, he could easily and passionately love having a child with her. But her nature was always to retreat — in fact, that was why he loved her — so he could hardly resent her for this central aspect of her nature. Still, he made one last attempt. "You know, we could try out the marriage thing... We could move to a new place."

"But where would we go?" she asked. "You know, I think having a kid is incredibly demanding. You'd come happily home from work only to find me totally frazzled and in a lousy mood, and it would be..."

"So how do other people manage, then, in your opinion?"

"They aren't like us," she replied, and pulled away from him. What this meant was: "They're not fiercely committed to being happy." He had nothing to say in reply. That evening, they went out and drank themselves silly. The next day, he planned to ask a friend of his for an address.

CHAPTER 22

The intern's face was stiff and ugly, filled with contempt. She couldn't tell if it was contempt for himself or for all the women whose sufferings he'd relieved, after a fashion, these last couple of years, to the modest tune of 80,000 francs apiece. He performed this service at their own homes, using no anesthesia, and he didn't come back if it turned out badly. He was scheduled to meet with Lucile the next evening, and she was trembling with fear and disgust at the mere idea of seeing him again. Antoine had borrowed the 40,000 francs that they didn't have from work, which had not been easy, and luckily for him, he hadn't gotten to see the great intern, since the latter, either out of some twisted moral principle or out of prudence, refused to meet "the guys". The alternative had been some Swiss doctor near Lausanne, but for that, one needed 200,000 francs up front, not to mention the expenses of the trip. That was out of the question; she hadn't even said a word about it to Antoine. The place was just too upper-crust. Not for her, the clinic, the nurse, and the shots. No, she was going to submit to this butcher, do her best to get through it alive, and, in all likelihood, be in wretched health for months thereafter. It was too stupid, too gruesome. And she, who had never before had second thoughts about her silly self-indulgences, now remembered with bitter regret her old pearl necklace, sold prematurely. She could just see herself winding up like the heroine of *The Wild Palms,* nearly dying of blood poisoning, with Antoine going to jail.

She paced back and forth in the little room like a caged animal, looking at her face and her slender body in the mirror, imagining herself disfigured, diseased, distressed, stripped forever of her brash young healthiness, which in large part lay at the root of her joy in being alive — and she started growing furious. At four o'clock she gave Antoine a call, but he sounded weary and troubled, and she just couldn't muster the courage to tell him of her fear. The truth was that at that moment, had he simply asked her to, she could easily have decided to keep the baby after all. But he seemed alien to her, unable to help her in any way, and all at once she felt a terrible yearning for someone, anyone, who could protect her. She felt very sad at having no female friend to whom she could turn for advice on these strictly female matters, to whom she could at least address her burning questions on crucial details that were terrifying to her. But she didn't know any women — indeed, her sole female friend had been Pauline. And as she softly spoke that name, she reflexively thought of Charles — Charles, the memory of whom she had squelched, since it gave rise to a lingering sense of remorse, since his was a name that could still make Antoine suffer. And in a flash, she knew for certain that she was going to ask for his help, that no one could keep her from doing so, that he was the sole human being on earth capable of doing something to make this nightmare go away.

She went to the phone and dialed the old number of his

office, saying a friendly hello to the switchboard operator. Charles was there. She had a strange emotional reaction to the sound of his voice and it took her a moment to regain her breath.

"Charles," she said, "I want to see You. I'm in a rough spot."

"I'll send the car for You in an hour," he replied, a calm head in the storm. "Is that all right?"

"Oh, yes — yes," she said. "I'll see You very soon." She waited a second or two for him to hang up, but then, as he wasn't doing so, she recalled his impeccable manners and did so herself. She got dressed as fast as she could, and as a result had to wait another three quarters of an hour, forehead pressed against the window, for the car to pull up. The driver greeted her joyously and as she sat down on the familiar seat, a feeling of limitless relief swept through her.

Pauline opened the door of the apartment and kissed her. Everything was still the same — warm, spacious, quiet — and the carpet under the English furniture was still that same blue, so soft on the eyes. For a moment she felt underdressed, and then she broke out laughing. It was a bit like the return of the prodigal son — but in this case it was he himself who was great with child. The driver had gone off again to pick up Charles, and she sat in the kitchen with Pauline just as in the old days, sipping a whiskey. Pauline muttered something about her having lost weight and having circles under her eyes, and Lucile felt like putting her head on Pauline's shoulder and handing over her fate to her. At the same time, she was appreciating Charles' thoughtfulness in having her come back alone to his place, as if it were still her own home, and in giving her a little time to refamiliarize herself with her past. It didn't occur to her that this might be skill on his part. And when he entered the hallway and shouted "Lucile!" in an almost jolly manner, she suddenly felt as if she had traveled back six months in time.

He too had lost weight and had aged. He took her arm and escorted her into the living room. Although Pauline protested, he asked her to bring in two scotch-and-sodas, then closed the door and sat down facing Lucile. All at once she felt intimidated. She cast a glance around the room, commented that nothing had changed, and he echoed her remark, saying that indeed, nothing had changed, even himself, in such a tender voice that she thought with panic that perhaps he was guessing that she was returning to him. She started blurting things out so quickly that he had to stop her and make her start over.

"Charles, I'm expecting a child, I don't want to keep it, I've got to go to Switzerland, I don't have any money."

Softly, he said that this was more or less what he had expected. "Are You very sure that You don't want to keep it?"

"I can't afford a baby. That is, *we* can't afford one," she blushed, correcting herself. "And also, I just want my freedom."

"Are You really sure that it isn't just a matter of having enough resources or not?"

"Completely sure of it," she replied.

He stood up, took a couple of steps, and then turned around with a sad little laugh. "Life is poorly designed, isn't it? I would have given almost anything to have a child with You, and You could even have had two nannies, if You'd wanted... But I suppose You wouldn't have kept a child of mine either, would You?"

"No."

"You really don't want to be burdened with anything, do You? Not with a husband, not with a child, not with a house... not with anything at all. It is really pretty strange."

"I don't want to own anything," she said. "You know that. I intensely dislike ownership."

He walked over to his desk, made out a check, and proferred it to her. "I have an excellent reference in Geneva. My only request is that You go there — I'd feel more at ease that way. Do You promise?"

She nodded timidly. She felt her throat tightening up, and she almost wanted to blurt out to him not to be so kind, so reassuring, not to bring her to tears — the tears that she felt welling up under her eyelids, tears of relief, bitterness, melancholy. She stared at the blue carpet, inhaled the mixed scents of tobacco and leather that still pervaded this room, heard the voice of Pauline downstairs, as she laughed with the driver. She felt she had come in out of the cold, to a shelter.

"You know," said Charles, "I'm still waiting for You. I'm terribly lonely without You. I know it's not very sensitive of me to say this to You today, but we see each other so very seldom." And he gave an awkward little laugh that completely undid Lucile. She quickly stood up and stammered, "Thank You" in a hoarse voice, and made a beeline for the door. She went down the staircase in tears, just like the time before, and she heard Charles cry out after her, "Will You get back in touch with me, or with my secretary, afterwards? Please!", as she headed out the door into the rain. She knew she'd been saved; she felt herself lost.

•   •   •

"I won't have anything to do with this money," declared Antoine. "Can you imagine what that man must think of me? Does he think I'm some kind of pimp? First I steal his woman from him and then I make him foot the bill for my escapades?"

"Antoine…"

"You've gone too far this time — way too far. I may not be a paragon of moral virtue, but I have my limits. You don't want my child, you lie all the time to me, you secretly sell off your pearls, you just do anything you damn well please. But I won't go along with you borrowing money from your ex-lover so you can kill the new one's baby. That's beyond the pale."

"But I take it that you'd find it perfectly moral for me to go get myself sliced up by a butcher as long as *you've* paid for it? Someone who'll operate on me in my living room, without any anesthesia at all, and who'll just leave me to die if there's the slightest infection? By your lights it would be moral for me to risk permanent damage to my body, just as long as Charles is kept out of the picture?"

They'd turned the red lamp off and were speaking very softly, as they were both so upset by the ugly things they were saying to each other. For the first time ever, they despised one another, they hated themselves for these feelings, and words just started bubbling out without check.

~ 190 ~

Chapter 22

"You're a coward, Lucile — a selfish coward. When you're fifty years old, you'll suddenly wake up and realize you're all alone, with nothing to your name. All that stupid charm of yours won't do a thing for you any more. There won't be a soul around to comfort you."

"Well, you're every bit as cowardly as I am. You're a hypocrite. What really gets you is not the prospect of killing this baby — it's that Charles would pay for the operation. Your honor comes ahead of my physical well-being. So tell me, where are you going to put this great honor of yours on display, for all to admire?"

They were both shivering, avoiding touching each other. They felt, weighing down on them, in this big bed — which for so long had been their only escape route — the weight of the world. They could foresee evenings spent alone, money troubles, wrinkles, they could see nuclear missiles being launched in a huge burst of flames, they could see a future filled with hostility and animosity, they could see life apart from each other, life without love. Antoine had the distinct feeling that if he were to let Lucile go off to Switzerland, he'd never forgive himself for it, that he'd resent her deeply for doing so, and that it would mark the end of their love. His intuition warned him that this intern was dangerous. His intuition also warned him that if he were to keep this baby, she would gradually be more and more overwhelmed by the daily grind, and she would lose interest in life and would stop loving him. Lucile was made for men, not for children — she would never be adult enough herself. And if, some day, she were to become an adult, she wouldn't like herself.

Part IV: L'hiver

All day long he kept on thinking, "This is crazy. Sooner or later, every woman goes through this — they all have babies, they all have money problems — that's just life. She's got to understand this. All it is is selfishness on her part." But then each time he looked at her again, saw that bright face, carefree and unreflective, he suddenly started feeling that all of this wasn't some shameful defect in her character but actually a deep and hidden animal power in her, which deflected her from engagement with life's most natural flow. And he couldn't keep himself from feeling a curious kind of respect for the very thing that, only ten minutes earlier, he had found contemptible. Unblemished; her intense craving for pleasure made her unblemished, made him relabel her selfishness as integrity, her indifference as detachment. And all at once a strange moan came forth from within him, a moan that felt as if it was drifting up all the way from his childhood, from his birth, from his entire destiny as a male human being.

"Lucile, I beg of you, keep this child. It's our only hope."

But she didn't reply. After a few minutes, he reached his hand out toward her and touched her face, where he found tears rolling down her cheek and onto her chin, and he awkwardly wiped them off.

"I'll ask for a raise," he went on, "and we'll scrape by somehow. There are lots of students who do babysitting in the evenings, and you can always put babies in day care all day long… It's not all that hard. And he'll get to be one, then two, then ten years old, and he'll be our kid. I should have said all this the very first day — I don't know why I didn't. We've got to try, Lucile."

Chapter 22

"You know very well why you didn't say any of this back then. You didn't believe in it — no more than I do." She was speaking in a calm voice, but the tears kept on rolling down her cheeks.

"We didn't start out this way. At the outset we hid what we were doing from our lovers, we pulled the wool over their eyes, we made them unhappy. You and I were made for the thrill of cheating and making passionate love, not to suffer together. We only got together because we wanted pleasure, Antoine, and you know that very well. Neither of us has the strength to... to be like all those other people."

She flipped over onto her stomach, nestling her head on his shoulder. "Sunlight and beaches, freedom and laziness — that's what we're made for, Antoine, and we're powerless to change that. It's part of our makeup, it's under our skin. That's just how things are. I suppose some people would say that we're spoiled rotten. But the only time I feel rotten is when I act as if I believed their words."

This time it was he who remained silent. As he stared at the spot of light cast by the streetlamp on the ceiling, the memory came back of Lucile's bewildered face when he'd tried to force her to dance that night at the Pré-Catelan. He remembered the tremendous wistfulness that her tears had induced in him then, he remembered how fervently he'd yearned that some night she would sob in his arms, so that he might console her. And tonight she *was* sobbing in his arms — he'd gotten his wish — but he was unable to comfort her, try as he might.

There was no point in lying to himself — he wasn't all that

interested in having this child, he was only interested in having *her* — alone, elusive, free as a bird. The most central thing in their love was how restless, carefree, and sensual they were together. A sudden feeling of tenderness surged up in him, and he took this crippled, irresponsible half-woman, half-child, his treasure, in his arms, and he whispered in her ear, "Tomorrow morning, bright and early, I'll go out and get us airplane tickets for Geneva."

CHAPTER 23

$\mathcal{F}ive$ weeks went by. The operation had been quick and successful, and as soon as she was home she called Charles to reassure him. But he wasn't at work and it was with a vague feeling of disappointment that she had left a message with the operator. Meanwhile Antoine was all wrapped up in a new literary series that he had been assigned, and his job situation was improving by leaps and bounds, thanks to one of the many upheavals that were taking place at that point in the publishing world. They ate out quite often with friends, co-workers, and acquaintances of Antoine's, and she was amazed and delighted to see the sway he seemed to hold over them. The two of them never spoke of Geneva, but simply took certain precautionary measures from then on. Actually, doing so wasn't particularly difficult, as she was often tired and he was often preoccupied, so that many nights they would just kiss tenderly before going to sleep, first facing each other, and after a while rolling over to face the other way.

One very rainy February afternoon, Lucile bumped into Johnny at the Café Flore. He was flipping through an art magazine somewhat distractedly because there was a very good-looking young blond fellow sitting at a nearby table, so at first she just walked by him discreetly, but he noticed her and called her over very warmly, so she joined him at his table. As was to be expected, he was sporting a most prominent tan, and he kept her in stitches for quite a while, recounting Claire's latest escapades in Gstaad. It also turned out that Diane had traded in her Cuban diplomat for an English novelist who was sleeping around behind her back with various youths — all of which clearly delighted Johnny. In a rather perfunctory fashion he inquired about Antoine, and she answered in a similar fashion. It had been ages since she'd had such a rollicking, laugh-filled gossip session, Antoine's friends being bright as a rule, but dreadfully humorless.

"You know that Charles is still waiting for You," said Johnny. "Claire tried to set him up with Clairvaux's girl, but it fizzled in no time flat. I've never in my life seen a man yawn so much. In the hotel, each time he walked from the lobby to the restaurant to the bar, he'd depress every soul he passed along the way. It was downright scary. What ever did You do to him? What kind of power do You have over men in general? I could use some tips from You!"

He smiled at her. He'd always been fond of Lucile, and it troubled him to see her in such a dowdy old suit and with her hair in disarray. She still had her same adolescent charm, with her eyes seeming both far away and yet twinkling at the same time, but he found her too pale and too scrawny. With concern, he asked, "Are You happy?"

She said yes, but very quickly — too quickly — from which he deduced that she was wasting away in boredom. And then it somehow crossed his mind that he could try to bring Lucile back to Blassans-Lignières, who, after all, had always been very well disposed towards him. Now that would be a good deed. And in thinking about why he was inclined to do this, he completely forgot about the intense pangs of jealousy that had overcome him eight months before, when he saw Lucile and Antoine gazing at each other, frozen and flushed with desire, at that trendy American's cocktail party, the very day after they'd first made love.

"You really ought to give Charles a call one of these days. He doesn't look at all well. Claire even suspects that he may have some frightful disease."

"Do You mean…"

"Oh, everyone bandies the word 'cancer' about so glibly these days. But in this case, I worry that there may be some truth to it."

He was lying. And he noticed with amusement that Lucile was growing slightly pale. Charles… Charles — so kind, so alone in his huge apartment. Charles, so abandoned by all those people that he didn't like and who didn't like him, by all those girls that people threw at him simply because he was rich. Charles, sick. She had to phone him. And this whole week, Antoine was all booked up with important lunches and dinners, anyway. She thanked Johnny for having let her know the situation, and only then did he remember, a bit on the late side, that Claire couldn't stand Lucile. She would doubtless be furious if Lucile were to get back together with Charles. But Johnny didn't mind playing an occasional dirty trick on his dear friend Claire.

Part IV: L'hiver

So one morning Lucile gave Charles a call and they agreed to have lunch together the next day. It was a beautiful, crisp, clear winter day, and he insisted that she have a couple of apéritifs to warm herself up while he did likewise. The hands of the *maîtres d'hôtel* were darting all about their table just like swallows, it felt wonderfully toasty inside, and the soft and — you could just tell — utterly empty chatter of all the patrons made for a most soothing background noise. Charles ordered their meals with his usual precision, flawlessly recalling her preferences. She, meanwhile, was watching him closely, trying to discern any telltale traces of his illness on his face, but the truth was that he actually looked somewhat rejuvenated since the last time she'd seen him. She wound up telling him this, in a somewhat resentful tone, and he replied, with a smile, "Well, I did have some little problems this winter. There was this bronchitis that I just couldn't shake for the life of me. Then I had three rough weeks skiing, but that was the end of it."

"But Johnny had given me to believe that You had some serious health problems…"

"Me? Not in the least!" replied Charles, quite cheerfully. "Believe You me, I'd tell You about it if that were the case."

"Do You swear this is all true?"

The look of surprise on his face was very sincere. "My goodness — of course I swear it's true. Do You still have this nutty thing about people saying things under oath? It's been a good long while since I've had to swear that something was true." He gave a tender little laugh and she laughed with him.

"Johnny had given me the impression that You had some

kind of cancer — that's the simple truth of the matter."

Charles stopped laughing instantly. "And so *that's* why You called me up? Basically, You didn't want me to die all alone?"

She shook her head. "Well, I also wanted to see You again." And to her great surprise, she realized that it was so.

"I'm alive and kicking, *ma chère Lucile*, deplorably alive, although the dead probably have more fun than I do. I'm still working, and since I don't have the courage to stay at home all the time, I go out now and then."

He paused and then resumed, in a softer voice, "Your hair is still every bit as black, Your eyes still just as gray as ever. Truly You're in bloom today."

It occurred to her that it had been a long time since anyone had complimented her on her eyes or her hair, or for that matter on any aspect of her appearance. Undoubtedly Antoine figured that his ardor precluded any need for compliments. But it really felt very satisfying to have this mature man sitting right across from her and admiring her despite her inaccessibility, rather than seeing her as an object of desire that he could possess at any moment...

"I was just wondering," he said, "if You might happen to be free this Thursday evening. There's going to be a lovely concert in the old La Moll mansion on the Île Saint-Louis. They're scheduled to be playing that Mozart concerto for flute and harp that You were always so fond of, and Louise Wermer herself has agreed to perform. But of course, I suppose it would be pretty awkward for You?"

"Why awkward?"

Part IV: *L'hiver*

"Well, I have no idea whether Antoine likes music, but more crucially, wouldn't an invitation to him from me very likely rub him the wrong way?"

This was Charles all over, this invitation. He was inviting Antoine along with her partly because he was just plain polite, but also because he would rather see her in Antoine's company than not see her at all. He would patiently wait for her and he would faithfully get her out of all her scrapes, whatever they might be. And she, in the meantime, had forgotten he even existed for six months, and it had taken her thinking he was at death's very door to come out of hiding. What was this due to, how could he stand this horrible asymmetry in their relationship, how did he manage to keep his love alive on so few scraps, with his generosity and his tenderness receiving so little in return?

She leaned over towards him and asked, "Why do You still love me? Why?" Her voice was fierce, almost resentful, and he hesitated a moment before answering.

"I could tell You that it's because You don't love me, and in fact that would be an excellent reason, although surely incomprehensible to You, with Your constant search for pleasure. But there's also something else about You that I'm so terribly taken with. It's…" He paused for a moment, then went on: "I don't quite know. Some kind of verve, the sense of somebody who's headed somewhere, though God knows that You don't have any desire to go anywhere. Some kind of greediness, though God knows that the last thing You want is material possessions. Some kind of perpetual bubbliness, and yet You seldom laugh. You know, people always seem overwhelmed by their lives, while

Chapter 23

You, somehow You've turned the tables on life, and it's You who seem to be on top. *Voilà.* I don't know else how to put it. Would You like a lemon sherbet?"

"It's certainly good for one's health," observed Lucile dreamily. "Antoine has a publishing dinner on Thursday," she said, which was perfectly true, "and so I'll come alone, if You'd like that."

He liked it very much; indeed, it was everything that he craved. They set their rendezvous for 8:30, and when he suggested meeting "at home", she didn't for a split second think of the Rue de Poitiers. Rue de Poitiers meant just a bedroom; it wasn't a home, and never once had it been one, even if it had been Paradise and Hell all swirled together.

CHAPTER 24

The La Moll mansion had been built in the eighteenth century by some long-forgotten minor dignitary. Its rooms were enormous and its woodwork exquisite, and the candlelight, which was harsh and soft at the same time (harsh, because it brought out the soul — or lack of soul — behind a face; soft, because it blurred age away), made the size and the charm of the grand salon seem even greater. The orchestra was at the far end on some kind of low stage and, if she leaned over a little, just barely missing the reflected candlelight in the windowpane, Lucile could see the waters of the Seine flowing by, luminous and black, no more than twenty meters below her. There was a feeling of irreality for her about this evening, for the view, the decor, and the music were all so perfect. One year earlier, she might have yawned; she might even have hoped to see some unhappy guest take a tumble or hear the tinkle of a breaking glass, but this evening, something in her appreciated almost desperately the serenity, the precision, and the beauty that were being offered, all thanks to the upstanding La Moll family's illegal trafficking in far-off French ex-colonies.

"Your concerto is coming up right now," whispered Charles. He was sitting beside her, and out of the corner of her eye she could see the bright white of his tuxedo shirt, the perfect cut of his hair, his slender manicured hand with its little spots, holding a glass of scotch that he would share with her any time that she expressed the desire for a sip. He looked handsome this way, in this vacillating light; he seemed sure of himself, and even a bit boyish; he seemed happy. Johnny had smiled on seeing them come in together, and she hadn't asked him why he had lied to her.

Now the old lady was leaning over her harp, smiling a little, and the young flutist was watching her, ready for a cue, and you could see his throat pulsating. It was a very elegant crowd and he had to be feeling intimidated. This was clearly a soirée à la Proust: it was at the home of the Verdurin family, young Morel was making his first appearance, and Charles was the wistful Swann. But Lucile felt there was no rôle for her in this splendid play — no more than there had been at *Le Réveil*, in that icy office three months earlier, no more than there would ever be for her, in her whole life. She wasn't a courtesan, nor an intellectual, nor the mother of a family — she was nothing at all. And the very first notes sweetly plucked from the harp by Louise Wermer made her eyes well up with tears. And this music would grow even more tender, she knew it, even more wistful, even more irreversible — despite the fact that this last adjective would not admit of degrees of "more" or "less". It was a detached, unearthly music for someone who had tried so hard to be happy, tried so hard to be kind, yet had only managed to make two men suffer, someone who no longer knew who she was.

The old lady was no longer smiling and the harp was playing so poignantly that Lucile, without any forethought, reached over and grasped the hand of the human being seated right next to her. This hand, this doubtless fleeting but very living warmth, this touching of two skins — this was the only thing that stood between her and death, between her and loneliness, between her and the unbearable suspense of the notes that were churning and swirling together, coming from flute and harp, coming from a timid young man and an aged woman, yet all at once perfectly matched in that stunning scorn for time that is evoked by Mozart's music.

Charles kept her hand in his. Every once in a while he would reach over with his free hand for a glass of scotch and would offer it to Lucile's other hand. And thus she drank a great deal that evening. And there was a great deal of music as well. And Charles' hand grew ever more confident, and it felt slender and long and warm in hers. And who was that blond man who had sent her off to distant movie theaters in the rain, who had insisted on her taking a job, who had arranged for her to be given an abortion by quasi-butchers? Who was this Antoine who proclaimed that these amiable people, this exquisite candlelight, the plushness of these old sofas, and the music of Mozart were all rotten to the core? Of course he hadn't spoken about these sofas or these candles or Mozart, but he had often said just that about these very people who, at this very moment, were offering her all this beauty, as well as this chilled and golden liquid that warmly flowed down her throat as smoothly as if it were water. Lucile was very tipsy, very still, and very happy, clinging to Charles' hand. She loved Charles, she loved this soft-spoken and gentle man, she had always loved him, she never wanted to leave him again, and so she was shocked by his sad little laugh when she told him all this as they were driving back.

"I would give anything to believe You," he said, "but You've drunk a lot this evening. It's someone else that You love."

And later, of course, when she saw Antoine's hair on the pillow and his long arm extended across their little bed to the spot where she usually slept, she knew that Charles was right. But in realizing this, she felt a curious twinge of regret. For the first time...

And then came quite a few other times. There was no doubt that she still loved Antoine, but she no longer loved loving him; she no longer loved their shared life, its lack of spontaneity due to their lack of money, the overall dreariness of their days. As for him, he could tell how she was feeling, and in reaction he stepped up the pace of his professional activities, practically ignoring her totally. Those idle hours that she once would pass in such excitement waiting for him to come home were now becoming ever more empty because his awaited return was no longer a miracle but merely a habit. She would drop in on Charles now and then, never mentioning it to Antoine, for what use would it have been to pile jealousy on top of the resigned torment that already filled those yellow eyes?

And at night, they engaged more in combat than in lovemaking. The science that each of them had so carefully worked out to prolong the other's pleasure was now almost imperceptibly turning into a crude technique allowing them to be over and done with it all the more quickly — and not out of boredom but out of fear. They each fell asleep reassured by their sighs and moans, forgetting how thrilled they once had been by them, long ago.

•   •   •

One evening when she had been drinking, for these days she was drinking a lot, she returned with Charles to his place. She barely realized what was happening. All she said to herself was that this had been bound to happen, and that she had to tell Antoine. She went back at dawn and gently woke him up. Nine months earlier, in this very same room, crazily in love with her, he'd thought he'd lost her forever — and it wasn't Lucile but Diane who had bid him adieu. But now he *had* lost her forever, lost her for keeps... He must not have been pushy enough or strong enough or something of that sort, but he couldn't figure it out and wasn't even going to try any longer. For too many days, the stubborn taste of defeat and helplessness had been rolling around in his mouth. He nearly blurted out that her concern for him made no difference to him, that she'd always been cheating on him with Charles, with life, with her entire soul. But then he remembered those summer months, he recalled the taste of her tears on his shoulder that last month of August, and he bit his tongue.

For over a month, ever since Geneva, he had been expecting her to leave. It may just be that there are certain things that cannot take place between a man and a woman without wounding them permanently, no matter how open they are with each other, and perhaps the Geneva trip had been such a thing. Or perhaps their fate had been predetermined from the very start, from that first explosion of laughter they'd shared at Claire Santré's. As he gazed at Lucile's weary face, at the rings around her gray eyes, at her hand touching his sheet, he realized that it would take him a very long time to recover from this. He knew every tiny corner of this face, every curve of this body; this was not a geometry that one could easily expunge from one's consciousness. They exchanged trite phrases. She felt shame but otherwise totally devoid of feelings, and doubtless, all it would have taken on his part was for him to exclaim, "Stay!", and she would have stayed. But he didn't do it.

"Well, anyway, you weren't happy any more."

"Neither were you."

They exchanged a strange sad smile of apology in an almost perfunctory fashion. She rose and walked out, and only after she had closed the door behind her did he start to moan, "Lucile, Lucile," and to hate himself. She walked all the way home, to Charles' apartment, to loneliness, sensing that she was now forever banished from any kind of life worth living, and that this was the fate she deserved.

PART FIVE

Plus tard...

$\mathcal{T}$ranslator, $\mathcal{T}$rader

An Essay on the Pleasantly Pervasive
Paradoxes of Translation

Douglas Hofstadter

BASIC
BOOKS

A Member of the Perseus Books Group
New York

A CIP catalogue record for this book is available from the United States Library of Congress in Washington D.C.

LCCN: 2009922415
ISBN: 9780465010981

2 4 6 8 10 9 7 5 3 1

À Caroline
qui m'a tant donné

Translator, Trader

An Essay on the Pleasantly Pervasive
Paradoxes of Translation

Scaling Mount Sagan

MANY gritty folks climb greater and lesser mountains; a few scale the loftiest peaks there are. Thus when, for the first time in history, Sir Edmund Hillary and Tenzing Norgay conquered the tallest mountain on earth, it made perfect sense that each of them would eventually write a book about their epic alpinistic achievement. But if someone were to climb a little-known peak in a less grandiose mountain range (without having a harrowing close shave with death), most people would find it rather odd if the climber chose to write a book about this feat, no matter how arduous the struggle or sweet the victory.

Analogously, if, after twenty years of intense and anguished struggle, the Chinese translator of *Finnegans Wake* — by anyone's lights one of the more Himalayan peaks of world literature — were to pen a joyous memoir recalling certain highlights of the exhausting oxygen-deprived upward trek and the final exultant planting of the Chinese flag at the volume's summit, one might not be terribly surprised. Some people might even consider such an accomplishment more heroic than the ascent of Everest!

However, the dozen or so novels penned by Françoise Sagan constitute but a smallish mountain range in the French literature of the twentieth century, and Sagan's 1965 novel *La Chamade* is

not usually regarded as the apex of the Sagan chain. And yet here am I, writing an essay that chronicles and comments on the intellectual voyage that I made in the act of climbing this little-known literary peak — that is, in translating this rather obscure novel into English, or rather, into American English, or even more specifically, into my own personal brand of American English. Why? Why not simply do what most translators of novels do — just get the job done as well as possible, and stay humbly in the background? Why such hubris?

Hubris?

I MUST admit that when I go into a good bookstore and look at the myriads of books that have been translated from all sorts of languages and in which, in nearly every case, the translator's name is exhibited only one time, on the title page (and that's all), then the fact that I'm writing this long essay to accompany my rather small act of translation makes me feel like I'm some kind of exhibitionist. I can't help asking myself, "Why aren't you meek and humble, like all those hard-working translators are?"

But then I imagine what it would be like if I *did* come across a translator's preface in, say, the French translation of Khaled Hosseini's extraordinarily gripping novel *The Kite Runner*. Would I be taken aback and turned off, immediately realizing that the translator suffered from the grievous character defect of an enormous ego? No, on the contrary, I would see such a preface as simply icing on the cake of the novel itself, as giving me a lucky opportunity to reflect on the work of literature, both in English and in French, in a fresh new way, and my curiosity would be aroused. In short, I would warmly welcome such a thing.

This reminds me of when, as a teen-ager, I discovered that the marvelous and eccentric pianist Glenn Gould had written the

Translator, Trader

liner notes for his famous recording of Johann Sebastian Bach's "Goldberg Variations". I was most excited to find out what this clearly brilliant individual had to say about Bach's work of genius, movement by movement. As it happened, I found much of Gould's prose to be convoluted, obscure, and even opaque at times, but obviously that was just a personal quirk of Gould's and not an inevitable trap whenever someone writes about how they have interpreted a work of art.

And when I attend a live piano recital, I am always pleased as punch when the performer, instead of remaining 100 percent mute for the entirety of their sonic performance (quite an irony, when you think about it), first turns toward the audience, opens their mouth, and actually speaks to us, letting down their guard and telling us about the pieces they are about to perform, unveiling for us some of their humanity, and giving us a very special light in which to consider what we are about to hear. I am always grateful for such a verbal "performance"; in fact, I find it to be disarming. For me, at least, it makes the performer, who as a virtuoso musician is so incredibly skilled that at times they seem to belong to a different species from us mere listeners, seem friendly and approachable rather than alien and remote.

Lang A to Lang B — Big Deal!

AND thus I'd like to think that my writing of this essay is not an act of hubris but merely a modest personal attempt to spur thoughtful people to reflect more deeply than perhaps they have on the subtle art of translation. I chose to make this attempt because in the course of doing this translation, and especially in the act of revising and polishing it, I myself was forced to confront very intimately, almost brutally, the question of what on earth I was doing. I became more and more aware of just how

strange, even paradoxical, it was to use my native language —
and, more specifically, my own deeply personal style of crafting,
manipulating, and savoring phrases in my native language — to
rewrite someone else's book. As translation's paradoxes started
to haunt my thoughts ever more intensely, I felt a growing desire
to make them as vivid as I could for other people.

I believe that most well-educated people, perhaps especially
in my native land, the United States, have an unconscious image
of translation as a quite straightforward, rule-driven act carried
out nearly mechanically by individuals who for one reason or
another simply happen to be bilingual. Indeed, to be quite frank,
I myself had just this impression for shockingly many years. In
my teens and twenties, the sight of a book sitting on someone's
shelf with words on its spine that said "The Trial / Franz Kafka"
or "Remembrance of Things Past / Marcel Proust" or "Crime
and Punishment / Fyodor Dostoevsky" never once struck me as
paradoxical, miraculous, or even interesting in the least. It
seemed no more surprising that such books could move from one
language to another than that I myself could move from the town
of Palo Alto to other towns, like Prague or Paris or Petersburg.

Sure, it had taken some drudge a lot of work and time, but
that was all. So they took all those sentences in language A and
put them into language B... Big deal! I remember that even
when I thought about translating wordplay and other tricky
linguistic structures, my first reaction was that anybody bilingual
could do it, or at least anybody bilingual with a modicum of wit.

Then a couple of decades passed and one day, on a lark, I
sent out a challenge to many friends and colleagues to translate a
charming and intricate miniature poem by the sixteenth-century
French poet Clément Marot. I received many responses, and
they ranged incredibly in quality, with perfectly bilingual people
often stumbling terribly and coming out with what struck me as

atrocious products, and conversely, non-fluent speakers of either the source or target language coming up on occasion with truly brilliant solutions. As I came to see how few people, whether bilingual or not, could carry out such tasks at all well, my respect for translators of literary works in which form and content are intricately fused shot up enormously. And yet, I must once again confess that there remained in my mind a kind of disinterest in the act of translation of "ordinary" literature, a lack of respect for "ordinary" translators. They still felt just like airplanes carrying passengers from one city to another — most impressive but nonetheless perfectly mechanical.

This reminds me of a period in my life when I was filled with admiration for the jazzy kinds of typefaces designed mainly for advertising ("display faces") but I found so-called "book faces", such as Baskerville, the typeface that you are now reading, utterly pedestrian. I was totally convinced that the former were rife with creative spark while the latter were devoid of it. But one day, on a friend's suggestion, I took a more careful look at Baskerville and began to notice the grace of its curves and the unexpected number of subtle decisions that had gone into its design:

abcdefghijklm
nopqrstuvwxyz

Note, for example, the elegant way the loop of the "a" hits the vertical diagonally, or the graceful unclosed lower swirl of the "g", or the gentle curves of the upper serifs of the "b", "d", "i", "j", and others, or the cute little "droplet" capping the curves of the "a", "c", "f", "j", and others, and on and on.

Needless to say, the scales fell from my eyes shortly thereafter. I came to realize that coming up with an excellent book face takes just as much of an artistic eye and a creative mind as coming up with an excellent display face. The skills in these two forms of design are not the same, but in neither art form are they smaller or less worthy of respect.

At some point in my life, analogous scales fell from my eyes and I came to realize how deeply artistic, even creative, is the act of translating "ordinary" works of literature — "mere" novels, so to speak. The strange thing is, though, that I can *still* quite easily slip back into the mindless mindset of thinking of the translation of "ordinary prose" as being a mundane, spark-less act, and since I myself am so susceptible to this illusion, I find it easy to imagine that many other people, perhaps most, also have an unconscious presumption that what translators do, especially translators of "mere prose", is no big deal. To do my bit to combat this widespread but subterranean prejudice, using this particular novel as my main source of examples, is the main reason that I am writing this essay. I hope that is not seen as hubris.

Four Pleasantly Pervasive Paradoxes

IF THE act of translating novels is in fact riddled through and through by paradoxes, then what are these paradoxes? Here I'll give a short list to get the idea across in broad brushstrokes, and then in what follows, we will see these paradoxes crop up over and over again.

The Wrong-Tongue Paradox: How can Dante Alighieri have written a book in English, a language that didn't even exist when he was alive, or William Shakespeare a set of sonnets in Russian, when he knew not a word of that language? Or else take these "quotes" by three illustrious names from antiquity:

Euripides: *"Onwetendheid van tegenslagen is een duidelijk winstpunt."*
Plutarch: *"Wind je over de feiten niet op, ze hebben schijt aan de kwaaie kop."*
Confucius: *"Laat de zon geen tranen drogen die je kunt wegvegen uit het oog van degene die lijdt."*

Here are three famous gents of yore, all speaking impecccable modern Dutch (and Plutarch, that sly old imp, is even rhyming!). I found these "quotes" all on a Web site, quote marks and all. Is this not crazy? Well, maybe or maybe not, but quite obviously the claim of authorship is profoundly muddied up by the act of changing from one language to another.

The Wrong-Style Paradox: Since writing styles are every bit as different as are faces or fingerprints, how can Person B rewrite Author A's book from top to toe and then not cringe in claiming that the resulting sequence of words is still "by Author A"? This paradox, please note, need not involve language-jumping; just think of Person B paraphrasing an essay by Author A while keeping the language fixed. I certainly know that when essays of mine are given to others to copy-edit or shorten, modified sentences often stand out like a sore thumb, at least to my eye. "I could never have written such a thing in a million years!", I'll exclaim indignantly. And yet B, my well-meaning paraphraser, thought it said exactly the same thing as what I'd written (or even said it better!). Replacing one person's literary style by another's is clearly a deep violation of authorship, and yet what alternative is there, if translation is to be carried out at all?

The Wrong-Place Paradox: When characters in a story speak, the language they use is informal and colloquial, so their lines are inevitably peppered with colorful words and idioms that come from the streets of their land and the history of their people. And any other people has a different history, different traditions, and scads of different colorful ways of expressing itself. Therefore,

when idioms of culture B are placed in the mouths of individuals from culture A, the result is incoherent. And yet as readers, we are expected to skip right over that — and the curious thing is that we usually do! The incoherence passes invisibly right through our filters, and we often see nothing wrong at all. But behind the scenes, the authenticity of the geographical and temporal setting of a story is constantly being threatened by the most mundane acts of translation — already somewhat in the narrative passages, but especially in the characters' conversations.

The Don't-Trust-the-Text Paradox: What an author really means is often not transmitted by their words alone. Indeed, the act of reading is a process of converting words into ideas and then of largely (though not totally) forgetting the words involved. As readers-in-depth, translators particularly have to respect ideas more than words (although I suspect the public generally thinks it is the reverse). Of course it is the words on the page that *lead* one to the ideas, but paradoxically, keeping one's trust in the words after one has found the ideas that they stand for amounts to a knee-jerk preference for letter over spirit, and this Literality Trap amounts to a death sentence for high-quality translation.

I hope my paradoxes strike you as plausible, intriguing, and provocative, even if here they've been given as blurry generalities sans context. Since I always prefer concrete examples to abstract generalities, in the rest of this essay I will discuss these paradoxes in down-to-earth ways, mostly though not wholly in the context of my translation of *La Chamade* into my own brand of English.

Authors at the Mercy of Translators

WHEN my son Danny was a senior in high school, he had to write an essay on a short story by Gabriel García Márquez. The story was handed out to his class in a photocopy in English, and

on those sheets, no mention was made of the work's country of origin, let alone its original language, the name of the translator, or the fact that some of the words on some of the pages perhaps had something to do with someone other than the named author. Now I didn't know his teacher personally, so I have no idea whether she gave any thought to the quality of the translation, or whether she had considered that a different translation might give a radically different impression of the work or the author, but in any case, I suspect that such notions never crossed any of her students' minds. It certainly wouldn't have crossed mine at that age, even though I spoke two languages well (English and French) and was passionately fascinated by language in general.

At some point around the year 1970, when I was in graduate school, I heard an interview on the radio with Alexander Solzhenitsyn about his book *A Day in the Life of Ivan Denisovich*, which takes place in a Siberian work camp, and I was so impressed with Solzhenitsyn's forceful character and powerful ideas that I went right out to buy it. Of course, "it" was not the original work in Russian, but "its translation" into English (as if there could self-evidently only be one such). So… some drudge had taken all those sentences in language A and had put them into language B — big deal!

I didn't give this matter a moment's thought but simply purchased a paperback copy that I found in some random bookstore and went home to read it. Well, it didn't take long before I started to squirm. To my confusion, the book was filled with down-home American idioms, American swear words, and American slang, so much so that to my ears, it sounded exactly like it was taking place in a California prison! The more I read, the more I was jarred, and pretty soon I could take it no longer. This book was not at all like the book I had hoped to read, and so, extremely disappointed, I shelved it forever.

It took two more decades before I encountered a different translation of *A Day in the Life of Ivan Denisovich*. The one I had purchased twenty years earlier turned out *not* to be "the" English translation; rather, there were several such — and they varied enormously in style and feel. The troubling pervasiveness of American slang was a feature only of that first version I had picked up, and the others were free of that flaw. One, however, erred in a different but unfortunately analogous fashion — it came across as extremely British, and to me, that was just as serious a sin as sounding too American. But there were a couple of translations that seemed to come much closer to the mark, and at least from my point of view they preserved and conveyed much of the essential Russianness of this work. Thus, with a sigh of relief, I was able to read Solzhenitsyn's novel without feeling it had been stripped of much of its Russianness and made less alien in order to be more acceptable to American palates, a bit like Taco Bell's diluted Mexican fare.

The Localized Nature of Words

WHAT discombobulated me in my first encounter with *Ivan Denisovich* was that the novel had been more than translated; it had also been *transculturated* halfway around the world. This was my first exposure to the Wrong-Place Paradox. But had the translators (it was done by two people working together) actually *set out* to subtract Russianness from the novel? Was their act of transculturation deliberate and conscious? I didn't ask myself this question at the time. As I think about it now, however, the issue seems very subtle.

Whenever one tries to express anything, whether in speech or in writing, whether in creating an original work of art or "merely" in crafting a fine translation, one's brain is a boiling

cauldron of largely instinctive and unconscious mental processes that are simultaneously seeking appropriate grammatical pathways and appropriate words, as well as longer standard expressions, and as a result of this seething activity, various candidate phrases eventually come bubbling up out of the murk and duke it out, and at the fight's end the victor gets sent on to the "output channel" (the vocal cords, the typing fingertips, whatever). The degree to which one's verbal output winds up imbued with the unique flavor of a specific culture is an unplanned, emergent outcome of this frenzied competition. The many facets of who you are, of your current mood, and of the context in which you currently find yourself all constitute conscious or unconscious pressures that collectively determine what will come out of your cauldron. But the target language itself is the landscape in which this battle takes place.

Any language has a very large number of words and phrases that feel essentially timeless and placeless, for what they denote is simply part and parcel of the eternal, universal human condition. For example, here are a few eternal, universal words in English:

> and, but, with, maybe, food, drink, sun, old, daughter,
> sand, shut, pith, baby, mood, pink, run, cold, water.

Of course the list of timeless-sounding expressions denoting human universals includes untold thousands of compound words and longish stock phrases, such as these few:

> sailboat, schoolhouse, lighthearted, bittersweet, remarry, oversleep,
> notwithstanding, nevertheless, give up, make do, shove off, eat out,
> up early, bad luck, rotten apple, sweet victory, play favorites, get away
> with it, never again, all of a sudden, most of the time, out of control,
> on the other hand, as far as the eye can see, and so forth and so on...

— and so forth and so on, *ad infinitum* (or nearly *infinitum*). Every language on earth is filled to the brim with such "culture-free", "universal", "unflavored" expressions.

On the other hand, every human language also has just as many deeply "flavored" or "localized" words and phrases that powerfully exude a particular era or cultural setting. English, for example, has these few, among untold myriads of others:

gee willikers; yee-haw; shucks; dagnabbit; gonna grab me some grub; buffalo gals; the bee's knees; take a spin in the flivver; Mom, Dad, Bud, and Sis; before you could say "Jack Robinson"; get off your duff; you betcha; darn right; the real McCoy; and I'm like wow; gag me with a spoon; goy, shmoy; you vant bagels, I got bagels; yo' motha bad!; all systems go for liftoff; toot my horn; leaner and meaner; smashed to smithereens; knock 'em dead; I kid you not; couch potato; eye candy; that's a no-no; he's one cool dude; I'll just pop off to the loo; blimey; jolly good fun; it's your go!; stiff upper lip, my good man!

I'm sorely tempted (and note that phrase) to try to extend this list forever, but I'll restrain myself.

Although many of the *ideas* in this third list are themselves timeless and universal (thus, "gee willikers" simply expresses a kind of naïve surprise, "get off your duff" expresses impatience or urgency, "that's a no-no" expresses disapproval or warning, and so on), the *expressions* are so richly, quaintly flavored that somehow they localize the imagery they evoke, pinning it down to a particular era, place, subculture, or cultural perspective.

Between these two extremes there is a vast spectrum of words and phrases possessing various intermediate degrees of flavor or localization. Needless to say, "degree of flavor" is a very blurry notion, so that given a random phrase, it would be absurd to try to state *precisely* where it lies along the spectrum, but here are a

few sample English phrases that strike me as lying roughly half-way between the ones in the previous two lists:

> big deal; part and parcel; swan song; smashed to bits; in broad brushstrokes; few and far between; two-timer; make a hit; can't put my finger on it; the genuine article; frightened to death; a black-and-white matter; what's up?; you don't say; duke it out; don't have the foggiest idea; to my chagrin; hanky-panky; the nitty-gritty; beats me!; the girl next door; have a ball; up in the air; and — last but not least.

It's self-evident that in any novel, many thousands of "eternal, universal" words and phrases (as in the first two lists above) will appear. Some will occur in the narrator's descriptions, others in the characters' dialogues. And then, depending on the subject matter and the author's style, there may also be hundreds or thousands of mildly or highly localized phrases.

Now, universal words and phrases are usually not too hard to translate — thus, "the sun was setting" and "she opened her eyes" are so generic that it's pretty cut-and-dried what to do with either of them. On the other hand, partially or highly localized expressions give a translator headaches. How localized should the expressions in the receiving language be? And localized in which culture? And how does this depend on whether the expressions are found inside *descriptions* or inside *conversations*?

Dans les Ascenseurs de Paris

THE last thing in the world that translators of novels wish to do, unless they are into playing special kinds of intellectual games, is to carry a work of literature across the seas and re-set it in another land and culture; nonetheless, because vast numbers of words and phrases give off subtle aromas of which one is not

always aware, this can happen, at least to some extent, despite their best intentions. The most insidious problem is that every single tiny act of translation, no matter how innocent-seeming, involves some degree of transculturation. This happens even with highly universal, vanilla-flavored words, such as "house", "door", "dog", "walk", "happy", "thanks", and so forth.

To take a concrete example, how does one say "elevator" in French? If one uses the dictionary equivalent *ascenseur* (and there really is no alternative, so it's a forced move), that word will tend to conjure up in the mind of a native French speaker an image formed over the course of thousands of experiences with French elevators (strictly speaking, to be self-consistent, I should have written, "with French *ascenseurs*"). To be sure, the images of *ascenseurs* that jump to a French mind have much in common with the images of elevators that jump to an American mind, but there are also many differences, as anyone who has spent any time in the two countries knows very well.

For instance, American elevators are usually quite large and frustratingly slow. They tend to have very thick walls and very thick, multi-layered doors that, on opening, slide out of view and, often after quite a long wait, slide back shut. They are rather silent (except for beeps at every floor), they have lots of lights, and they "intelligently" or "politely" stop at intermediate floors, if someone has pushed a button there. By contrast, European elevators (especially those of a few years ago) are often small (sometimes just a couple of people can squeeze in), their manual doors swing open outwards (and often there are two sets — one inner and one outer). They move fast and are often "dumb" or "impolite", blithely ignoring people on intermediate floors, who simply have to wait till all current passengers have disembarked. And then there are those wonderful antique elevators with cages instead of actual walls, where, as you ascend or descend, you can

see the spiral staircase winding around you, and woe to anyone who sticks their finger through the iron grillwork of the cage.

The contrast between these kinds of images is enormous. Although both the American elevator and the French *ascenseur* serve the function of vertically transporting people, animals, suitcases, and other items in some tallish building, the "vibes" that they emanate are radically different. Therefore, if a French translation of an American novel taking place in Richland, Washington replaces the word "elevator" by the word *ascenseur* all three times it occurs, there will result a tiny, microscopic, almost undetectable effect of transculturation in the minds of French readers. (To be sure, many French people have traveled to America and are perfectly familiar with American elevators, but human nature being what it is, even they will still have a subconscious tendency to visualize described scenes in the easiest, laziest, most mindless fashion, and that tendency will somewhat cancel the effect due to their worldliness.)

The effect of just this one particular word-substitution is very small, but since this kind of "innocent" replacement is inevitably going to be carried out thousands of times, with bread in a Richland grocery store being replaced by *pain*, cars driving down Richland streets by *voitures*, sidewalks by *trottoirs*, high schools by *lycées*, mountain climbing by *alpinisme*, songs sung in American English by *chansons*, hoodlums by *voyous*, coffee by *café*, kisses by *bisous* and *baisers*, cigarettes by *cigarettes*, giggles by *fou rire*, and so forth, the novel will perforce become, to some extent, a novel rooted in France, no matter how much care is taken by the translator not to transculturate. The mere act of shifting these "universal" words from language E to language F already amounts to a non-negligible act of transculturation, and one can do nothing about it. In short, some amount of the Wrong-Place Paradox is an inevitable effect of any act of translation.

"Traduttore, Traditore"

WITH this, we find ourselves square in the territory staked out by the celebrated and hugely negativistic Italian slogan *Traduttore, traditore,* which literally means "Translator, betrayer" or "Translator, traducer" — or then again, "Translator, traitor." The irony residing in the final one of these three possibilities is that it beautifully undermines its own claim. The pithy slogan "Translator, traitor" shows very clearly that a translator need *not* be a betrayer or traitor, for it beautifully preserves the key quality that makes the original Italian phrase so memorable — namely, its catchiness, which is due to the fact that the two nouns inside it sound so much alike. There is no important aspect of the phrase *Traduttore, traditore* that is missed by "Translator, traitor", and so this English translation is a checkmate in response to the strong-seeming check tendered by the Italian opponent.

I am not in the least a believer in the extreme pessimism expressed by *Traduttore, traditore* (or its perfect English counterpart "Translator, traitor"), no matter how catchy this famous phrase may be and no matter how often it is repeated like a clever mantra by supposed literary sophisticates. I hear it as a cute sound bite rather than as a serious thesis about translation. In fact, I am far more inclined to believe in a rival (and also cute) sound bite — namely, "Translator, trader" (or if you wish, I can spell it out more explicitly as "Translator, phrase-trader").

The philosophy of this alternative motto is self-evident: that in translating from language A to language B, one always has to sacrifice some aspects of the original passage in language A, but in exchange one gets brand-new but comparable aspects of the resulting passage in language B. You lose a little here, you gain a little there, but as long as you are in the hands of a sufficiently skilled translator/trader, in the end it all balances out pretty well.

One Phrase-trade Examined Up Close

LET'S explore the philosophy expressed in the sound bite "Translator, trader" by taking a close look at a fine example of phrase-trading — namely, the rendering of *Traduttore, traditore* by the English phrase "Translator, traitor".

To begin with, the skeptical and cynical meanings of the two slogans are identical (at least as identical as anyone could ever hope), so there's no loss or gain there — it's a precise tie game in the semantics department. To be sure, some wet blanket could trot out the argument I just gave about the untranslatability of even the simplest words, such as "elevator", "sidewalk", "bread", and "kiss". Yes, yes, all right — in some nitpicky sense, a *traduttore* might not be exactly to speakers of Italian what a translator is to speakers of English, and likewise a *traditore* might not be quite the same thing as a traitor. The cultural models for both concepts might be ever so slightly distinct. I don't recall how I learned about traitors in history classes in school, but surely there was some specific American cultural component, and presumably when Italian children learn about *traditori* in history, they are given different people as canonical examples. But to claim that "translator" is an inadequate translation of *traduttore* or that "traitor" is an inadequate translation of *traditore* amounts to claiming that nothing can ever be translated at all — a most silly pose that, in my view, cannot be taken seriously.

The other side of the coin is, of course, the question of the phonetic catchiness of the two slogans. In Italian, both words have four syllables, whereas in English one has three and the other has two. Some people might consider this inequality to be a slight *loss* in the passage from language A to language B. In compensation, though, the English slogan boasts a precise two-syllable rhyme ("lator"/"traitor") whereas the Italian features a

double "t" contrasting with a single "t". These are not identical sounds. Not only do the Italians savor the beauty of their double consonants, but they exploit them to distinguish between words. For instance, whereas *molti anni* means "many years", *molti ani* means "many anuses" — so watch out! To enjoy as precise a rhyme as its English counterpart, the Italian phrase would have to be either *Traduttore, tradittore* or else *Tradutore, traditore*, either of which grates against the Italian ear.

All in all, then, in the phonetic-catchiness department, there might be a tiny *gain* in the passage from language A to language B, though that's debatable. I won't insist either way. The main point is, a tiny bit has changed, with perhaps a slight gain here and slight loss there, but overall, it's very close to a perfect balance. Some people might feel that the original Italian phrase is superior, some might prefer the English version, but in any case a pleasing trade has taken place, with some virtues and faults disappearing and other ones taking their place.

This little example reveals the essence of the art of translation, showing it to be the art of trading X for Y, pondering what constitutes the best possible trade, and refusing to settle for a bad deal. And most fortunately, translation, unlike trading in a bazaar, is not an act of bargaining or haggling with an adversary, because there is no adversary. It's merely a careful search for a sufficiently good trade, and it's the skill of the trader alone that will determine the quality of the results turned up in the search.

Now suppose that someone had the temerity to propose "Translator, trader" not just as a fun new slogan but actually as a *translation* of the classic phrase *Traduttore, traditore*. Well, that would carry the whole game one step further, since this move not only trades in the dark pessimistic meaning of the original Italian phrase for a cheery optimistic meaning, but it also simultaneously alludes, via near-perfect homonymy, to the more obvious English

translation "Translator, traitor", and in so doing, the cocky new slogan amusingly thumbs its nose at its snooty, pessimistic rival. By trading so much for so much at once, "Translator, trader" takes a far larger risk than does "Translator, traitor". But since he believes his cute new sound bite hits the nail on the head, your friendly translator/trader will take the risk any day. In fact, he's adopted it (and please forgive him for this!) as his trade mark.

Françoise Quoirez Sagan and her Novels

BEFORE I plunge into the nitty-gritty of my translation of *La Chamade*, I would first like to say something about the novel itself, and then to recount in brief how I came to read it and what impelled me to translate it.

Françoise Quoirez was born in 1935 in the tiny village of Cajarc in southern France, and she wrote her first novel, *Bonjour tristesse* (literally, "Hello, sadness"), when she was eighteen. It was a mildly scandalous but sensitive novel about a teen-age girl's first explorations of sexuality, love, and jealousy, and as soon as it was published in 1954, under the pseudonym "Françoise Sagan" (the last name was borrowed from the Princesse de Sagan, a character in Proust), it received rave reviews from the French press as well as the prestigious Prix des Critiques, and it enjoyed an enormous success in France. Soon it was translated into many languages and was also made into a movie, and thus Sagan skyrocketed to international fame. Writing *Bonjour tristesse* was a remarkable achievement for someone so young, and there is no doubt that Françoise Sagan was a prodigy both in terms of her insight into the human psyche and in terms of her ability to tell a powerful story in elegantly flowing, compelling prose.

Over the next couple of decades, Sagan wrote several more novels that were generally well received, although her first novel,

for better or for worse, remained the one that people most strongly associated with her name. She also branched out into drama, writing several successful plays in the 1960's and 1970's, and producing yet more novels and a couple of memoirs in the 1980's and 1990's.

Like many people who grew up when I did, I often heard of Françoise Sagan when I was a teen-ager, but I never read any of her novels. *Bonjour tristesse* sat on my parents' bookshelf for years, and yet, despite my love for the French language, I never picked it up. At some point when I was in my late twenties, my parents went to Paris for a couple of weeks, and one evening they were invited by Serge Gorodetzky, a French physicist from Strasbourg who was an old friend of theirs, to a small dinner party with two friends of his, one of whom turned out, to their surprise, to be Françoise Sagan. Since I knew that Sagan was a very famous writer, it was with considerable interest that I heard about this dinner on my parents' return. My mother, to whom I always looked up as an extremely avid reader of serious fiction, told me that Sagan had grilled her nonstop about all the latest American writers but that, to her great chagrin, she hardly knew a thing about any of them. But all in all, Sagan had left her with a good impression. Well, the only concrete effect on me of my parents' dinner with Sagan was to spur me, the next time I was in a French-speaking city, to buy copies of several of her books.

Two more decades passed, and in early 2002, while spending a year in Italy, I was scheduled to give several lectures in Paris. On my various flights between Bologna and the City of Light, I read *Un certain sourire* ("A Certain Smile") and I enjoyed it a great deal. I particularly savored the smooth flow of her words and the way in which she would often place herself inside her characters' heads, affording strongly flavored snapshots of the world from various inner perspectives.

It took another couple of years for me to get around to reading the remainder of my small Sagan collection, which consisted of *Aimez-vous Brahms* ("Do You Care for Brahms?" — and don't ask me why, but the question mark is always left off the French title), *Bonjour tristesse*, *Les Violons parfois* ("Occasional Violins") and *La Chamade*. I read the first three during the Christmas vacation of 2003, and as before, I found them all engaging and gracefully written, but none of them left me reeling with a sense of tremendous power.

However, when I returned home after the vacation, I picked up *La Chamade*, which was the last one on my shelf, and the experience of reading it was extremely intense. I know I could never articulate precisely what it was that so touched me about this novel. All I can say is that I found myself deeply moved by living inside Lucile's soul and feeling how torn she was between two complex men who were completely different from each other, and I was just as moved by witnessing, from very close up, the power of these two men's feelings for Lucile. When the novel came to an end, I was indeed quite overwhelmed, and I felt very sad to say good-bye to these people forever.

One time earlier in my life, I had had a similar feeling about a novel in a foreign language, and as a consequence, I had wound up translating that novel into English. I am speaking of Alexander Pushkin's remarkable novel-in-verse *Evgenij* (or *Eugene*) *Onegin*, and the year I spent translating it from Russian verse to English verse (1998) will forever remain in my memory one of the most vivid, vibrant, and rewarding periods in my life. Well, with such a memorable experience as precedent, it is perhaps understandable that the idea of translating *La Chamade* into English came flashing to me, and it took me no time at all to decide to take on this challenge. I loved French immeasurably and I had been deeply touched by this novel, so what better way

to savor both at the same time than to make the events in the story all take place once more, but this time in English?

Transcription and Translation

FOR some odd reason, I have always been very drawn to the physical act of writing with pen or pencil, and so, just as I had done with *Eugene Onegin*, I decided to do my translation in some blank notebooks that I already had, using ballpoint pen, with crossing-out very welcome at any time. Each session always consisted in an alternation between two modes, the first of which was literal *transcribing*. I would copy a few pages of the French text line by line onto lined sheets in my notebooks, always leaving two blank lines below each line of text. For some ill-defined esthetic reason, I chose to make my line breaks coincide exactly with those of the printed text, and it gave me great pleasure thus to make the original work my own, in some sense.

Incidentally, this act of homage — or of love — toward the original has a close counterpart in my personal engagement with *Eugene Onegin* — namely, it corresponds to my memorization of stanza after stanza of the novel, all in the original Russian. At my peak I knew 75 stanzas by heart, amounting to well over a thousand lines. It was in that fashion that I internalized *Eugene Onegin* and made it my own. Although copying the entire text of *La Chamade* was far less intense than that, it played a similar psychological role in deepening my involvement with a book that up till then I had only read. I did not notice this analogy at the time I was translating *La Chamade*, but now, after the fact, it jumps out at me, clearly revealing how I tend to seek to "marry" beautiful books that have a powerful emotional effect on me.

The other mode in each session was, of course, that of *translating* what I'd just copied. I always used different colors of

ink for the two languages, and I tried to think out each line of English very carefully before committing anything to paper, hoping thus to produce a full handwritten sheet without a single crossed-out word or even letter. But if crossing-out was called for, I didn't hesitate in the least, and as a consequence, there aren't more than a dozen or so pristine sheets out of the 500 or so that I penned.

Every morning during the first three months of 2004, I would spend several hours in this fashion, alternating between copying a page or two from the book and then rendering that passage in English, going back and forth between transcribing and translating. Now if you happen to know some molecular biology, this pair of words may ring familiar: the *transcription* of a strand of DNA results in a strand of RNA, and it is soon followed by the *translation* of that very strand of RNA into one or more proteins (via the genetic code). This is called "gene expression". This two-stage process lies at the very heart of all life on earth. Though purely coincidental, it is a pleasing parallelism.

If anyone had asked me, during my transcription–translation period, why I was spending so much time in this activity, I would have replied, "It's very simple — out of love." And if they had further pressed me as to whether I would like to have my version published, I would have said, "I guess so, but publication isn't my purpose. I just want to do this because I was so touched by this lyrical and poetic novel."

Robert Westhoff: Lover, Translator

SAD TO say, *l'amour,* although it may make the world turn 'round, is seldom the *raison de traduire* a novel from one language to another. Most of the time, a publisher in language B hires a respected A–B translator to translate a particular novel out of

language A, and since money talks in any language, the job gets done. The translator may or may not fall in love with the novel, but that's hardly the point, and love is seldom the spark or the outcome. In my case, though, it was just a personal choice coming from a powerful inner flame. I did it only for myself. But since many of my friends were curious if I was intending to publish my translation, I wound up devoting some thought to the question, and soon decided that it would be very desirable. I had found the book truly rewarding, so it was only natural that I would hope to afford a similar pleasure to other people.

This led to the natural question of whether *La Chamade* had ever been translated before. In this day of the Web and Google (that's not the name of a pub!), answering such questions is a piece of cake, and I quickly found out that indeed, an English translation by one Robert Westhoff had been published in 1966. I also found out that it was long out of print. What did that imply? I knew that several translations of a single novel could coexist (as was the case for *Ivan Denisovich*), but I didn't how common it was for a publisher to give the green light to two or more rival translations, or to a new one when an old one was out of print. All these things seemed blurry to me, so eventually I contacted the original Parisian publisher of *La Chamade*, and the people there were very friendly and said a second translation was fine with them, as long as I could find an American publisher.

These were all bureaucratic matters and held little interest for me, but what did intrigue me was who this Robert Westhoff was, and what his translation was like. Actually, although part of me was very curious to see his translation, another part of me didn't want me to read even a single sentence of it, out of fear that my own translation might possibly be contaminated by someone else's style. In any case, I was driven by curiosity to explore this fellow a bit more.

A little Web sleuthing revealed that Robert Westhoff was an American who was not just Sagan's translator but had been married to her for a year or two and was the father of her only child, Denis Westhoff. It seemed as if translation and love had indeed gone hand-in-hand, at least in the case of this novel! Despite divorcing, Sagan and Westhoff remained close friends for their entire lives, and he translated a couple of her early novels. And a little more sleuthing revealed the sad fact that Bob Westhoff had died rather young — in 1990, roughly at age sixty.

It was obvious to me that it would be foolish not to obtain a copy of Westhoff's translation, because certainly one day, sooner or later, when mine was done, I would want to look at it and see how his and my versions compared. So, through a used-book dealer on the Web, I was able to track a copy down and I had it sent to me. I remember how, the day it arrived in the mail, I tore open the package and pulled out the hardback volume, which, as it turned out, had once belonged to the Public Library in the small burg of Richland, Washington, of all places — a town whose fifteen minutes of fame are due, in part, to the fact that its elevators and doors, its kisses and cars, its giggles and its cigarettes are all subtly different from their Cajarc counterparts.

I did my very best not to read one single sentence, but in the end I yielded to the tiny temptation of reading what Mister Westhoff had done with the novel's first sentence, "Elle ouvrit les yeux." He had written "She opened her eyes." Well, what do you know — so had I! And so, having obtained that amusing but almost totally uninformative clue as to Westhoff's style, I quickly slammed the book shut and said to myself, "No more peeking until you are all done, my friend!" And I adhered religiously to this edict except in one tiny but crucial fashion, and that, for obvious reasons, was the matter of the title that Westhoff gave to his ex-wife's novel in English.

Translating the Novel's Title

WHAT do the words *la chamade* mean? One might hope to get a clue from the title of Westhoff's translation, but he, or perhaps it was his publisher, chose the easy way out — they left the title in French. That sort of begs the question, doesn't it?

If I look up *chamade* in my huge Collins–Robert unabridged French–English dictionary, I find this indication: "NF ⇒ battre". Frankly, this kind of thing drives me batty. Now I have to go look up *battre* instead, and since it's a very high-frequency word, I'll have to scan down dozens and dozens of randomly-ordered phrases in several long columns of very fine print in order to find *battre la chamade*. Most frustrating.

But all right. If one is sufficiently patient, one will eventually find, way down in the entry for *battre*, the sentence "son cœur battait la chamade", and its translation is given as "his heart was pounding/beating wildly". And so it turns out that *chamade* is a feminine noun ("NF") that is used in only one phrase in the French language (*battre la chamade*), and it basically suggests a wildly beating heart, a powerful throbbing of the heart, caused by intense emotions such as fear or anticipation or thrill.

Given this, why didn't Bob Westhoff call his translation "Heart Throb"? Well, I guess it's obvious — someone's latest heart throb is their latest flame, and that isn't at all what was meant by the French title. Then why not "Heartbeat" or "Wild Heartbeat"? Or then again, why not "Pounding Away", or perhaps "The Throb"? Well, your guess is as good as mine. All we know is that somehow, the decision was made to leave the title in French, perhaps because it sounds more enticing that way. Remember that Françoise Sagan was very well known in America in the sixties, so her name alone was already quite a draw. Perhaps "La Chamade" sounded mysterious and sexy to

an American public. And of course, the title "Bonjour tristesse" had been left in French, so this was just extending a precedent.

I'm not saying it was a bad decision to leave the title of *La Chamade* in French, but it isn't what I myself would have chosen. In fact, as you know, I took another pathway. One day, I was just looking at the word *chamade* and, as often happens when my mind is idling, I started juggling the letters around a little bit, and what popped out but "mad ache". This felt a bit eerie. After all, the whole story is about the mad ache in the hearts of several different people, all of whom are desperately searching for love or think they have found it. Something about this felt very right to me, and at that moment it occurred to me that this would be a delicious way to translate Sagan's title "La Chamade". It took a bit more thought about whether to say "A Mad Ache" or "The Mad Ache" or "That Mad Ache" or even just plain "Mad Ache", but in the end I settled on "That Mad Ache".

An amusing footnote to this is that my friend Daniel Kiechle (about whom more below), on hearing about my proposed title, started searching for English anagrams involving all nine letters in "La Chamade", and he came up with "A Calm Head", which, though a nice phrase, is pretty nearly the diametric opposite of the meaning of the original title. What a curious coincidence! Needless to say, I didn't go for Daniel's anagram, ingenious though it was.

What should one think about such a brazenly redone title as "That Mad Ache"? Is it reasonable? In particular, what does the playful game of anagrams have to do with this novel or with Françoise Sagan's style? Admittedly, nothing at all. But even so, I think there is something charming about tipping one's hat to one's author by making the translated title through nothing more than a rearrangement of the very same "raw materials" that constituted the original title. But then I'm biased.

In any case, the most common thing in the world is for books, plays, and films to have their titles radically redone in other languages. An example that springs to my mind is the French-language title that was given to Khaled Hosseini's above-mentioned novel *The Kite Runner* — namely, "Les Cerfs-volants de Kaboul", which means "The Kites of Kabul". Salinger's title "The Catcher in the Rye" was rendered as "L'attrape-cœurs" ("The Heart-catcher"), and Steinbeck's "Cannery Row" as "Rue de la Sardine" ("Sardine Street") — and so on. And going in the other direction, Proust's title "À la Recherche du temps perdu" became "Remembrance of Things Past" (instead of "In Search of Lost Time"). Hundreds of examples could be adduced, but the point is clear — titles are up for grabs.

But if it is generally accepted that titles can be radically modified in their passage from one culture to another, does this not suggest that *any* aspect of a piece of literature can be modified with pretty much the same degree of freedom? Why should a novel's title, certainly among the most carefully considered choices in the whole book, be more tamperable-with than the sentences inside the book? Indeed, why isn't the title sacred — absolutely sacred and untouchable? And if the title isn't sacred, then what is? Or to be more specific, how much liberty does a translator have to play around with the various elements on all the different scales inside a novel — words, phrases, sentences, paragraphs, sections, and chapters?

Let me make this question a little more pointed, since here we are coming to the crux of the matter: Not only how much liberty *may* a translator take, but how much liberty *must* a translator take, in order to do a good job? This pair of questions haunted me all through the process of translation of *La Chamade,* and I will make a stab at answering them in what follows, though there are never any final answers.

Translator as Dog-on-a-Leash

IT'S my suspicion that we translators of novels are all would-be novelists ourselves; it's just that most of us lack the wonderful imagination to come up with deep and fascinating characters, strange intrigues that intertwine the characters' lives plausibly but ever surprisingly, and occasional glimpses into their hearts' secrets, all carried out in an artistic fashion featuring a natural and graceful rhythm in which events, meditations, and descriptions all meld together harmoniously and pleasingly. Architecture on that grand a scale is, sad to say, just too much to ask of most of us — but we still love admiring it and we wish to savor its magic as intimately as possible, and so if life grants us the chance, we select some favorite book and we then take its small-scale local components — sentences, images, thoughts — and one by one we recast them, using our love for our native language's special ways of phrasing things, into our own personal mold.

Whenever I am translating something that someone else carefully wrote, I feel like an unleashed dog taking a walk with its master through a forest or a huge park. It's a marvelously joyous feeling, a subtle blend of freedom and security. I run around on my own, but despite all my seeming freedom, I am in truth always invisibly tethered to my master and to the unpredictable pathways that my master chooses to take. Locally, I am captain of my own fate, but on a larger scale, I am slaved to my master's whims. It's a comfortable thing, a comfort zone, giving a sense of security. And fortunately, even if we translators are doomed to serve our novelist masters, some of us have *chosen* those masters for their benevolence — in fact, we've chosen them precisely because of the wonderful strolls they take through parks we know and enjoy. So between translator and author the partnership is a happy one, as hopefully it is between dog and master as well.

Living Vicariously in the Novel

AND now, in order to bring us down to earth from these airy metaphors, here is a short excerpt from Chapter 12 of this book, first in the original and then in my rendition. It is not by any means an example of virtuosic translation intended to show off clever tricks — I don't think there's anything clever here at all. It is just a passage that came to mind when I thought about how I put myself into the scene whenever I translate.

Le gravier crissait sous le pied des garçons, des chauves-souris rôdaient autour des lampes sur la terrasse et un couple congestionné avalait sans dire un mot une omelette flambée à la table voisine. Ils étaient à quinze kilomètres de Paris, il faisait un peu frais et la patronne avait posé un châle sur les épaules de Lucile. C'était une de ces mille petites auberges qui offrent une chance plus ou moins sûre de discrétion et de bon air aux Parisiens adultères ou fatigués. Antoine était décoiffé par le vent, il riait. Lucile lui racontait son enfance, une enfance heureuse… Il sourit, il tendit la main à travers la table, serra celle de Lucile.

The gravel was crunching under the waiters' feet, some bats were swooping around the lights on the terrace, and at the next table, a couple with very pink faces was wordlessly gulping down an *omelette flambée*. They were fifteen kilometers outside of Paris, it was a bit chilly, and the lady who ran the place had solicitously wrapped a shawl around Lucile's shoulders. This was one of a thousand similar small inns that offer adulterous or simply weary Parisians an almost failsafe privacy as well as fresh country air. The wind had done a good job of messing up Antoine's hair, and he was laughing. Lucile was telling him about her childhood, a happy childhood… He smiled, reached out across the table, and squeezed Lucile's hand.

As I read, transcribed in pen, and finally translated this passage, I felt transported to another place and time. It was *I* who was sitting in the little garden terrace of the restaurant located fifteen kilometers outside of Paris, and it was *I* who, firstly as Lucile, felt the cool night air, heard the crunching gravel, saw the pink-faced couple, watched those bats and their flitting shadows — and then it was *I* who, now Antoine, reached out and touched and squeezed Lucile's hand — although what the name "Lucile" denoted in my mind was a subtle, nebulous, tenuous, ephemeral amalgam of a hundred different people I have known (mostly women, but not all of them) — and much the same could be said for that restaurant, for those bat-swoops, that gravel-crunch, those pink faces, that *omelette flambée,* those waiters, and that night air. They were all made of raw materials drawn from my life, but freshly rearranged in a new fashion catalyzed by Françoise Sagan's artfully chosen words.

Trusting Memories over Words

NOW I'd like to give an example of the Don't-Trust-the-Text Paradox by focusing in on a tiny part of the above passage — just one word. The verb Sagan chose to describe the bats' flight is *rôder,* which my big heavy Collins–Robert renders as "roam, wander, loiter, lurk, prowl". Well, I suppose I could have used any of those English verbs in my translation, but on what basis would I have selected just one of the five? Which one would *you* choose to describe what the bats were doing near the lights?

Luckily, I don't have just a dictionary in my head; I have a lifetime of memories in there as well. In it, there are memories of seeing bats on many occasions, and to my mind, none of those five verbs does a good job of capturing what bats actually do. The first two suggest to me someone walking about rather idly

and aimlessly, and the last three suggest someone hanging around suspiciously or sneaking around under cover, probably with criminal intent. (Of course, there's far more to each verb than that; this is just a crude, quick take for our purposes here.) By contrast, the visual image that came to me, especially in the context of outdoor lights surrounded by small swarms of insects (who ever mentioned insects? not Sagan — but we all see them swarming there anyway, don't we?), was that of crazy flittings and zigzaggings in the air, and that led to a completely different set of candidate verbs, including "flit", "flutter", "zigzag", "swoop", and so on. Eventually I settled on "swoop".

By the way, so did Robert Westhoff (I just checked), and I find our agreement quite fascinating. Why did he, too, trust *himself* over all the English words in the authoritative dictionary, and over the French word on the novel's "author-itative" page? By trusting ourselves over these authorities, did Westhoff and I thereby betray Françoise Sagan? I don't think so; we simply trusted our personal images, which had been evoked by the words on her page, over the literal word *rôder*. In fact, I would go further and assert that for me, to have trusted Sagan's word over my own images would have been to betray her.

Poetic Lie-Sense

IN MY Translator's Preface to my "novel versification" of *Eugene Onegin*, I wrote a passage that I think is key in this context, but few of this essay's readers are likely to have seen that work, so here I'll take the liberty of quoting it in part. It said this:

> The truth of the matter is that the name of the game is *para-phrasing*. But I would propose an alternate name for the art of compromise in poetry translation — I would say that poetry translation is

the art of "poetic lie-sense". Yes, one is always lying, for to translate is to lie. But even to speak is to lie, no less. No word is perfect, no sentence captures all the truth and only the truth. All we do is make do, and in poetry, hopefully do so gracefully.

To be sure, this was written about poetry translation, but to me, *La Chamade* is definitely a kind of poetry, as are most novels. And I see no way around the fact that expressing ideas is always some kind of distortion, for words are only crude approximations and simplifications, and re-expressing someone else's ideas is also always some kind of distortion, but the second layer of distortion need not be less faithful than the first layer.

Or perhaps I should say that being in love is a kind of lying, a wonderful kind of lying to oneself, and since, while I was translating them, I was deeply in love with both *Eugene Onegin* and *La Chamade* (and, in fact, still am), it was very important to me — it was crucial to me — that I lie as beautifully as I knew how in rendering them in my own way in my native tongue.

What matters, as I see it, is that the compromises that emerge in the end — the final results of the trading process — should be sensible, should be comprehensible, should share the tone of the original, should evoke imagery close to that evoked by the original, and so on. That's the meaning of my phrase "poetic lie-sense", and it's the credo of translation to which I subscribe.

If Dogs Run Free, Then Why Not We?

BACK to our short passage for a few last comments. In my rendition of it, I gratuitously injected the word "solicitously", impudently rendered *bon air* by "fresh country air", and even had the chutzpah to say that the wind had "done a good job" of messing up Antoine's hair, instead of simply saying that his hair

had been messed up by the wind, as the French says. Why did I do all of these nonmechanical, subjective things, like a free dog running far from its master? The answer is quite simple: "If dogs run free, then why not we, across the swooping plain?"

Of course Bob Dylan's sweet lyric is not the real answer to the question, but I couldn't resist quoting it, once my friend Scott Buresh had pointed it out to me. The real answer is that I am not a translating machine but a human being filled with millions upon millions of dormant memories, and I felt that as a lover of this book, I had been assigned (by myself) the task of writing this passage in English, partly under the influence of the literal words Sagan had chosen (and in the precise order that she had chosen them), but just as much (and probably a good deal more) under the influence of the enormously rich, partially conscious, mostly unconscious, set of images that her words and turns of phrase had collectively churned up in the vast sea of my memories. Caught in this complex crossfire of mental pressures, I tried to find a midway path that tipped its hat, and with deepest respect, to both sides of this extremely blurry competition.

I think it's interesting, in this connection, to cite a passage in *La Chamade* itself (or rather, in *That Mad Ache*). It's in Chapter 14, and Charles has just proposed to Lucile that they take a trip together to southern France. One word has a striking effect inside her head:

> "The Riviera," she repeated dreamily, "the Riviera...?" And behind her stubbornly closed eyelids, she could see the sea rushing up onto the beach, she could see the color of the sand in the evening when the sun abandons it.

And I'm sure that you too, whether your eyes are closed or open, are now mentally seeing "exactly the same things" (in a

manner of speaking) as Lucile did. There's nothing complicated about what's going on here; such sound–mind transactions are a dime a dozen. Words trigger thoughts, and thoughts trigger words. This little loop is really the most central facet of what makes us human beings. If you eliminate the thought part of the loop, though, and insist that in translation, *words* must trigger *words* without *thoughts* intervening, then you are denying what makes us human, and any translation based on such a philosophy will turn out arid and wooden at best, and absurd and incomprehensible at worst.

If you want to see very concretely what I mean, let's submit the original French passage — not a particularly elusive or subtle passage, I might add — to a quintessentially non-human translator — namely, Google's translation engine (and since that venerable beast is a moving target, I'll state that in this case I'm talking about its incarnation on the date of October 12, 2008). First the original French, then Google's English:

> « Le Midi, reprit-elle, d'une voix rêveuse... le Midi ?... » Et sous ses paupières obstinément closes, elle vit se précipiter la mer sur la plage, elle vit la couleur du sable, le soir, lorsque le soleil l'abandonne.

> "The Midi," she said, a dreamy voice... the south..." And its stubbornly closed eyelids, she lives is precipitate the sea on the beach, she saw the color of the sand in the evening when the sun abandons.

Incidentally, in a subsequent version, the "same" engine changed the strange phrase "its stubbornly closed eyelids" to "his closed eyelids stubbornly". I can't say I think it's much of an improvement! What this of course reveals is that there is not the least attempt at understanding — that is, the production of imagery or thoughts — going on here.

M'amie

ALL through the winter and spring of early 2004, I worked diligently and faithfully, transcribing and translating *La Chamade* at the rate of about two pages a day, and slowly but steadily turning it into *That Mad Ache*. As per my resolution, I never took the tiniest peek into Westhoff's translation, even though it was sitting around tempting me all the time.

While I was engaged in this process, I savored countless evening reading sessions, over countless varieties of tea, with my friend Caroline Strobbe, who grew up in the city of Lille, a couple of hundred kilometers north of Paris. Our ritual was that Caroline (for whom one of my nicknames was "*Fille belle Ca Stro*") would read aloud (from my handwritten transcript!) a few pages of the French original, and then I would go back and read "between the lines", since that was where my translation had been penned. There were invariably discussions about just what such-and-such a phrase meant (in either language), or what a particular character must be thinking or feeling behind the scenes, and so forth. Some of these discussions were about passages in French that I found mysterious, but just as many were about the complex events and the people themselves, and how to think about them. Sometimes Caroline would tell me that in her opinion I had misinterpreted something Sagan had written, and once I'd heard and reflected on the alternative inter-pretation, I usually realized that she was probably right. These delicious evening tea-to-tea tête-à-têtes were crucial to the quality of my translation and to the quality of my life as a whole, and they are the loveliest memories of my *La Chamade* days.

The next phase, after filling up all the notebooks with printed words in colored ink, was typing everything into my computer. On nearly every page of each of my nine notebooks, there were

all sorts of alternative renderings of words and phrases, and I had assumed that in the typing-up phase, I would simply read the rival possibilities each time, ponder them a little, and then make a choice, thus producing a manuscript that was much closer to the final version. However, when I came to this stage, I found that making those choices was not nearly as easy as I had expected. Very often I was totally stymied, and so I actually wound up leaving most of the alternatives in my typed-up text, just putting them in boldface so they would jump out at my eyes.

Mommy

ONE awful day in the middle of May, 2004, my aging mother out in California suffered a serious stroke. Shortly after this happened, I flew out there to be with her for several weeks. She was physically greatly reduced, but luckily her mental faculties were as acute as ever, and since she was unable to hold books, she was delighted to have other people read to her. I asked her if she would like to hear my translation of *La Chamade*, which she had heard about over the phone, and to my gratification, she said she would love to. So during parts of June and July she heard the entirety of my text, which I read out loud to her straight off my computer screen.

What about all those choice points? Well, whenever I could, I would make a rapid choice without missing a beat, and on the screen I'd quickly highlight my choice, in order to remember it later, figuring that most likely this instinctive snap decision was somehow right. But of course there were many very stubborn spots where I found myself completely torn between two or three or even four wildly different rival phrasings, and in such cases I would stop and read these rivals aloud to my mother, one by one, then ask her for her opinion. She invariably had one, and it

was always interesting to hear the reasoning behind her choice. Often I would take her suggestion and choose that version, although sometimes I'd take another route.

In this fashion, the manuscript for *That Mad Ache* grew quite a bit leaner and meaner, but still it was far from totally polished. I wanted and needed more feedback, and at this point my friend Kellie Gutman in Boston volunteered to help. I shot my manuscript off to her by email, and after she'd read it through from beginning to end, she, too, gave me insightful comments on all of the difficult choice points, as well as on many other aspects.

Well, as a result of incorporating (or respectfully disagreeing with!) the insights of three of my favorite people in the world — Caroline, my dear old Mom, and Kellie — I found myself slowly converging down on a final version… or so, at least, I thought.

Out of the Blue

THERE were still a number of extremely sticky points that I just couldn't figure out — syntactic ambiguities in the French, mysterious phrases that I couldn't make head or tail of, even passages in which I felt that Sagan (or one of her characters) was saying exactly the opposite of what she (or they) should mean. This was driving me crazy when all of a sudden, out of nowhere, a calm head bubbling with ideas appeared on my screen, via email — Daniel Kiechle, born in Switzerland, a native speaker of French and German, a superb speaker of American English (he had lived in the U.S. for fifteen years, and he had married an American, to boot), and someone fascinated to the nth degree by languages and translation. *Deus ex machina!*

From his home on the French Riviera (I could just picture it, with the sea rushing up onto the beach, and the color of the sand in the evening when the sun abandons it), Daniel had written me

a very kind letter about my books *Gödel, Escher, Bach* and *Le Ton beau de Marot,* but he'd never expected his note to lead to much. However, there was an instantaneous resonance between the two of us, and even though we'd never met face to face, we found ourselves all of a sudden in an intense flurry of email exchanges about all sorts of fine points concerning *La Chamade.* Daniel went to a local library (well... to a *bibliothèque*), took out a copy of the original book, read it from cover to cover, and proceeded to give me detailed comments on all the points where I was stuck.

The amusing thing is that in many cases, as a result of all this analysis, the fog remained or even grew thicker, rather than being dissipated. It seemed that some of the points I had found tricky were just as tricky to native speakers of French like Caroline and Daniel, and the more they thought about them the trickier they got. Concerning one of the most confusing points, Daniel and I were completely at odds with each other's views, while Caroline saw it as I did, and so he resorted to the device of taking an electronic poll of his co-workers. They turned out to be split as well, which amused both Daniel and me, since each of us was convinced that this was a black-and-white matter that should have had total clarity.

During our e-flurry, it came out that Daniel's comfort zone for translation is a little more conservative than mine, or as Scott Buresh put it, if I lean toward the "hot", Daniel leans towards the "cool", which translates to the idea that if Daniel were a dog, he would opt for taking walks on a rather short leash. This does not mean, however, that his "translation temperature" is Everest-cold or that mine is Sahara-high. I would say that on a scale from 0 to 100, my style is a comfortable 70° Fahrenheit, but it fluctuates from passage to passage, once in a while dipping down momentarily to a chilly 50°, other times briefly soaring as high as a blistering 90°. Perhaps Daniel's average temperature is closer

to 60° — a bit spartan, but good for you (especially when you're trotting briskly alongside your master).

In any case, the meticulous concern that Daniel devoted to all my questions was incredibly gratifying to me, and I think it provided him with just as much stimulation, for as a matter of fact, all this intense involvement with the translation of a wonderful novel led him to the thought of translating one of *his* favorite novels, and over the course of the next few months, that's exactly what he did: he translated *Die Brücke,* a famous novel about World War II by the German author Manfred Gregor, into English. How could I ever have guessed that my decision to translate *La Chamade* into English would one day catalyze someone else to translate a German novel into English?

I Compare Notes with Mr. Westhoff

SURELY, you must be thinking, my translation was coming in for a landing. So I thought, too. But one key factor has been left out of the equation — Robert Westhoff. This, after all, was a man who not only had translated the same novel but had once been married to the novel's author! If anyone should be authoritative, it should be Mr. W!

And so, now that just about all my *i*'s had been dotted and all my *t*'s crossed, I figured I could finally allow myself to peek inside Westhoff's version, not only in order to see what he had made of all the foggy passages (perhaps he had the key to them all!), but more generally to see how the whole book felt in someone else's phrasing. And so one day I sat down at page 1 and started going through our two translations sentence by sentence, even word by word. It was an extremely arduous experience, one that I wouldn't like to repeat. It took me many weeks, and as I did it, I was absolutely bowled over by the

immense chasm that I discovered between our styles. It was like night and day.

I hadn't been expecting anything like the rift I encountered, and I documented it in a very detailed fashion. I won't bore you with most of my findings, but a few examples will, I think, jazz up this discussion of translation in an entertaining fashion. But first I will need to describe, for the benefit of those who haven't yet read the novel itself, its main characters, all of whom are very well educated but also all unmarried. So here's the cast:

> Lucile, about 30 years old, unemployed, bright but flighty;
>
> Charles, exactly 50, in real estate and very well off, cool but warm;
>
> Claire, a bit over 50, a socialite, a maker and breaker of romances;
>
> Diane, around 45, unemployed, very rich but very needy;
>
> Antoine, 30 or so, employed in the publishing world, smart and intense;
>
> Johnny, probably around 50, no clear employment status, gay and droll.

Lucile doesn't need a job since she lives with Charles, who is rich from his business dealings. Diane is also very well off (she has a Rolls and a chauffeur, for instance), and Antoine, roughly fifteen years her junior, is her current romance, or as some would put it, her gigolo. Johnny is a rather jolly and generous friend of Claire's who takes great interest in all the romantic goings-on around him. All of the characters wind up attending some of Claire's slightly pretentious and highly exclusive Parisian soirées, and indeed those are where much of the action takes place.

Letting the Dog off its Leash

ONE OF Françoise Sagan's most typical story-telling devices is that of slipping imperceptibly out of a purely "objective" third-person narrative into a passage that, although remaining in the

third person, is actually a "recording" of the private thoughts of some character — and then gliding imperceptibly back out to pure narrative. Here is a snippet taken out of a long internal monologue of Diane's in Chapter 8, where she's reflecting on some of her fellow guests at a party of Claire's. First we have the original French, then Westhoff's translation, and then mine.

C'était agaçant, cette manie qu'avaient les gens richissimes de ne faire jamais, jamais que des affaires. D'avoir des réductions chez les couturiers, des prix chez Cartier et d'en être fier. Elle avait échappé à cela, Dieu merci, elle n'était pas de ces femmes qui cajolent leurs fournisseurs quand elles ont les moyens de faire tout autrement.

It was irritating, this mania that the ultrarich had for always, always getting the better part of an affair. To have a rebate from the dressmaker, a discount at Cartier's, and to be proud of it. She had escaped all that, thank Heaven; she was not one of the women of means who haggled with tradespeople.

God, it was a drag, this obsession of the super-rich for doing nothing but swinging deal after deal. Wangling discounts from dressmakers, cousin prices at Cartier's, and being pleased as punch with themselves for these trivial accomplishments. At least *she*'d not fallen into this trap, thank the Lord — she wasn't one of those coy rich dames who finagle each and every seller into giving them sweeter deals when they don't in the least need to do so.

I must emphasize that I selected a passage that highlights our stylistic differences as sharply as possible. In reading Westhoff, I often feel a pretty tight tether connecting him to Françoise Sagan. Sometimes he even seems to be choking on his leash, although here it's not that bad. Or, to switch metaphors, I'd say

that in this particular passage, Westhoff's translation temperature, though not freezing, is pretty nippy (say, 40°, give or take a few), while mine is about as high as I ever let it get (say, 90°).

Such a super-high temperature means that in rendering this little snippet, I took unusually many liberties. For instance, I baldfacedly threw in the interjection "God", and I used the quite-warm-to-very-hot expressions "a drag", "swing a deal", "wangle", "cousin prices", "pleased as punch", "coy", "finagle", and perhaps others. What's my defense? I'd like to quote Bob Dylan once again, but I'll refrain. Instead, I once again plead guilty to being a human being and not a translating machine. I plead guilty to trying to get inside the head of Diane and trying to feel things as she feels them. I plead guilty to going beyond the words and to going behind the scenes. I plead guilty for saying things in the way that I think that somebody whose native language is American English would say them (or rather, would think them), and for not just slavishly copying the words and their order that Sagan used when expressing herself in French.

In short, while doing this passage, I was an unleashed dog with its master strolling in the English Gardens, exploring them as a lively dog will, joyously dashing here and there but being sure never to stray out of hearing range of its master's call. Or perhaps in this case I strayed a little too far. But as I said above, this passage is one of my "hottest" moments in the whole book.

Rendering Sentences with Two Meanings

ONE example gives but a first impression, so let's go on and take a look at another, which will bring up some new issues. This time Sagan is in more of a pure-narrative mode, although to tell the truth, between her pure-narrative mode and her internal-monologue mode the line is often tremendously blurry. In any

case, this passage, taken from Chapter 20, describes some of Lucile's vaguely annoyed reactions to the inane bubblings of an overenthusiastic co-worker of hers at *Le Réveil,* a small Parisian newspaper where she has just started working:

> Elle travaillait avec une jeune femme nommée Marianne, enceinte de trois mois, très aimable, très efficace et qui parlait avec la même vigilance attendrie de l'avenir du journal et de celui de son rejeton. Et comme elle était persuadée que ce dernier serait du sexe mâle, il arrivait à Lucile quand Marianne proférait une de ces sentences optimistes telles que : « Il n'a pas fini de faire parler de lui » ou : « Il ira loin », de se demander un instant s'il s'agissait de *Réveil* ou du futur Jérôme.

> She worked with a young woman called Marianne; three months pregnant, very likable, very efficient, who spoke with the same moving vigilance of the future of the newspaper and the expected child. She referred to them both in the masculine gender, certain that the baby would be a boy, and it sometimes happened that Lucile, when Marianne proferred an optimistic remark, such as, "They won't stop talking about him," or, "He'll go far," wondered for a moment if she meant the Réveil or the future Jérôme.

> She worked together with a young woman named Marianne, who was three months pregnant, very likable and efficient, and who spoke in equally tender and concerned tones about the future of the newspaper she worked for and that of the child she was carrying. Indeed, Lucile often had to wonder, when her colleague would come out with some corny cliché like "Paris is going to go crazy over this one!" or "*This* baby will knock 'em dead!", whether Marianne was speaking of the next issue of *Le Réveil* or of her imminent offspring Jérôme.

In Sagan's French, Marianne's two sentences are intrinsically ambiguous, since the reader, like Lucile, cannot tell what their subject — the masculine pronoun *il* — refers to. Does it refer back to the inanimate (but masculine-gendered) newspaper *Réveil*? Or contrariwise, does it refer to the animate embryo in Marianne's womb, which she is convinced will turn out to be a male? To Lucile, this bivalence is a bit annoying, but to us readers, it's rather humorous. What to do about this in English?

I decided to go for an ambiguity not based on pronouns, because I didn't want to have to explain two things — one, that *Le Réveil* would naturally be referred to as "he" in French, and two, that Marianne has decided that her unborn child will be a "he". So after a while I came up with two English sentences that could easily be heard as applying to either entity but that sidestepped the use of pronouns.

By contrast, Westhoff followed Sagan far more closely, but to do so he had to insert the explanatory remark that Marianne "referred to them both in the masculine gender" — and even with this advance warning, the two English sentences he gives don't sound as if they could possibly apply to a newspaper. Why would anyone call a paper "he"? Probably most readers will realize this has to do with the existence of gendered inanimate nouns in French, but even so, it feels heavy to me to have to insert such an explanation and then to use two sentences that don't sound appropriate in English. If there is going to be an amusing, even punlike, passage of this sort, I feel it's best if it sounds normal and can be understood without any explanation.

Knockin' 'em Dead in Gay Paree

I WAS reasonably pleased with my footnote-free, pronoun-less solution to this translation problem (which, obviously, is related

to the much larger issue of the translatability of wordplay and of humor in general), but along another dimension, I can see that someone might well raise their eyebrows at the idea of a French woman exclaiming, "*This* baby will knock 'em dead!" The question is, what language is this woman speaking? What, in particular, is that humorous slangy phrase "knock 'em dead" doing inside a supposedly French sentence?

It is, after all, a curious thing to read a novel about French people who are in theory speaking French to each other but where all their remarks are being reported in English, and in quotation marks to boot, suggesting that *these are the exact words that they used.* A reader must engage in a strange kind of suspension of disbelief here, a bit like the suspension of disbelief that takes place when one reads fables or comic books in which animals talk and dress just like people, or when one watches a musical in which, every so often, people spontaneously break out in song and dance and then stop all at once, as if nothing out of the ordinary had taken place! We humans are amazingly capable of dealing with this kind of incoherence — we've grown up with it from childhood — but even so, it looks rather strange when one points a bright spotlight straight onto it. But the suspension of disbelief involving humans speaking in language B when they are in fact speaking language A is, I think, somewhat subtler.

It's relatively easy to accept the idea that Marianne is actually speaking French when she is reported by Westhoff as saying the words "He'll go far", because it doesn't sound like any of those words *per se* really matters. We think only of the *meaning* behind her statement, not of her *words.* But "knock 'em dead" is a horse of another color.

The question is, did Marianne use *that idiom*? Did she really say " 'em", dropping the initial "th" sound? How in the world could Marianne have done that, when speaking French? Well, of

course we know that she didn't say *that*, but rather, something French that was "essentially the same" (in the way that *une autre paire de manches* — "another pair of sleeves" — is essentially the same as "a horse of another color"), but on the other hand, we have been told that this is what she really said (after all, it's in quotes), so we're in a bit of a dilemma.

With this dilemma, we have crashed headlong into the "Wrong-Place Paradox". By giving Marianne a fairly American-sounding remark, I seem to have taken her out of France and replanted her in America — at least a little bit. I seem to have committed the same sort of sin as those brazen translocators, those shameless transculturators, who inserted so many American swear words into the mouths of Russian prisoners in the gulags in Siberia that they de-Russianized the prisoners and ruined the whole feel of Solzhenitsyn's novel, at least for me. So why am I, of all people, committing the same sin?

Well, my defense is that such alleged sins come in many shades, and the lighter shades are actually not sins at all. The question is, at what point does a phrase start to sound absurd in the mouth of someone whom one envisions as speaking a different language? If I had put into Marianne's mouth the words "By cracky, this lil' ol' baby will blow them Parisians' ever-lovin' minds sky-high!", then I think everyone would agree that this would have fallen well beyond the proverbial pale — a blood-red transculturation sin.

Or I could instead have had her say, "Now I bet this one will make a hit!" This phrase still uses two American idioms, but I think most native speakers would say that they are not nearly as "far out". There is a blurry collective sense of how far someone is pushing the limits, and this sentence is far safer in that regard. And so what shade of transculturation sin are we dealing with here — pink?

Then again, what if I had had Marianne say, "This will probably appeal to many people"? I doubt anyone would accuse me of even the mildest transculturation sin here, but because it takes no risk at all, the phrase is as flat as a pancake (or a *crêpe*), as dull as dishwater, colorless. If one never ventures out at all toward that risky pale of transculturation, if one always tries to stay on very safe territory, one thereby runs a different kind of risk — that one's translation will come out sounding like pablum.

Translation is a risky, paradox-grazing, sin-tinged business. A phrase-trader has to have an intuitive sense of where the pale is — what's well within it, what's well beyond it. But the pale is so ethereal, so elusive, so intangible, so impalpable — so pale — that no one can actually see it. The pale is something determined collectively by the masses that speak the language, and no one person can pinpoint it. When a phrase seems to scream out its land of origin (or its era, or its subculture), and when that does not match the land (or era or subculture) of the person allegedly uttering it, then one has clearly gone beyond the pale — but usually things aren't that screamingly blatant; usually it's not such a black-and-white matter; usually it's a judgment call.

One last point here. To render Marianne's other ambiguous cliché, I wrote, "Paris is going to go crazy over this one!" What made me decide to transcribe it that way instead of as "Paris is gonna go crazy over *this* one!"? Well, that verb "transcribe" is the key to the answer. Whenever I see the word "gonna" in a piece of text, I understand it to be an attempt to capture the actual phonetics of the person speaking, verging on an attempt to capture the *accent* or even the *voice* of the speaker. If one puts "gonna" into the mouth of a French speaker, one is blatantly violating that convention, and that's why I avoided it.

But why, then, did I feel okay about putting "it will knock 'em dead" in Marianne's mouth? Does this not also look like a

phonetic transcription in which Marianne really drops the "th" of the word "them" (an image that is obviously nonsensical)? Yes, admittedly, it does look that way, but I thought that it was necessary because the tamer, blander version — "This baby will knock them dead" — doesn't sound like something that anyone would say in English, or at least not like what I think *Marianne* would have said — *if* she had been speaking English.

In a word, we are dealing with a counterfactual situation here — "What if Marianne had been speaking English?" — and that's an incoherent notion to begin with, since she's French and she's speaking French with a French colleague about a French newspaper in the French capital. But we *have* to accept this incoherent counterfactual situation, because that's what translation is in(co)herently all about, and as translators we have to do our best, in our individual ways, to deal elegantly with these elusive and ineffable *would*'s and *would have*'s. That's the name of the game. Once again, it's poetic lie-sense.

Good Gravy — Americanisms Galore!

WHILE I was struggling to put a final polish on my translation, I was simultaneously hard at work on this essay, and as a consequence of this temporal overlap, I became hypersensitive to the fact that quintessentially American words and turns of phrase could be found in large numbers on every single page of my translation. I started to panic about the Wrong-Place Paradox.

At one point, I worriedly went through a hefty chunk of the printed manuscript with pen in hand and circled in green each phrase that seemed to me to be in some sense redolent of these shores and not of France. Of course, as I said above, the distinction between "guilty" and "innocent" lexical items was anything but crystal-clear, but since I was suddenly very con-

cerned with getting some feel, no matter how vague, for how dense these potentially incriminating words and phrases were in my text, I just plunged ahead and green-circled madly.

Well, the end result was that the number of Americanisms in *That Mad Ache* was on the order of twenty per page, and when I extrapolated this trend to the whole book, it came out at a few thousand Americanisms, at least. Part of me was horrified, because it seemed that, against my own will, I was turning into a perfect reincarnation of the translators who had ruined *A Day in the Life of Ivan Denisovich*. How could I be doing this to myself?

To give you a sense of the kind of thing that troubled me, here is a sampling of some of the most worrisome phrases drawn from a dialogue spread over a couple of pages in Chapter 22 (there were many less worrisome phrases that I've skipped):

> I won't have anything to do with it… some kind of pimp… make him foot the bill for my escapades… you've gone way too far this time… I have my limits… anything you damn well please… I won't go along with you doing that… it's beyond the pale… go get myself sliced up by a butcher… by your lights it would be moral… just as long as he's left out of the picture… all alone, with nothing to your name… all that stupid charm of yours won't do a thing for you any more… there won't be a soul around… you're every bit as cowardly as I am… what really gets you… overwhelmed by the daily grind… it's our only hope… we'll scrape by somehow… there are lots of students… it's not all that hard… he'll be our kid… we pulled the wool over their eyes… it's part of our makeup… it's under our skin… we're spoiled rotten…

To provide a reference point for readers, I have just gone to the same section in Westhoff's translation and excerpted all the parallel phrases, which I exhibit below:

I don't want it... a pimp... make him pay for my blunders... it's far too much... there are limits... no matter what, just so long as it pleases you... I won't have you doing that... it's not possible... be mangled by a butcher... you think it moral... so long as it isn't he... alone, with nothing... your damned charm won't work any more... you'll have no one... you're as much of a coward as I am... what bothers you... exhausted by the wear and tear of time... it's our only chance... we'll get along somehow... there are plenty of students... it's not so difficult... he will belong to us... we deceived them... it's in our minds... it's under our skin... we're rotten...

I think anyone would agree that there is a huge difference in tone here. However, my worry was not prompted by this kind of comparison between myself and Westhoff. It came solely from looking at my own handiwork in isolation and stewing over it. I kept on asking myself, "Could these kinds of phrases realistically belong to a dialogue taking place in Paris, France? Could a reader really imagine French people saying 'these things', in some blurry sense, to each other? Is suspension of disbelief possible in this case?"

The strange phenomenon that I noticed was that when I flagged these phrases and read them out loud to myself one after another, the needle on my "transculturation meter" shot way up, yet when I went back and read them in context, things seemed to flow naturally and the transculturation meter's reading sank back down to nearly zero, which left me wondering if I'd blown a molehill up into a mountain. The fact that my judgment could flip back and forth like this was in itself a paradox, and I'm not sure that I can explain it at all. Nonetheless, over time, I gradually came to the conclusion, hopefully not fooling myself, that despite all the green-circled "sinning" on a local level, the overall feel of *That Mad Ache* is perfectly consistent with a story

taking place in France and with its characters speaking to each other in their native French.

This conclusion came as a great relief to me, but of course it is not something that I, who here stand accused of being a phrase-traitor, can objectively judge, and I even worry that by drawing attention to this issue so explicitly in this essay, I am raising the chances that people who would otherwise never have given it a moment's thought will suddenly sit up and fiercely declare me guilty of several hundred counts of Sagan-violating treachery. And then I will be sentenced to twenty years of literal translation at zero degrees (brrr!), with my leash pulled as tight as possible, choking my neck at all times. (Dante would approve!)

If this essay were to provoke such a harsh backlash against its own author, that would be a pity and an irony, but I trust that my readers are more sympathetic than that. The point is, though, that honesty compelled me to bring up this issue, which involves both the Wrong-Place Paradox and the Wrong-Style Paradox, and to shine a bright spotlight thereupon, since in my view, these constant battles form the very core of translation.

Doug on a Hot Long Leash

I'LL try to give a richer perspective on this messy issue by discussing a few more examples. In Chapter 11, a somewhat bewildered-feeling Antoine concludes an outburst of internal monologue with "C'est le comble!" Very literally, this means, "That's the peak!", but on this occasion, it's an idiom meaning "This is too much!" That's almost exactly what Westhoff has him think to himself ("It's really too much!"). However, if *I* had been Antoine in this context, my silent words would never have been that bland. *I* would have been thinking, "If that doesn't take the cake!" And since that was by far the top contender

among the possibilities in *my* mind, I stuck it right into Antoine's francophone stream of consciousness. Unfortunately, though, some friends who I've asked about this phrase have been a bit skeptical, saying that I'm pushing things with it. How can a French person be using our American idiom "take the cake"? Maybe they're right — maybe this is putting too American a mask on Antoine — but hopefully I do such things seldom enough that I don't go beyond the pale. It's a tug of war between ego-dog and superego-leash, where my ego's drive to write with flair and punch is eternally at odds with my superego's warnings that I must always be cautious and never go overboard.

Here's another example. In Chapter 12, Antoine and Lucile are having a very pleasant conversation, but all at once he twists an innocent question of hers around and starts grilling her about the importance of money to her. Although she answers him twice without getting angry, she's feeling besieged and she asks him, "Pourquoi toutes ces questions?" — literally, "Why all of these questions?" Those five English words are the exact line that Westhoff has Lucile say to Antoine, but once again, I find them to be much too bland for the context.

When I translated this passage, temporarily becoming Lucile myself, I felt far more upset than that and I gave myself several possible things to say to Antoine, three of which were: "What's the inquisition all about?" "Why the sudden Spanish Inquisition?" "Why this third degree out of the blue?" However, even though I couldn't put my finger on why, the first two struck me as going just a little too far out on a limb — too high a temperature — and so I threw them out, although with some regret, because I liked their flair, I liked their punch. After a while I didn't like "out of the blue" very well either, so I borrowed "sudden" from one of my rejected phrases, and in the end I settled on "Why the sudden third degree?" I admit that

this sentence's temperature may be as "hot" as 80°, but then again, why not? After all, some like it hot.

A good question, however, is why *I* felt compelled to stray so far from a literal translation ("Why all these questions?") when, as I said, Westhoff was perfectly satisfied with one. Couldn't one argue that if Sagan had wanted Lucile to use an idiom expressing great outrage, she would have had her do so, and therefore that Lucile's non-use of an idiom in the original suggests that she *isn't* quite that outraged, after all? Not having Lucile use an idiom was Sagan's choice — and doesn't Françoise Sagan know Lucile Saint-Léger better than Douglas Hofstadter does? Yes or no?

I admit that this is a crucially important objection to what I did, but I can't help it if I believe that this is how Lucile is really feeling — and given my firm belief on that score, then I really have no choice but to have her express herself as I did.

Could it be that, though not intentionally, I am actually slightly modifying Lucile and Antoine (and others) a very small amount, by twiddling the knobs that determine their personalities? I admit that this is conceivable, although I'd like to think that it's not the case. Perhaps by making them use more idioms in English than they use in French, I am making them just a tad bit "bigger than life" — blowing them up by, say, 1 percent. I don't know, but for the sake of argument, let's suppose that this is the case. Consider, then, my versions of these characters as contrasted with their cinematic versions, for indeed, in 1968 a film was made of *La Chamade*, with Catherine Deneuve as Lucile and Roger van Hool as Antoine. Since I have not seen it (that's an intentional choice), I can't say too much about it, but one thing I can say for sure is this. The cover of the paperback edition of *La Chamade* shows a still shot from the movie, and one sees that Antoine's hair and eyes are jet-black; by contrast, in the book, Antoine's extremely fair blond hair and his unforgettable "yellow

eyes" are described over and over again, mostly because Lucile is extremely taken with these physical traits of his. Now isn't the movie's blatant rejection of these salient traits a far more radical betrayal than my simply giving Sagan's characters a few more idioms in English than she gives them in French? And yet Sagan, in her 1998 memoir *Derrière l'épaule,* recalls how she herself worked very hard on the movie, and she warmly praises it. One thus gets the impression that she permits, even encourages, considerable twiddling-about with the knobs that determine the identity of her characters. That's food for thought.

Reined in by the Leash

ONE last example of this kind of thing. In Chapter 13, Lucile is replying with indignation to a question Antoine has asked her. She thinks the answer is self-evident, and where Sagan has her say, "Bien entendu" (meaning literally "of course"), Westhoff has her say, "Of course." That's fair enough. My first inclination, however, was to go much further than this — namely, "Well, what do you think — is the Pope Catholic?" Once again, though, some little voice inside me protested, for two reasons. One is that what Lucile actually said in French was much shorter and simpler than this sarcastic retort, and the other is that the rhetorical question "Is the Pope Catholic?" might sound too American. I don't quite know why that would be, since popes and Catholics are hardly limited to America, but perhaps there's a down-home American sense of humor lurking inside that remark, and perhaps it's that hidden flavor that sounds a bit un-French. In any case, none of my friends who read this phrase thought it belonged in Lucile's mouth, and so I threw it out and settled for just, "Well, what do you think?", and as I did so, my translation temperature fell from 100° to 75°.

Throwing out that idiom bothered me, but I bowed to the combination of pressures. Still, I couldn't help wondering what would be so very wrong about putting it in Lucile's mouth. So what that Sagan had her say just "Bien entendu"? Is Lucile exclusively Françoise Sagan's character? Isn't she at least a little bit *my* character? After all, who has been choosing her words for the past hundred pages or so? Me, that's who! So why can't I choose her words in my own way *this* time? How long a leash am I on, anyway? What is the exact nature of this leash, this bond, this intangible thread, linking me to Françoise Sagan?

Missed My Chance

INDEED, the whole time I was translating *La Chamade,* I felt there was some kind of special link between me and Françoise Sagan, partly because I loved this novel so much and was so painstakingly and meticulously trying to reconstruct it in English, and partly because my parents had, through some weird fluke, chanced to have dinner with her some thirty or more years earlier. I nourished high hopes of showing her my translation and getting her reaction to it, and I assumed that this was bound to happen one way or another. It seemed that an encounter between us was somehow fated.

I didn't actually have any direct contacts to Sagan, however, Serge Gorodetzky being the only one I could think of, and he had died a few years earlier. In the spring of 2004, I sent some emails to various friends in France to see if, by some coincidence, any of them had a direct avenue to Sagan, but I made white cabbage — that is, *j'ai fait chou blanc* — which is to say, I struck out. This didn't particularly bother me, though, because I wasn't in a big hurry; I wanted to wait until my translation was completely ready before showing it to the author herself.

A couple of months later, when my mother had her stroke, many new pressures swarmed down on me, and for a few months, *La Chamade* was placed on the back burner. When fall arrived, I returned to Bloomington, classes started up again at Indiana University, and my work routine more or less resumed. I was hoping to get back to my translation and to put the finishing touches on it, which would allow me to send it to Sagan. One day in late September, though, quite out of the blue, I got a sad, terse little email message from my sister Laura out in California, telling me that Françoise Sagan had died. That was a sad blow for me. I felt as if I had lost a potential friend, and as if Sagan, too, had lost a potential friend in me. I guess my intuition had been wrong; it was fated not to happen.

Translator as Copy-editor

WHEN I was growing up, my mother subscribed to *The New Yorker,* and in my late teens I greatly enjoyed flipping through each issue of that august journal, looking for cartoons and other amusing tidbits, one of which was the sporadic feature called "Our Forgetful Authors". Here one would find two passages gleefully quoted that directly contradicted each other, both taken from the same book, with the page numbers cited, invariably followed by some wry comment at the hapless author's expense. I always savored these little jabs that were pointed at various writers the world around, some very well known.

I suppose that all authors make blunders of this sort — *errare humanum est.* Even though I knew this, I was a little surprised to find a couple of glaring errors in *La Chamade.* One of them had to do with Diane's last name. In Chapter 3 she is called "Diane Merbel", but in Chapter 15 she is called "Diane Mirbec". Those are the only two places where her last name is given. I wasn't

sure what to do with this. I certainly didn't want to have two different last names appear in my translation, even if that had happened in the original. It would make both Sagan and me look stupid, at least to those readers who happened to catch the inconsistency. So unless I was going to fall into the Literality Trap, I would have to override my author. But should I choose "Merbel" or "Mirbec"? I was stymied until it occurred to me that I could blend them, making either "Merbec" or "Mirbel". I liked the sound of the latter more, and so I opted for that. I later asked Google how many occurrences of each of these it could find on the Web, and it reported back to me 783 for "Merbel", 31 for "Mirbec", 38,100 for "Mirbel", and 77 for "Merbec". I was pleased with my intuition, and stuck with my choice.

In Chapter 9, Lucile is thinking to herself that it's ten in the evening and that she'll see Antoine in seventeen hours. Well, that would mean three o'clock in the afternoon. However, one page later, she continues her musing and says to herself that she'll see him at five o'clock in the afternoon. Who made the mistake — Lucile or Françoise? I don't know, but once again, I saw no reason to leave this kind of slip-up in my translation, so I changed "seventeen" to "nineteen", figuring that of the three figures, the one gotten by subtraction was by far the most likely one to be wrong. It seems to me that carrying out this patch was not only a *permissible* liberty I took, but the kind of liberty any dutiful translator *must* take (this is the old Don't-Trust-the-Text Paradox again). Sagan wouldn't wish a careless arithmetical goof-up to mar her book (or rather, our joint book).

A similar arithmetical goof-up involves ages. At one point, Diane is described as being 45 years old, and at another point she is said to be ten years older than Lucile is, while at two points, Lucile is said to be 30 years old. This just doesn't add up! Since, once again, I put more stock in Sagan's use of absolute

numbers than in her subtraction, I changed the ten-year age difference to a fifteen-year age difference. This kind of repair work is just part and parcel of a respectful translator's duty.

A somewhat different type of error occurs where Sagan is describing how a remark by Lucile suddenly relieves Antoine's tension. She writes, "Et, comme un reflux, la tranquillité envahit l'esprit d'Antoine…" Now the word *reflux* means "ebb tide" — that is, a tide flowing *out*, not in — but Sagan tells us that this ebb tide of tranquillity is *invading* Antoine's soul, which does not compute. At this juncture, Robert Westhoff, liberating himself elegantly from his ex-wife's words, wrote, "And like an ebbing tide, apprehension left Antoine…", making a semantic double flip that I find rather clever and charming. I, too, felt compelled to free myself from Sagan's erroneous word-choice, but my maneuver was quite different. I wrote, "And the sense of relief that came flooding into his soul was so powerful that…", replacing the dangerous ebb-tide metaphor with the less risky metaphor of a flood, which poses no directional problems.

A very different type of author error (if "error" is even the word) occurred in Chapter 14, where on one page Sagan writes:

> elle le subissait avec un mélange d'ironie et de désespoir

and just three pages later she writes:

> elle le subissait avec un mélange de bonheur et de désespoir.

Whether you know any French or not, you can see that these two long phrases, both describing Lucile but in very different circumstances, differ in just one word. This nearly verbatim repetition jumped out at me one morning as I was transcribing those pages into my notebooks, and I made a note to myself to be

sure to avoid using nearly-identical phrasing in these two spots. I felt that leaving the two phrases almost identical would make Françoise Sagan sound like she was in a rut.

Some people might fault me for this choice, saying that since Sagan re-used (nearly) the same phrase, I should have slavishly done the same thing — but speaking as a dog free to trot about, I would adamantly disagree. It was my desire that Sagan should sound always fresh and never rut-stuck, so in the first spot I wrote that Lucile "had just accepted its frenzy with a mélange of irony and despair", and in the second spot that she "would submit to it in a weird blur of joy and desperation". As for Westhoff, in the first spot he wrote, "she had supported it with a mixture of irony and despair", and in the second one, "she bore it with a mixture of happiness and despair". This is all right, but it only slightly diminishes the sense of repetition.

It was my intention with my modification to try to do Sagan a small favor. It's not as if *La Chamade* were a poem in which near-echoes had been deliberately inserted from time to time a few pages apart, intended as subtle artistic touches. Rather, this repetition was just a bit of careless writing, and I, acting as Sagan's anglophone proxy and solicitous copy-editor, felt it was my job to fix things up so that no one would have grounds for chuckling at her obliviousness. To leave the repetition would have been to fall timidly into the Literality Trap; to get rid of it was to welcome and to savor the Don't-Trust-the-Text Paradox.

Clarity, Vividness, and Logic

HERE'S another tiny error that I patched up without any qualms. We're in Chapter 24, and one autumn morning Lucile has turned up at Antoine's apartment at daybreak. Facing her, Antoine, filled with complex emotions and in a swirl of intense

memories, reviews in his mind the summer that they just spent together, particularly its final month. In the French, however, it says "il revit le mois d'été", which means "he resaw the summer month". This singular doesn't make sense, since summers have three months, and they spent nearly the whole summer together. In fact, in the following clause Sagan has Antoine zeroing in on one particular month — August. I would guess the use of *le mois* rather than *les mois* was a typo rather than an author error, but whatever it was, I felt compelled to fix it. The first clause should have said, "il revit *les* mois d'été" — "he resaw the summer *months*"; then Antoine's thought would have flowed logically.

FS: Il faillit lui dire que son geste n'avait aucune importance, qu'elle l'avait toujours trompé de toute façon, avec Charles, avec sa vie, avec sa propre nature. Mais il revit le mois d'été, il se rappela le goût de ses larmes ce dernier mois d'août sur son épaule, et il ne dit rien.

RW: He almost told her that her act was of no importance, that in any case she had always deceived him, with Charles, with life, with her own nature. But he relived that summer month, he remembered the taste of the tears she shed on his shoulder that August, and he said nothing.

DH: He nearly blurted out that her concern for him made no difference to him, that she'd always been cheating on him with Charles, with life, with her entire soul. But then he remembered those summer months, he recalled the taste of her tears on his shoulder that last month of August, and he bit his tongue.

We're not done with this passage yet; there are more issues of logical flow in it that I wish to discuss. The last few words — "et il ne dit rien" — tell us that the power of Antoine's memories has

made him refrain from saying something harsh to Lucile. Westhoff copies these words very literally, writing "and he said nothing". I, by contrast, stray a little bit further from Sagan, and write "and he bit his tongue". Now French has the same stock metaphor (*se mordre la langue*), but Sagan didn't use it. So why did I, then? Because *biting his tongue is clearly what Antoine did*, and because using that very common metaphor makes it just a little bit clearer and more vivid. But do I, a mere translator, have the right to turn up the clarity and vividness knobs?

Well, the fact is that I'm naturally inclined to turn these knobs up high no matter what I'm writing, because clarity and vividness are, in some sense, my religion. I would be betraying *myself* if I didn't allow myself to be as clear and as vivid as possible when I translate. Indeed, were I told that I had to adopt the principle of such rigid "faithfulness" to the author, then I would just give up translating, for it wouldn't allow me to use my own mind. It would turn me into a dull automaton, and it would remove all joy from the act. And why would I wish to translate anything if doing so was emotionless from start to finish, or worse yet — and far more likely — if it was painful from start to finish, as I constantly and slavishly suppressed one after another of my carefully considered judgments?

Some critics might say that I shouldn't allow myself (or be allowed) to use my own style — the Wrong Style — no matter how much I personally revere clarity and vividness; I simply have to "copy" what the author did. That is, after all, the translator's sacred duty. Well, I would retort that "copying" one's author is anything but a mechanical act. For example, look at how Robert Westhoff — Mister Low Temperature himself — "copied" Sagan's phrase "le goût de ses larmes" (literally, "the taste of her tears"): he refers to "the taste of the tears she shed". But Sagan has no such clause as "she shed" in her original sentence. Does

Translator, Trader

this turn Westhoff into a traitor to his ex-wife? Absolutely not. I would vehemently defend his right to play around at this level. He felt that adding those two words made it *flow better* in English. That was his artistic judgment, and using one's artistic judgment is what a good translator *has* to do. The fact is, we make such judgment calls in every single sentence we translate, often doing so many times in a single sentence, and in many cases entirely unconsciously, just taking the winning phrase that bubbles up from the roiling, boiling murk in the cauldron of our mind.

In my case, I opted for using an idiom that carries the reader just an iota more into Antoine's head than does the rather bland phrase "and he said nothing". You may also have noticed that I opened my rendition of this same short passage with a similar gesture countering blandness, replacing "Il faillit lui dire" ("He nearly told her") by "He nearly blurted out". These two choices of mine are two sides of the same coin. First Antoine nearly "blurts something out", but in the end he "bites his tongue" — this in contrast to his "nearly saying something" and then "not saying anything". Why not make things come more alive, when it's possible to do so with a minuscule tweak like this? It's not as if I were rewriting the plot of Sagan's novel, or changing her characters' characters; I am just being myself.

"Performer, Perverter"

AND SO, what about this idea of "being oneself" when one translates? Is that a legitimate part of the game? Is being oneself allowed for a translator, or is it a taboo no-no? Most translators seem to believe that it is evil and *verboten*, and that, quite to the contrary, it is their sacred duty to suppress their own selves as much as possible. This, to be sure, is all in the noble aim of serving the author faithfully.

I am reminded of a couple of recordings of preludes and fugues by Dmitri Shostakovich that I purchased in the 1960's. Over time, I came to love these works very dearly, so much so that in 1969 I even wrote a glowing fan letter to the composer (to which he never replied, to my disappointment). Each of the records contained several preludes and fugues (out of twenty-four in his full Opus 87), and on one of them the performer was Shostakovich himself, while on the other the performer was the famous Soviet pianist Sviatoslav Richter. The two records had a couple of preludes and fugues in common, so in those cases I got to hear the "authentic" version versus an "interpretation" by someone else. Well, I don't think anyone will be too surprised to hear that I far preferred Richter's way of playing Shostakovich's piano music to Shostakovich's way. Richter made the music flow, made it sing, made it dance, made it come fabulously alive. Shostakovich did an okay job, but on the whole his renditions sounded pretty wooden and flat. Would purists, however, object, saying that Richter had taken impermissible liberties, and that he should instead have paid strict attention to how Shostakovich himself performed every note and that he should have imitated Shostakovich slavishly, in order to be more "authentic", more "true", in order not to "betray" the master?

I am also reminded of a famous set of recordings made by Ella Fitzgerald in early 1956 of some thirty or so songs by Cole Porter (still available, incidentally). In each of these songs, Ella takes the original melody as written down and all over the place adds to it highly idiosyncratic, uniquely Ella-ish twists, heightening its beauty with her trills and mordents and swirls and grace notes, turning it into an immortal work of art in which her spirit and that of Cole Porter are magically joined. (By the way, I am neglecting the fantastic contribution of Buddy Bregman and his orchestra, also *sui generis,* but taking that into account would only

make my point even stronger.) Would we want to hear just Cole Porter's own piano-playing accompanying his own rather lovable but also very squawky voice every last time we listened to "Begin the Beguine"? I think not. Ella's myriad artistic choices, most of them made spontaneously and unconsciously, make this album a priceless treasure, a landmark in my life and many friends' lives, and in the lives of thousands of others. It is a magical marriage between Porter and Fitzgerald, and one to cherish forever.

At this juncture, I feel compelled to recall to the reader's mind the harsh verdict "Translator, traitor", which prejudges all translators of all works of literature of being guilty of some kind of crime, without even putting them on trial. If we were to apply this same kind of mindless "reasoning" to music, then we would have to declare about both Richter and Fitzgerald, without once having listened to a single note by either, "Performer, perverter."

"Transistore, Traditore"

HOW IS musical performance any different from translation? Unless you want to entrust everything to a machine, translation requires a human performer. Sometimes I get the impression, though, that many people want the process of translation to yield something that is essentially mechanical — they want (or they seem to want) to read "pure Sagan in English" without any human intermediary, or at least without any subjective human choices getting in the way between them and Sagan's French.

In fact, to my bafflement, that seems to be the holy grail of many, perhaps even most, of the members of the translating profession. Many of them state explicitly that their dream is to be "invisible", so that their author will come through perfectly, without any "interference" — a humble stance that is virtually the diametric opposite of that of musical performers, who for the

most part aspire to be maximally in the limelight, and often, if at all possible, more so than the composer.

Well, all right then — if neutral mechanicalness is what we want — that is, untouchedness by human hands — then let's go for it. I have just carried out a little experiment to see what is possible along these lines. I began by opening *La Chamade* to a random page (page 134 in Chapter 17, if anyone cares) and I copied down the first sentence that my eye lit upon (and I swear this is true — I didn't choose the most challenging sentence of two or three or ten; I literally chose a totally random sentence from a totally random page of the book). Here it is:

> *Original version:* En attendant, ils regardaient, comme fascinés, se dérouler le présent, se lever le jour qui les trouvait réunis dans le même lit, jamais rassasiés l'un de l'autre, descendre le soir qui les voyait marcher dans un Paris tiède, tendre, inégalable.

Then I fed this rather complex sentence into Google's mechanical translation engine, to see what a wholly disinterested, unbiased party might make of it:

> *Google's version:* While waiting, they looked at, as fascinated, to be held the present, to rise the day which found them joined together in the same bed, ever satisfied one of the other, to descend the evening which saw them going in tepid Paris, tender, incomparable.

There can be no denying that this piece of verbal garbage is a very literal translation (essentially just dictionary lookup plus some grammatical rearrangement). Although it's "objective" by virtue of being mechanical, it's hard to imagine anyone who would ever suggest or believe that this untouched-by-human-hands rendition faithfully represents Françoise Sagan in English.

A couple of explanatory notes: *se dérouler* unfortunately got replaced by "to be held", which it sometimes indeed means (in the sense of a conference or a concert being held), but certainly not in this context, where it means "to unfold", and *jamais* got replaced by "ever", the exact opposite of what it means here. Well, that's par for the course when zero intelligence is brought to bear on translation. Zero intelligence yields a freezing-cold, zero-degree, zero-sense translation (and even applying the word "translation" to such output is being overly generous, I think).

By the way, the bulk of this essay having been written in 2005, the garbage shown above was produced by a now-obsolete version of Google's translation engine. In the past year or so, the engine has been overhauled totally (dictionary lookup has been replaced by a much fancier kind of phrase-level lookup that takes context into account, for anyone who's interested), and so, in the interests of scientific accuracy and literary honesty, here is the translation that Google produced for me on October 12, 2008:

> *Google's October 2008 version:* Meanwhile, they watched, fascinated as is this place, stand on the day that was gathered in the same bed, never satisfied one of the other, get off the evening which saw them walk in a Paris warm, tender, incomparable.

As you can see, this garbage is quite different from the 2005 garbage (but it's hardly any better — in fact, it's probably worse). So much for the idea that a translation done by machine is "neutral" and "pure". What this shows is that it is very hard indeed to produce a good translation without any thinking — and for better or for worse, thinking is what makes a good translation extremely human, and anything but mechanical.

It seems to me that a helpful, pithy summary of my simple experiments with machine translation is the following brand-new

sound bite: *Transistore, traditore.* If you don't understand it, then just ask Google to translate it for you. It'll do a perfect job of it!

Many a Choice Results in a Voice

LET'S GO on with our discussion of the ideal of "pure" or "neutral" translation, devoid of subjectivity. Having explored machine translation and found it wanting, I decided to render the same sentence very literally myself, thus bringing in a modicum of human intelligence (essentially just a bit of common sense in choosing word senses) but trying to avoid any genuine artistry. In my product, shown below, I explicitly indicate a fair number of choice points where further choices — judgment calls involving at least a little artistry or personal taste — would be required. If I were to make any of those choices, then of course my own ego — my personal style and taste — would necessarily be intervening, so I stayed out of the picture.

> *Choice-littered literal version by DRH:* [Meanwhile/in the meantime], they [watched/were watching/would watch/used to watch/looked at/were looking at (etc.)], as if fascinated, the present [unrolling/unfolding], the day [arising/breaking], which [found/was finding] them [reunited/collected/gathered/combined (etc.)] in the same bed, never [satisfied with/having gotten enough of] [each other/one another], the evening [fall/falling], which [saw/was seeing] them [walk/walking] in a [tepid/lukewarm/warm/balmy], tender, [matchless/unmatchable/incomparable] Paris.

Next, I decided to turn this choice-littered literal translation into a (hopefully) high-quality literal translation by using my own judgment calls, thus trying to get as close to a "pure Sagan" (*i.e.,* untouched-by-human-hands) version of this sentence as I could:

DRH literal version: Meanwhile, they were watching, as if fascinated, the present unfolding, the day breaking, which would find them reunited in the same bed, never having gotten enough of each other, the evening falling, which would see them walk in a warm, tender, incomparable Paris.

To me, the above reads in a very wooden fashion, despite the artistry that I tried to bring to bear in making choices. In fact, it strikes me as hopelessly clunky. The reason is that there is really very little room to maneuver if one begins with a choice-littered literal translation and one's hands are tied by that fact. The raw material was badly wanting, so that calling the making of such choices "artistic" is really a kind of bad joke.

My next step was simply to copy Robert Westhoff's translation of this sentence out of his book:

Westhoff's published version: Meanwhile, they watched, fascinated, the present unfold, the day break to find them together in the same bed, never wearying of each other, the sky darken at twilight to find them walking about a warm, tender, incomparable Paris.

In most of this sentence, Westhoff just stays on his usual short leash. In fact, it is striking how close my literal version and Westhoff's version are. But there are a couple of spots where he pulls out a little farther from the literal, with phrases like "never wearying of each other" and "the sky darken at twilight". Those phrases are not "pure Sagan in English", which is a pipe dream, but Sagan–Westhoff, and it's precisely where Westhoff starts to exploit his own artistic taste that it starts to sound more like something someone might actually want to read. Arf arf!

Finally, I simply cut-and-pasted my own long-leash final version of this same sentence from Chapter 17 into this essay:

DRH final version: And so, in the meantime, they were watching the present with fascination as it unfolded, with each day as it first broke finding them tightly joined in their little bed, never getting enough of one another, and with each evening as it fell finding them walking side by side in the mild, sweet, magical Parisian air.

As advertised, this was done by a much freer dog. The two occurrences of "each", for example, help make it clear that this is not a one-time scene but an oft-repeated one, a fact that is subtly suggested by the original French (largely by the imperfect tense of the verbs *trouvait* and *voyait*), but which a literal translation fails to convey. Other small touches, such as "And so", "tightly joined in their little bed", and "the mild, sweet, magical Parisian air", came purely from my own head — a head that has lived sixty years in the same world that Françoise Sagan had spent thirty years in when she wrote this passage. I think that having lived in the world brings a great deal of life into one's translation, provided that one *allows* oneself to dare to admix one's own life with the life of the author.

This passage, in short, is by no stretch of the imagination "pure Sagan in English" — a pipe dream, I once again repeat — but it is Sagan–Hofstadter, an abstract entity a bit like Porter–Fitzgerald (if I'm allowed to make such a bold analogy). You cannot — I repeat, *cannot* — get "pure Sagan in English", and I won't even add "sad to say", because the idea is just incoherent. It would be like saying, "You can't get a square circle, sad to say." There's nothing sad about its nonexistence because it's just a contradiction in terms. What you *can* get is various people's styles of rendering Françoise Sagan in English, just as you can get various people's styles of singing "Begin the Beguine". Some of them may turn out to be sublime works of art, others may not. But each one will unavoidably bear its performer's unique stamp.

Flow-words and the Author's Voice

THAT little word "and" buried two-thirds of the way through my final version above ("never getting enough of one another, *and* with each evening...") merits a bit of commentary. To me it helps the sentence flow more smoothly and clearly. Try reading it aloud without the "and" and see if you agree. Perhaps you will agree, perhaps you won't, but in any case, for a combination of intangible reasons, I myself felt the flow was improved, and so I took the liberty of adding it.

As this shows, one of the characteristics of my style is to try to make the "logic" of what I write flow smoothly. For that reason, I am particularly concerned with "flow-words" like the conjunctions "but", "so", "as", "since", "although", "because", and so forth. Although I usually render Sagan's rather bland word *et* by the literal choice "and", there are spots where, in the interests of smooth, clear flow, I will render *et* by less bland words, such as "but" or "and so" or "and then". Indeed, there were a few spots in *La Chamade* when a sentence with *et* had such a screamingly "but" feel to it that for me there was no choice at all but to use "but" instead of "and". You might ask, "Well, if it so blatantly called out for 'but', then why didn't Sagan say *mais* in French?" Good question. I can only reply, "Beats me!"

Stern and severe purists would say that I should always respect Sagan's decision to say *et* instead of *mais,* and I believe I understand this sentiment very well. Indeed, respect for the original wording is certainly one of the pressures — the many pressures — that I feel asserting themselves and tussling with each other inside my brain whenever I translate. But, though it is always strong, it is often not the *winning* pressure. Always following the literal route is being too much the dog on the short leash, and leads invariably to a graceless, wooden outcome.

"But what about Sagan's *style?*", I hear some people protest. "Aren't you killing her style and replacing it with Hofstadter style?" Another excellent question, going right to the heart of the matter, which is, of course, the Wrong-Style Paradox.

I once heard a talk by John Nathan, a gifted translator from Japanese to English, in which he emphasized how crucial it is to preserve the author's "voice" or "soundprint" in one's translation. His point was that he doesn't want his English translations of three different Japanese novelists all to come out sounding like *him*; he wants them to have three recognizable, individual, unique voices (or soundprints), so that anyone who read a little bit of his translation of a piece by author X would immediately recognize the characteristic "X voice" and would be able to identify the author as X almost instantly. This is certainly a noble aim, I agree — so the question is, am I diluting Françoise Sagan's personal voice by superimposing on it my own desire for clarity or flow or logic (or whatever you want to call it)?

My answer to this subtle question is that it all depends on the extent to which the "Sagan voice" demands what I would call a "misuse" of flow-words like *et, mais,* and so forth. If Françoise Sagan consistently used *et* where I felt something else (such as *mais*) was called for, and if she did this so frequently and so reliably that people felt that this was really a deep hallmark of her style, then I would surely back away from replacement of *et* by "but" in English. However, this is not my take on Françoise Sagan. It seems to me that most of the time, she uses flow-words in a very normal, reasonable fashion, corresponding exactly to my expectations and my own writing style. But once in a while, it seems to me that she carelessly slips up, and I suspect that if an editor had said to her, "Why don't you switch this *et* into a *mais?*", she would have reread the passage and then said, "Sure! It flows better!" (in French, of course, despite my quote marks). I

don't know this for sure, and of course I can't prove it, but it is my very strong intuition.

Françoise Sagan was not into surface-level affectations of the sort whereby an author becomes famous for some strange and idiosyncratic way of using common words. To the contrary, she used words in a very straightforward and reasonable way, and in fact that is one of the reasons that her prose appeals to me so much. The special flavor of Sagan's voice does not in the least depend on a weakened sense of flow or logic, thanks to repeated abuses of words like *et* and *mais*; Sagan's special novelist's voice comes from a much larger-scale way of portraying people and events through descriptions, dialogues, and especially inner monologues. If I were to betray her at *that* level, then people could, and people should, complain that the Sagan voice had disappeared in the Hofstadter translation. But I do my very best to respect her at that quintessentially Sagan level.

I do, by the way, think that there are many jazz artists — in fact, almost all of today's jazz musicians — who knowingly replace the composer's voice by their own when they improvise on a tune not of their own invention. By the time one is but a minute or two into the piece, the composer's voice has been completely drowned out, as has all trace of the original melody. Ironically, however, this kind of liberty is not looked down upon by music critics — instead, it is warmly saluted as exhibiting creativity at the highest level. If it works that way in music, then why not in literature as well?

Distinct Voices inside the Novel

WHILE we're on the topic of voices, I feel it is important to point out that in any novel there is more than one voice. There are the voices of the individual characters. Thus in a scene

where Claire, Diane, and Johnny all speak, hopefully one will be able to tell them apart easily and one won't simply say, "Oh, this sounds like Françoise Sagan speaking once again." Just as J. D. Salinger's characters in, say, *The Catcher in the Rye* should not all sound like just one person (especially not J. D. Salinger himself), so should any novelist's cast of characters sound like separate, truly distinct individuals.

But what are the elusive signs that would serve as signatures of a particular person in a novel? If the author doesn't resort to simplistic gimmicks (a lisp, a stammer, dialectal usages, frequent repetition of a particular pet word, constant use of very short or very long sentences, and so forth), the crux of the answer has to be that it is mostly the flavor of the *thoughts* that the person comes out with, and not so much the surface-level qualities of their syntax or word choice. Most native speakers of any language use words in a fairly similar fashion, though some people have pet words that give them away (a couple of mine are "jolly" and "droll", for instance, but you won't find them riddled throughout everything that I write).

My belief is that most of the telltale signs that distinguish one person's written "voice" from another's, whether we are talking about a novelist's voice or the voices of characters inside a novel, reside on a level that is far higher than the rather low levels at which I, as a leashless translator-dog, feel free to manipulate the text I am translating.

If I am right, then the liberties that I have taken in this novel and described in this essay have not destroyed the authenticity of the various voices in it. If, however, I am fooling myself — if Sagan-ness is truly gone from my translation and if I am unaware of this fact — then that means I have produced a poor translation, which would certainly be a shame, but unfortunately there's nothing I can do about it at this late date.

The Translator's Voice, Every So Often

THAT having been said, I do not feel that I must religiously suppress in every last instance the kinds of linguistic touches and turns of phrase that might allow someone to recognize *my* voice peeking through every now and then. Just as Ella Fitzgerald can make distinctly Ella-like gestures without taking away much if any Coleness from a lovely Cole Porter melody, so I allow myself to indulge in some of my own characteristic gestures every once in a while, although I make sure to keep this high-temperature "here's me!" tendency down to a very low volume.

For instance, there is a spot in Chapter 9 where Sagan describes Lucile's first, unexpected sense of Antoine as a genuine stranger to herself:

> Pour la première fois surtout, elle pensa qu'Antoine était un « autre », et que tout ce qu'elle savait de ses mains, de sa bouche, de ses yeux, de son corps n'en faisait pas forcément son indissoluble complice.

The word *autre,* meaning "other", is the key word here, as one sees from Sagan's having placed it in quote marks. Well, when I translated this sentence, I happened to notice a curious coincidence involving the English words "an other", and so I exhibited it to my readers explicitly, as follows:

> And most of all, for the first time it hit her that Antoine was not like her, but was another — an other, a not her — and that all her intimacy with his hands, his mouth, his eyes, his body, did not mean he was her irrevocable soulmate.

There is no wordplay in Sagan's French, and so this little interpolation is me, not her. It may mar the translation if all one

wants is a very obedient dog heeling constantly, suppressing its own nature at every moment, but I like to think that it adds a little touch of interest. Think of an Ella grace note.

And then, in Chapter 18, Lucile smiles at an old woman to whom she has just relievedly given away her bus ticket, and Sagan writes, "Lucile lui renvoya un sourire incertain" ("Lucile re-sent her an uncertain smile"). Perhaps, being so immersed in Sagan's writing at the time, I was unusually sensitized, but in any case, I could not help seeing in the final three words an allusion to the title of Sagan's second novel (dating from 1956) *Un certain sourire,* which means "A Certain Smile", and so one part of me was strongly tempted to keep those literal words "uncertain smile", but there were several other pressures, and in the end I wound up spurning this choice and opting instead for "Lucile flashed a shaky smile back at her." It saddened me a bit, but it just worked better overall.

However, I unexpectedly made up for this lost opportunity a few pages later. In particular, in the next chapter Sagan writes about Antoine, "il tourna vers elle un visage souriant, indécis" ("he flipped towards her a smiling, indecisive face"), and I thought a good way to render this was "he turned towards her with a sweet, uncertain smile", thus managing, after all, to squeeze in my little allusion to *Un certain sourire,* albeit at a few pages' remove from the more obvious spot in which to do so. Sticking this small and nearly invisible wink at one Sagan novel inside another one certainly made me smile.

My final sin of translator's self-indulgence involves a passage in Chapter 12 where, as I was translating it, I noticed that two or three English words that begin with "fl" happened to appear, by pure chance, near each other. All these words were subjective, artistic choices on my part — another translator might not have used a single one of them (indeed, Robert Westhoff didn't use

any of them). But be that as it may, I had used a few and I noticed that I could easily extend this pattern over the rest of the sentence, giving me in the end a total of seven such words (out of 37 in the whole sentence). I was pleased with the alliterative quality that this gave to the sentence, but once again, a critical reader might say, "What are you *doing* here?! There is no such playful pattern in the original French sentence! You are just arbitrarily sticking Hofstadter-ness into this Sagan novel, where it doesn't belong at all! You are a traitor!"

My first line of defense would be the same old Ella-sings-Cole line that I have trotted out above (her trills and grace notes add terrific Ella-ness but don't diminish Cole-ness by one whit), but almost surely that wouldn't satisfy the hypothetical critic.

In this case, however, I happen, by sheer luck, to have a second possible line of defense. At the very end of Chapter 17, the following sentence occurs (in an inner monologue of Antoine's): "Il savait bien que l'*été était* fini et que ç'avait *été* le plus bel *été* de leur vie" — which, translated word for word, means this: "He knew well that the *summer was* over and that it'd *been* the most beautiful *summer* of their life." I have italicized four words in the French sentence and four in its literal anglicization. Although only two of the English words sound alike (being identical!), all four of these French words sound alike, except that *était* ends with a slightly different vowel. The point, though, is that there is a clearly audible phonetic pattern here. Now whether Sagan *intended* to make a sound pattern here, or even noticed that she had done so inadvertently, is another matter, admittedly. We will never know, now that she is gone, but the existence of one undeniable phonetic pattern *somewhere* in her novel could be said to provide at least a plausible pretext for a translator's inserting an audible phonetic pattern somewhere or other in their translation. If you can't do it in the last sentence of

Chapter 17, then why not do it somewhere in the middle of Chapter 12? And so I would say that this shows very clearly that I am *not* a traitor; I'm just a trader.

Translating the Translator

I HAVE just listed all three of the passages in *That Mad Ache* where I deliberately inserted a little taste of my own personal style. I don't think that, by indulging myself in these very few tiny ways, I let overly much of the Wrong Style creep in.

Nonetheless, at this point, a skeptic might well ask me, "How would you like it if somebody translated *you* in such a free-and-easy fashion, putting words in your mouth that you never said?" To this my unhesitating answer would be, "Why not? Turnabout is fair play!" As a matter of fact, right after each of my first two books came out, I wrote long, detailed cover letters to the then-unknown future translators of these books, and I requested them — indeed, ordered them! — to take precisely these kinds of liberties, over and over again, to the max. As long as my ideas are not betrayed, changing my language radically is fine with me.

The skeptic might well reply, "Well, that's very inconsistent of you! Your letters to your future translators gave a *carte blanche* invitation to radically transculturate your books in exactly the fashion that you so deplored in the case of *A Day in the Life of Ivan Denisovich.* How can you possibly justify such inconsistency?"

Well, all right. I can see how my letters could seem, at first, like the height of hypocrisy on my part, but I think I can explain. My books, unlike Alexander Solzhenitsyn's or Françoise Sagan's, are not novels — stories that by definition are deeply rooted in a particular place and time. My books are, rather, nonfiction, meaning that there is no story being told and no set of characters rooted in a specific location or culture. My books consist

primarily of essays that explore *ideas*, such as sexist language, quantum mechanics, meaning in music, the nature of consciousness, and even translation. There is no suspension of disbelief required in the case of such essays. For that reason, one doesn't need to worry very much about the Wrong-Place Paradox.

If a nonfiction essay becomes more vivid when the translator replaces an idiom in language A (say, "To have your cake and eat it too") by its counterpart in language B (here, "Avoir le beurre et l'argent du beurre", which literally means "To have the butter and the money for the butter"), the translator has not betrayed the rootedness of the essay in culture A, because the message of the essay was not a local one to begin with. The essay wasn't ever intended to be rooted in culture A as opposed to culture B; its message was more objective and universal to begin with. In a word, when one is translating a *novel*, transculturation is one's most insidious and worrisome enemy; by contrast, when one is translating a work of *nonfiction*, that is seldom the case.

Of course there are all sorts of twists and complexities that I am ignoring here (such as the fact that the line between fiction and nonfiction is anything but sharp), but this essay is not the place to go into all that. I do, however, talk about these things in quite some detail in Chapter 6 of my book *Le Ton beau de Marot*, entitled "The Subtle Art of Transculturation".

Transculturation? Yes! (Occasionally)

ABOVE, I gave a few examples where I put into French-speaking mouths American idiomatic phrases like "*This* baby'll knock 'em dead!" and "If that doesn't take the cake!" It was in those spots that I most worried that I might be crossing a subtle line and (at least locally) transculturating *La Chamade*. Though aware of such dangers, I was willing to take the risk. There are a

few other cases like this that fall into a little family that I find particularly fascinating, so I will now discuss them all in one fell swoop. They have to do with numerical measurements or units, and the words with which they are described.

In Chapter 20, Antoine blurts out angrily to Lucile, "Il ne t'ont pas payé un centime" — literally, "They didn't pay you a centime." Robert Westhoff rendered this as "They haven't given you a penny", whereas I converted it into "And they never paid you one red cent." My concern here is the degree of blatant un-Frenchness lurking in the phrase "red cent", but since one could ask a similar question about "penny", let's consider that first.

What is a penny? It could be a British coin or it could be an American coin, but it is certainly not (and never was) a French coin. And thus it would seem that by this little word we are being carried, if not across the Atlantic, then at least across the Channel. Or are we? Could it be that the word "penny" slips completely undetected below an average anglophonic reader's transculturation radar? Hard to say. In any case, the analogous question also has to be posed for my "red cent". I have no way of knowing how red a flag will be set waving in an average reader's mind by the word "penny", let alone by the phrase "red cent", but I decided to stick my neck out with this familiar idiom, intuiting (or at least hoping) that it would not trigger any loud alarm bells.

Scott Buresh reacted to this choice of mine by saying that he would prefer to have the original word simply remain in place — thus, "They didn't pay you a *centime*", perhaps with "centime" in italics to emphasize its Frenchness. Scott, who speaks no French, explained that this would give *him* the chance to do at least a tiny bit of the translation into English himself. In his mind, he could substitute "penny", "red cent", "blasted centime", or whatever he wanted when he encountered the raw word *centime* on the

page. He would prefer this open-endedness to having the characters' dialogue being predigested and spoonfed to him in too-smooth, too-idiomatic English. Basically, in the context of a translated novel, Scott says he would savor an occasional sense of floating in fog or mist — a kind of impressionistic haze — because, he says, this would give him the sensation of reading an alien language rather than his native language.

Well, all I can say is that I genuinely understand Scott's feeling, and part of me genuinely sympathizes. Perhaps that's the difference between being a reader and being a translator. As a translator, you want to carry things as far as possible out of language A and into language B, but as a reader, you resist this kind of push, at least once in a while. Something in you instinctively combats the overzealousness of a translator who overdoes things. The question is, how much translation is too much, and how little is too little?

In Chapter 16, Johnny is giving Antoine his impression of a mood Lucile was in a while earlier, and he says, "cela se voyait à vingt pas, sans la connaître" — "it was visible at twenty paces, without knowing her." Here, a bit bumpily, Robert Westhoff has Johnny say, "it could be seen from twenty feet, even if one didn't already know." Now I had to scratch my head when I first saw this. Why had "twenty paces" become "twenty feet"? To me, a pace is about two-and-a-half feet, so twenty paces would be more like fifty feet. Not that I think the distance in this metaphor should be taken *au pied de la lettre* (that is, literally), but why bother to convert "twenty paces" at all? Why not simply leave it as is? Everyone can relate to a pace. Moreover, having Johnny say "twenty feet" moves him out of the metric system and into the Anglo-Saxon measurement system, which is a dead giveaway that he is *not* speaking French. Or is it? Once again, does the English-speaking ear necessarily detect this transgression, or

could it be that "twenty feet" sounds so familiar to us that it slips entirely unnoticed right under our radar?

Now if you thought Robert Westhoff sinned here, well, *my* translation of Johnny's view of Lucile's mood should shock you considerably more. I have him say, "anyone could see it a mile off, even without knowing her." Wouldn't you agree that my use of the "m"-word here is, at least on the surface, even more risqué than Westhoff's use of the "f"-word? What could be more Anglo-Saxon than a *mile*? The French haven't talked about such things for hundreds of years! And yet in the end, I decided to leave "see it a mile off" in Johnny's francophone mouth because I decided it was probably a sufficiently dead metaphor that its key word, "mile", doesn't really make native English speakers think of the literal meaning at all. It was a close call, but that's how I decided to go.

In Chapter 18, Sagan mentions a Paris bus that would bring Lucile to within 300 meters of Antoine's place, and Westhoff converted this distance to 300 yards, whereas I, in this context, wouldn't touch a yard with a ten-foot pole; my move was to leave the distance intact, at 300 meters. Now why on earth should I act so skittish of *yards* when I was perfectly willing to embrace a *mile*? The answer is that "see it a mile off" is just a metaphor for "pick up on it very easily", and no physical distance is involved, whereas the gap from bus stop to apartment is a *genuine* distance. Although a yard is so nearly a meter that the trade might seem almost irresistible, the concomitant shift into the Anglo-Saxon measuring system struck me as a subtle but nontrivial slide down the slippery transculturation slope, so I resisted it.

As this little contrast makes clear, each translation question, whether large or small, sets up a unique and unpredictable combination of mental pressures, so that simple, hard-and-fast rules seldom yield insightful answers. This is why I feel very

uncomfortable with attempts to develop a scientific or precise or rigorous "theory of translation". In my opinion, translation is a subtle, subjective, esthetic art, not a precise science or set of rigid rules. To the contrary, it involves *thinking* and *judging* without ever any letup. And the final example in this little family will, I think, bring this out very nicely.

In the book's last chapter, Lucile and Antoine find themselves seated near each other at a party. Sagan writes, "Antoine et Lucile étaient à un mètre l'un de l'autre" — literally, "Antoine and Lucile were a meter away from each other." As one might expect, Westhoff writes, "Antoine and Lucile were only a yard from each other." Once again, he crosses the Atlantic (or at least the Channel) in order to give us a distance measurement, even though any literate English speaker knows roughly how big one meter is. This time, however, I *didn't* stick with the metric system but made a more radical shift: "Antoine and Lucile were only an arm's length from each other." Not only does this avoid the quagmire of meters versus yards, it also sounds less scientific and more poetic. It's a trade I thought was very much in my favor. Just think, though — I blew my chance to say, "Antoine and Lucile were only 39.37 inches from each other"! But somehow, I don't think that's what Sagan would have wanted this trader to say, even though it is an impeccable literal translation.

Imitate or Clarify Emotional Blur?

FOR ME, one of the harder sentences in *La Chamade* comes inside a long inner monologue of Lucile's in Chapter 14. She is in profound emotional turmoil and feels as if she is being crucified, but by spears that are poking through her heart instead of through her hands or feet. The next fragment of her thought, as reported by Sagan, goes like this:

> Elle s'étonnait alors de sentir son cœur se retourner, se vider sous le choc, devenir à la fois vide et affreusement encombrant.

Literally rendered, this sentence would give something like this:

> And it amazed her then to feel her heart turn over, emptied by the shock, emptied and yet horribly cumbersome.

Actually, I cheated a little — I gave you Westhoff's rendition of this sentence — but it will do pretty well as a literal translation. The problem is that it still strikes me as very hard to understand. Or maybe this isn't a problem at all — maybe that's what Scott Buresh meant when he said that he likes to have some fog, some mist. Could Sagan's fog here be desirable to some readers? If so, fine — but I personally rebel at the idea of outputting a verbal fog that I don't understand simply because I gave up too early, didn't think hard enough about the input sentence. I wouldn't be content with just making a literal translation on the basis of image-free words, in the manner of Google's translation engine.

Instead, I felt compelled at least to *try* to reach behind the words and to fathom the actual feelings. What could it mean for one's heart to turn over and empty itself? What could it mean for one's heart to be both empty and cumbersome at the same time? Is there anything tangible here, or is it all metaphorical?

Since I felt blocked, I turned to Caroline for her perspective, and after we had talked it over, I felt pretty sure that she had put her finger on Lucile's pulse, and so, borrowing her imagery, I rendered Sagan's sentence in English as follows:

> At such times, reeling in shock, she was astounded to feel her heart tip over and her emotions drain out, leaving it empty yet still unbearably heavy.

The sentence is still not totally clear, but I think it's about as clear as it can get. We are, after all, dealing with the eternal mysteries of the human heart, and the prospect of translating such mysteries precisely into words in *any* language is well-nigh hopeless.

The question I would raise here is whether I have done Francoise Sagan a service or a disservice in trying to "decode" and spell out, at least roughly, what she had said in a cryptic and elusive, although undeniably poetic, manner. Or perhaps the question is whether I have done *readers* a service or disservice in doing this. To my mind, though, there is no question. I *had* to do it, and I am happy to have done it. That's how I see my duty to Sagan and to our readers.

Some people may prefer the more literal approach, which would result in an ambiguously swirling verbal fog, and that's fine with me. There's plenty of room for more than one singer of a lovely song, and plenty of room for more than one translator of a lovely book. Or as they used to chant back in Mao's day (and perhaps they still do), "Let a hundred flowers bloom!" But I admit, they probably didn't chant it in English...

What on Earth did She Mean?

SOME of the more ambiguous spots in *La Chamade* use French phrases that I couldn't make head or tail of, and after tearing my hair out, I found out, to my relief (and also frustration), that both Caroline and Daniel were as baffled as I. One of these spots, found in Chapter 6, refers to Lucile's half-hearted attempts, in questioning Charles, to get to the bottom of a mystery.

> *FS:* Elle n'aurait pas insisté : ses quêtes de vérité, « ses moments russes » n'allaient jamais très loin.

RW: She would not have been insistent: her search for truth never went very far.

DH: She wouldn't have asked for more clarity; her quests for truth, her *moments russes,* were never terribly long-lived.

The French original uses "ses moments russes" as an appositive phrase to "ses quêtes de vérité", but what Lucile's "Russian moments" might be I had no idea. Do Russians have some unique mode of truth-seeking (or do French people suppose that they do?)? Do Russians go into a Dostoevskian or Tolstoyan trance of some obscure sort? Was this some profound, if cryptic, literary reference? Neither of my native French-speaking friends was sure what Sagan meant, and so my solution was not terribly brilliant — I just kept this elusive French phrase intact, leaving it to each reader's imagination to decide whatever it might mean (if the reader had any desire to do so). To my surprise, however, Westhoff, who had direct access to the passage's author, dropped it like a hot potato. I wonder why he didn't simply ask her!

Almost exactly the same scenario re-enacted itself in Chapter 8, where Antoine is musing about a certain "après-midi rouge et noir" — that is, a "red and black afternoon". At first I had no idea what this was about, but eventually I recalled that Antoine's room was always very dark (*noir*) and he always lit it up with a red lamp (*rouge*). Then it hit me that Sagan was perhaps alluding to the colors of Antoine's room by quoting the title of Stendhal's famous novel *Le Rouge et le Noir,* thus killing two birds with one stone. I wasn't sure of this, but it seemed a Sagan-like move, and since neither Daniel nor Caroline seemed to have any clearer ideas than I did, I just wrote "the whole *Rouge et Noir* afternoon", with the capitals suggesting a literary allusion. Westhoff, in case anyone is interested, sashayed around the issue, writing "yesterday afternoon". Why didn't he just phone up his ex-wife?

Laisser des mots français dans le texte ?

THESE two examples show that I occasionally leave French words in my English text. In fact, I do so quite often, and for the obvious reason, which is that having French words scattered throughout the text can only intensify the *ambiance* of Frenchness.

In Chapter 9, for instance, I leave an occurrence of *Je t'aime* intact, assuming that nearly all readers will have run across the French for "I love you" somewhere before and will thus be able to handle it effortlessly. Similarly, toward the end of Chapter 15, at a particularly wrenching moment, I leave the words *Au revoir* in their original language in order to emphasize the drama of the parting. It's unimaginable to me that any reader of this book would be thrown by this phrase, and to me that is sufficient justification for keeping it, especially in this poignant spot. And one other salient use of French terms is the names of the five major parts of the novel, which I left in French, presuming that they are pretty transparent to educated readers of English.

You may recall the *omelette flambée* devoured with gusto by the pink-faced couple. Well, there are dozens of other French terms sprinkled throughout the English text, including these:

> adieu, adroit, apéritif, aplomb, autoroute, bagatelle, banquette, brasserie, cabaret, café, camaraderie, carafe, chaise longue, chauffeur, confidant, coquette, coterie, dossier, douceur, élan, ennui, entourage, entrée, façade, faux pas, frisson, joie de vivre, liaison, maître d'hôtel, mélange, négligée, pique, première, protégée, rendez-vous, rêverie, rive gauche, savant, soirée, tête-à-tête, voilà.

Our language is well known for its willingness to gulp down foreign words whole, and as this list shows, many of the words I have called "French" are by now perfectly normal English.

"Tu" and "Vous" in English?

ONE OF the most fundamental ways in which English differs from French is that it has only one second-person singular pronoun — "you". French, like most European languages, has both an intimate or informal "you" and a respectful or formal "you". Among adults, the informal "you" — *tu* — is generally used within families, between close friends, between lovers, and so forth, whereas the formal "you" — *vous* — is used between people who don't know each other well, or who wish to maintain a cautious or respectful distance from each other.

These pronouns' usages have drifted a bit over the centuries, but in 1965, when this novel was written, they were much the same as they are today. Whereas some European countries have drifted or are drifting towards a universal *tutoiement,* France has definitely not gone that route. In any case, back in the sixties, much as today, French lovers virtually never said *vous* to each other; to do so would have sounded bizarrely chivalrous, vaguely aristocratic (or hankering to be so), and it would have evoked the flavor of an era long gone.

And yet, in this novel, *vouvoiement* between lovers occurs frequently, and is thus a very striking feature to any French-speaking reader. Indeed, the contrast between the couples that say *tu* to each other and those that remain at the *vous* level is almost the plot of this novel, boiled down to its essence. And so, for a translator merely to dismiss it and say, "We don't have this distinction in contemporary English — so too bad!" would be a serious betrayal of the fabric of this novel. On the other hand, I certainly wasn't about to turn back the clock a couple of hundred years and stuff the antique Anglo-Saxon pronoun "thou" into the mouths of chic contemporary Parisians! Talk about betrayal — that would have turned my translation into a laughingstock.

What to do, then? Was there any escape hatch at all? I ruminated on this quandary for quite a while, eventually hitting on an unorthodox idea that pleased me. I decided that since this is a work of written English rather than oral English — it's not a play that one hears spoken aloud but a novel that one reads with one's eyes — I could exploit this fact and invent an inaudible but visible English counterpart to the *vous/tu* distinction. Thus was born, at least for the duration of this novel, the "You"/"you" distinction. When capitalized, "You" would represent a formal, respectful, second-person singular form of address, wheras "you" written with lowercase "y" would represent an informal, intimate second-person singular form of address — the *tu* that is expected among lovers. And that's the convention I follow throughout my translation. (Note: I always use the lowercase "you" when two or more people are being addressed, since French makes no formal/informal distinction in the plural, and since it's always very clear in the novel when a plural "you" is being used.)

Needless to say, the capitalized word "You" coming in the middle of a sentence may look somewhat jolting, perhaps a bit stuffy and pompous, to English-speaking readers — but that's not a bad thing at all; indeed, it's just the effect I want, because in *La Chamade* the use of *vous* between lovers will strike French-speaking readers as precious and affected. Actually, it's a little subtler than that; there is also a kind of touching quality in this extra degree of respect for one's romantic companion — a kind of quaint, old-fashioned reserve, even gallantry, that contrasts with the easy, almost mindless shift to *tu.* A couple that resists this natural slide will only do so very consciously, and I think that the capital "Y" somehow may also convey this elusive flavor, at least a bit.

In retrospect, I would say that of all the risks that I took in creating *That Mad Ache* out of *La Chamade,* introducing this curious "You"/"you" distinction was among the greatest, but I

took this risk very happily because I felt it was a major help in conveying accurately the flavor of this novel as experienced by a reader of French.

Immense Care Taken with Tone

FOR ME, one of the most touching sentences in the book was the following extremely short remark (I won't reveal here who said it to whom, nor when nor where): "Vous êtes très en beauté." I must have gone back and forth dozens and dozens of times in trying to figure out how best to render, in English, the subtle feel of this very tender, intense, yet offhand remark. Among the candidates were the following sentences, with "You are" and "You're" always vying for primacy, and with the word "today" always an optional add-on at the end: "You're very beautiful"; "You're very radiant"; "You're looking so radiant", "You're truly radiant"; "You're really in bloom"; and so forth and so on. There are at least a hundred ways of taking the elements listed above and making plausible versions from them.

To some people, such nitpicky details as the microscopic difference in flavor between "You're" and "You are" wouldn't matter in the least; they'd say it was six of one and half a dozen of the other (which in French becomes "Bonnet blanc ou blanc bonnet", to translate which literally into sensible, acceptable English poses a mean challenge!). Well, such nonchalance is fine if you feel that way, but to me such fine-tuning choices matter enormously. After all, when I first read the book, this remark had been among the most telling moments in the whole story — a hingepoint, I would call it — and so I desperately wanted to get it *just right*, and of course I had only one try at it, since all the rival versions would necessarily remain forever invisible and silent in the wings, never to be seen or heard by anyone but me.

It's quite probable, I admit, that when Françoise Sagan came up with this sentence, she just tossed it off spontaneously without trying out a hundred close variations on the theme and picking the best of them. It would never have occurred to her to do any such complex, cerebral exercise. That's because she, in the manner of most novelists, was living intensely inside the heads (and hearts) of her characters, and of course this particular character just came out with this remark, just like that, without a lot of prior calculation. But I am not the original writer (let alone the character in her novel), and the only way I know to seek the best counterpart in English is to come up with a fair number of alternatives and to weigh them against each other. And I think it's a good challenge for anyone who's interested in translation. So, reader, given just one chance at it, how would *you* render this tender, touching, hingepoint sentence?

Breaks and Breath-marks

I HAD no idea, when I started translating this novel that I so love, that I would wind up asking myself over and over again whether or not I have the right to impose my personal sense of where breaks and pauses — metaphorical breath-marks — belong in the book. In other words, would I be overstepping my bounds if here and there I were to add, delete, or shift various markers that delineate the boundaries of all sorts of structural units of Sagan's elegant prose?

At a very microscopic structural level, for instance, dare I insert commas where Sagan has none (or dare I remove commas where she has them)? Well, of course I do — insertion or removal of commas here and there is hardly a great sin; I'd put it on the same level of sinfulness as swiping a paper clip from a friend's desk.

On a slightly higher level, dare I break some of Sagan's longer sentences into two or more pieces, or vice versa? Once again, yes, although I try not to do this too often. Perhaps this is the analogue of sneaking a popsicle from one's friend's freezer.

Jumping to a higher structural level, dare I break Sagan's paragraphs, some of which are unbelievably long, into more bite-sized chunks that have their own logic? To be concrete, in several chapters there are paragraphs two full pages long, and in Chapter 14 there is a paragraph nearly three pages long. As I transcribed such paragraphs, they felt mighty bloated to me, and I felt each of them crying out to me to split it up into more digestable pieces. Thus once again I wound up being lenient toward myself — and indeed, I took pity on all of these giant paragraphs and broke them into three, four, or five smaller ones, inserting breaks wherever my sense of esthetics and logic felt they belonged. Doing this was perhaps presumptuous on my part, but I felt it was needed. Perhaps this sin was on the same order as filching a few roses from one's friend's garden?

But we are not done; as in any novel, there are higher levels of structure than just paragraphs. Sagan explicitly breaks her chapters into what I will call "sections" (signaled by blank lines in the original French, and in my translation by lines with three centered bullets), and of course there are the chapters themselves, which have numbers but no names.

In general, I was very hesitant to insert (or delete) section breaks inside chapters, but in Chapter 4 there was one spot, right after Antoine and Lucile make a break from one of Claire's soirées and head out into Paris, "dark, glowing, and seductive", which strongly suggested that there should be a parallel break in the narration, and so I went right ahead and inserted it. And I admit that there are two or three other spots in the book where I had the gall to introduce my own section breaks, but I did so

only after much pondering. Here, maybe we're talking about "borrowing" a detective novel from our friend's bookshelf.

It would have taken even more effrontery for me to tamper with Sagan's chapter boundaries — chopping one chapter into two pieces, fusing two chapters into one, or other types of amputations and graftings. Maybe such an act of revision would be comparable to stealthily walking out of one's friend's house with a Françoise Sagan novel hidden under one's coat. And precisely because I thought it was just too brazen, I didn't dare do that anywhere in this book; however, had I been Sagan's editor in French, I would have suggested to her that she consider doing so in a couple of cases. To my eye, the logic of the novel could have been slightly improved by such adjustments.

Of Seasons, Reasons, and Treasons

ODDLY enough, it was at the very highest structural level of all that I bumped into a most troubling anomaly, which gave rise to the most troubling *crise de conscience*.

Françoise Sagan broke her novel into three overall "parts" and named them after the seasons in which they take place: Spring, Summer, and Fall. This is a very appealing idea, except for the very unfortunate fact that Fall's part falls apart, and does so quite flagrantly, at the end. The action in that part starts out in the autumn, as advertised, but then for four of its chapters, it extends way out into the winter, at least through March and possibly even further. And then the very last chapter — still in the part she called "L'automne" — takes place two years later!

As I thought about this blemish, a tiny little puppy-like voice inside of me yipped, "So just pinpoint the dividing line, and go ahead and create another part called 'Winter' right there!" But then another, much sterner, voice in me boomed out, trying to

rein in any such brazen thoughts: "Breaking the book into more than its official three parts is out of the question; you simply cannot impose your own pet notions on someone else's book! End of story."

Although this stern, deference-counseling view sounded like The Voice of Reason booming down from on high, somehow it didn't quite convince me, and meanwhile that little voice grew bolder, insisting, "To claim that those four chapters take place in the fall is *false*, no two ways about it." I had to admit that it deeply bothered me to label a set of four chapters so wrongly.

And then the unsquelched, rebellious yipper — the Voice of Treason — impudently added, "A year has four seasons! Make the book have four seasons!" Instantly the stern Voice of Reason bellowed back, "No, no, and no. Françoise Sagan, for reasons of her own, chose to make her novel *La Chamade* have just *three* seasons. Someone else's quirky personal desires for 'logic' or 'esthetics' have nothing to do with it. This is a question of *respect for the creator.* No fourth part. Sorry."

But that uppity little puppy simply would not be put down, coming right back at me with a powerful parry: "Don't forget that the very last chapter takes place *two years later, in the spring.* Including that chapter in the part called 'L'automne' is not just a tiny blemish; it's a total lie, it's an absurdity, it's an outrage!"

All at once, a mental avalanche took place, and everything flipped around in my mind. Why not add *two* more parts? Why would that be disrespectful? It would make the book's high-level structure not only more symmetric but also truer. Maybe Sagan had her reasons, but maybe not. Authors make mistakes. People forget things. *Errare humanum est.* And so in the end, the stern master was disregarded, the yipping puppy had a lovely romp, and Parts Four and Five (L'hiver; Plus tard…) were inserted. The Voice of Treason had vanquished the Voice of Reason.

This was a very high-level decision, yes, but on the other hand it was a very, very small decision. It barely affects a thing about the book, when you come down to it, but to me it made it feel much truer at that highest structural level. Brazen? Perhaps. But sometimes brazenness is what is called for. As for the analogous sin, I would compare it to walking out of one's friend's house with a paperback Françoise Sagan novel whose front cover had been crudely torn off, returning the next day with a first-edition hardback copy of the same novel in perfect shape, and putting it back up on the shelf where the damaged one had been.

Co-creation and Procreation

I HAVE, in writing this set of reflections on translation, given much thought not just to my own paragraph breaks, but also to my section breaks, and to their titles. If someone someday were to translate this essay into another language (though the idea of doing so eludes all logic, as far as I can tell), I would not want them to blithely ignore all my breakpoint decisions, but if they disagreed with a few here or there, I would certainly be open to a spirited discussion about it, and I'm sure I could be persuaded to accept some changes. I wouldn't feel that a momentary whim I'd once had was imbued with papal infallibility. And although I truly admire Françoise Sagan's writing, she's no pope either. In fact, I feel she has something of a blind spot concerning the placement of breath-marks on all her different levels of structure, so I'm pleased to have had the chance to try to make her work a bit more artistic, at least along this minor dimension, in English.

For me, the bottom line in translation is the belief that a product of the highest artistic caliber is attainable, and I feel that just about any author, no matter how highly regarded, can benefit from occasional small editorial suggestions here and

there. In this regard, I always recall how much more beautifully Sviatoslav Richter performed Shostakovich's preludes and fugues than did Shostakovich himself. Though the notes were all the same, there was a world of difference in how they came out. Of course Shostakovich wrote the melodies and harmonies, and those were all absolutely fixed, but below that level, all was up for grabs. The analogy to a translator's re-performance of a piece of writing is simple, but it speaks to me.

To be sure, the novel's author is the primary author and must always remain the primary voice, but in the grand scheme of things, there remains room for local spice here and there, representing the artistic tastes of the translator. At least in my experience, that is what lends to the re-creative activity of translation a profound feeling — hopefully not illusory — of engaging in fresh creation.

The fact that two people are involved, in very different roles, in creating a translated work reminds me of the fact that two parents are required, also playing very different roles, in creating a child. The mother, of course, plays the greater role, because she is the one who actually *makes* the child. For that reason, the book's original author could be thought of as the translated work's metaphorical mother. But a father, too, is needed for procreation, and although his procreative role is certainly far subsidiary to the mother's, it is nonetheless indispensable. In describing the genesis of a particular child, no one would ever dream of relegating the father to a mere footnote; rather, the two parents are usually seen as equal co-creators, with the father often even being listed first (silly though that seems).

As in procreation, so in co-creation. The translator, though clearly the junior partner in the act, is indispensable in somewhat the same way as is a father, and thus deserves a similar level of recognition as a co-progenitor of the final piece of literature.

Concluding Musings

WHEN, some years ago, I undertook to translate *La Chamade* out of my passionate reaction, as a reader, to the novel, I wasn't sure, at first, what my ultimate purpose was in doing this translation. It was certainly not that I wanted to rival or eclipse someone else — indeed, at the outset I didn't know if any other translation had been done, and in any case, competition was the furthest thing from my mind. Nor did I want to produce a "contemporary" translation, for I've never understood, let alone agreed with, the oft-quoted thesis that a great book, no matter how well it has been translated before, always needs a new translation every twenty years, or for each new generation.

No, it was not anything like that. If anything, my motivation was just that, for a constellation of inarticulable and highly personal reasons, I found *La Chamade* beautiful and touching, and I yearned to re-experience as strongly as possible the emotions it had churned up in me. Merely re-reading the novel would not have allowed me that degree of emotional intensity and intimacy with its characters, but rewriting it in my native language did, and I am extremely glad that I decided to make the attempt.

The entire time I was working on my translation, all sorts of thoughts about the process I was engaged in were accumulating, and in order not to forget them all, I scribbled down dozens of pages of notes for myself. Nonetheless, I would never have guessed that a year later I would wind up writing an essay about the subtle traps and crazy paradoxes that plague the translation of novels in general, let alone that writing that essay would take me nearly as long as doing the translation itself. Although I initially thought of my musings as constituting a preface, I eventually changed my mind and relabeled them "Afterword", because I felt it was important to indicate that the novel itself is

the main course here. But then, as a result of discussions with my friends at Basic Books, my Afterword turned into a short book (or half-book) of its own — this very essay. So be it.

In a nutshell, my essay's goal has been to combat this wrong idea: "So, some drudge took all those sentences in Language A and put them into Language B... Big deal!" The *right* idea is that high-quality conversion of a novel from Language A to Language B reflects the depths of the translator's soul no less than Ella Fitzgerald singing Cole Porter reflects the depths of Ella's soul.

Ever since my long-gone teen-age years, when I started intensely listening to music and avidly reading about it, I have been delighted when I chanced across a record (or a CD) with liner notes written by the performer. After all, who could be more intimate with a work of music than someone who chose to perform it out of profound love? Such pieces of writing by musicians are, of course, not always very coherent, but they are unfailingly informative in some ways, and on occasion they are vivid and gripping and leave one with an unforgettable set of ideas about the piece, perhaps even with elegant turns of phrase that will reverberate over and over in one's mind down the years.

Wouldn't it be nice if skilled translators, too, gave us the benefit, once in a while, of their unique perspective on works of literature they love? For good translators are not just "humble servants" of their authors, but full-fledged artists; indeed, a fine translator, no less than a novelist or poet, is an artist of the word. And these artists — these translator–traders — have tales galore about trades they've made in the tropical trade winds of words.

Translator, Trader

CHAPTER 25

They ran into each other again two years later, at one of Claire Santré's parties. Lucile had finally married Charles; Antoine had become the director of a new publishing outfit, and it was in this capacity that he had merited an invitation. He was very much wrapped up in his work, and he was also rather fond of hearing himself talk. Lucile still exuded her old charm and cheerfulness, and a young Englishman named Soames was smiling at her a great deal. Antoine found himself seated next to her at dinner, whether by chance or by one last little joyful act of malice on Claire's part, and delicately, they spoke about books.

"I say, where does the odd phrase *la chamade* come from?", piped up the young Englishman at the far end of the table.

"According to Littré's dictionary, it was a solemn drumroll sounded to announce defeat," declared some savant.

"Oh, how terribly poetic!" exclaimed Claire Santré, clasping her hands together in delight. "Of course I know that Your language is richer than ours, my dear Soames, but You'll have to admit that when it comes to poetry, France remains queen."

Antoine and Lucile were only an arm's length from each other, but just as *la chamade* meant nothing to either of them any more, Claire's little quip did not evoke, on either of their parts, even the tiniest of titters.